"Scott creates one of the most compelling characters in a generation with Father Solomon Lancaster . . . [and] weaves a rich tapestry that keeps you on your toes up until the last page."

—Patrick Anderson, co-host of the *Modern Horrors* podcast

"I could not put this damn book down until I finished it. Gripped me from start to finish."

—Frank Kemp, writer for *SiftPop* and *Modern Horrors* podcasts

"Jeremy Scott revels in this edge-of-your-seat tale with experienced glee, clearly leaning on his history of living in the small-town Midwest, knowledge of insulated religious gatherings, and frequent consumption of regional-specific hot dishes. This story will grip you by the wrists from the very start, and you will NOT want it to let go until the final page. Never have I been happier to surrender to whatever ride this mischievous author will take me."

—Barrett Share, producer and co-host of the *SinCast* podcast

"Scott's unvarnished style lures the reader into a sublime sense of comfort with his fascinating and frank descriptions of law enforcement, Catholicism, and small town living before twisting the knife with shocking twists and staggering revelations . . . the story unfolds in unexpected ways, growing ever more chilling while building to a jaw-dropping conclusion. This is a killer who won't soon be forgotten."

—Jenn Adams, horror journalist and podcaster

"Jeremy Scott delivers his most intimate and powerful story yet . . . an enthralling story that leaves you guessing until the very last page. A little bit Coen Brothers and a little bit Fincher, this sharp-tack character study disguised as an expertly written murder mystery is a wholly unique thriller from a writer at the top of their game."

—Stephen Sean Ford, actor and filmmaker

WHEN THE CORN IS WAIST HIGH

WHEN THE CORN IS WAIST HIGH

BY JEREMY SCOTT

KEYLIGHT
BOOKS

Keylight Books
an imprint of Turner Publishing Company
Nashville, Tennessee

www.turnerpublishing.com

When the Corn Is Waist High

This is a work of fiction. All the characters and events portrayed in this book are either products of the author's imagination or are used fictitiously.

Cover design: M.S. Corley
Book design: Tim Holtz

Library of Congress Cataloging-in-Publication Data

Names: Scott, Jeremy (Writer on cinema), author.
Title: When the corn is waist high / by Jeremy Scott.
Description: Nashville, Tennessee : Turner Publishing Company, [2022]
Identifiers: LCCN 2021030556 (print) | LCCN 2021030557 (ebook) | ISBN 9781684426478 (hardcover) | ISBN 9781684426461 (paperback) | ISBN 9781684426485 (ebook)
Subjects: LCGFT: Detective and mystery fiction. | Novels.
Classification: LCC PS3619.C6657 W47 2022 (print) | LCC PS3619.C6657 (ebook) | DDC 813/.6--dc23
LC record available at https://lccn.loc.gov/2021030556
LC ebook record available at https://lccn.loc.gov/2021030557

Printed in the United States of America

I would like to dedicate this book to the tiny farming towns of Indiana where I grew up, and the warm and weird people who lived there. The book is a thriller with murders and such, but it is also a bit of a love letter to a specific time and place in my life that was very formative for me.

I'll always consider myself a Hoosier.

WHEN THE CORN IS WAIST HIGH

CHAPTER 1

THE LILY

My third murder was my first.

I had two prior, of course, but officials hadn't recognized them as homicides at the time, and so they'd been classified merely as deaths. It would be a while before anyone realized that those first two were actually also intentional murders and not just accidental: years, in fact.

Anyway, I'd had six deaths during my time as sheriff of Crooked Creek, Indiana. That was over a period of about ten years. But I'd never had a murder until now—again, not counting the two prior that weren't currently considered homicides. Actually, I've probably explained this enough already. Let's move on.

Tina Hillary was dead; there were no two ways about it. She looked dead; she smelled dead. She was fucking dead. She'd been found by her landlord, faceup on her kitchen floor. He usually checked on her once a day; and when he got no response one evening, he got worried and let himself in to find her expired.

Mrs. Hillary was eighty-four years old and lived alone. Ordinarily her death would have been ruled one of natural causes—we might not even have ordered an autopsy. Autopsies are rarer in rural Indiana than in the big cities. And Jerusalem County had only one medical examiner, and he lived all the way over in Perrington, thirty miles away.

Ordinarily, as I say, we had to find some significant question or mystery surrounding a death before we could order an autopsy. An old woman dead on the floor? Wouldn't have qualified. That is, had it not been for the white lily whose stem had been literally sewn into Mrs. Hillary's arm, the flower itself cradled gently in her left hand.

"That's something," I said in that half-drawl all Indiana transplants seem to end up with after living here more than ten years. Hoosiers—those folks who live in Indiana—speak a unique blend of Southern drawl and Minnesotan, and those who moved here tended to pick a bit of it up. I'd lived in-state for fifteen years and couldn't quite place the moment I'd slid into it myself.

"That's why I called you," Skip said. Deputy Skip Holmes was the youngest member of our police force. He was regularly teased for being green, as well as for having the same last name as a famous fictional detective while simultaneously being mostly a goof. But he was a good kid. A bit talkative. Local boy. Went to college, then the academy, barely graduated, and then came home to enforce the law.

As the newest member of the force, he was on call for the night shift.

I'd been wrist-deep in a plate of Indiana nachos when Skip called, but I'd pretended to be asleep. I guess I was embarrassed to be such a junk-food-loving night owl. And a deputy who thinks I'm sleepy and cranky might be quieter and allow me to think.

Even now on the scene, I yawned to keep up the ruse. "Hmm." I stared at the corpse, thinking.

"You think we ought to call the mortician guy? Dobbins?"

I said nothing, still taking in the scene.

Skip continued. "I don't feel like this here can be considered natural causes, you know what I mean?" He strung words together like Gomer Pyle, but the actual sound of his voice was deep and clipped. Like a lawyer on a television show.

"The death may yet prove to be accidental," I said, more to myself than in reply to Skip. "But that lily did not get there through any natural causes." I knelt to take a closer look, knowing it would soon cost me whatever part of my nacho dinner still resided in my stomach.

"You think she just . . . she just . . . died?" Skip wore his heart on his sleeve and said almost every thought that ran through his head, apparently even if he thought I was tired and cranky. "And then someone came along, found her, and did this here with the flower and shit?"

I stood up, sensing a possible teaching moment. "No, Deputy Holmes. What I'm saying is . . . don't make assumptions. Regular folk—the car salesman at Sandsman Chevy, the cashier at Clemmon's Grocery, the gas station attendant—they can afford to make assumptions. Hell, some of them get by in this life solely through assumptions.

"But you, me, Dobbins the medical examiner, the county sheriff, the docs at the hospital . . . we can't afford to make assumptions. All we know is that she is dead, and someone . . . did some disgusting shit with a flower and her arm. For now . . . that's all we know." With my pen, I tapped the camera he was holding. "How about taking some pictures while I continue investigating the crime scene?"

Cops in a small town do more than one job. We had only five people on the payroll at the Crooked Creek Police Department: myself, the sheriff; three deputies; and Maggie, the office manager/receptionist/ CFO. Tonight, Deputy Holmes was both a police officer and a crime-scene photographer.

So, upon finding Mrs. Hillary's body, her landlord called 911, and the call routed to the county dispatch, who then called Maggie and woke her up, and she called Skip to go to the scene. We didn't usually have an officer on-duty overnights; just one on call.

Crooked Creek had only a couple thousand citizens, so our police force was actually pretty large when compared to other small towns in the Midwest. Usually you figure a farm town has about one officer per thousand citizens, so we were fortunate. The local chamber of commerce functioned as a shadow city council and kept plenty of funding funneled to law enforcement. It had been this way for at least nine or ten years, ever since the Lindy girl went missing in 1978. The folks in Crooked Creek with money seemed intent on preventing any repeat incidents.

Snap. Snap.

Skip took pictures on the police force's Polaroid while I continued assessing the crime scene and pretending I knew what I was doing.

I didn't consider myself much of a detective. I didn't consider myself much of a police officer, actually. Hell, I'd only run for sheriff ten years ago because the church board seemed so interested in it. All three of my deputies had gone to the police academy, but I never went. Something a lot of folks forget, especially in small towns: sheriffs are politicians, not cops.

I wasn't sure how to look for clues. The last two deaths in this town had been ruled accidental or natural causes, so I hadn't had to investigate much at all. I began looking for fingerprints on windows and shiny surfaces, only to immediately realize that neither I nor Skip had gloves on.

"Oh, shit!" I yelled.

"What?"

"Gloves! Gloves! Put the camera down. What did you touch?! What did I touch?! Never mind, let's go to my truck; I have gloves. We need gloves."

"Shit, sheriff. I touched a bunch of stuff," he called, running after me.

I felt so amateur. Because I was. Most of the crime I dealt with here was small stuff: domestic disputes, petty theft, the occasional pot bust, some light vandalism. Murder was something I was wholly unprepared for. But even though I didn't know what I was doing, gloves should have been obvious, even for a high schooler.

I grumbled unintelligibly to myself as Skip and I tugged the latex gloves on, one at a time. How many fingerprints had we already left in this place? Jesus.

As we walked back through the threshold of the front door, a familiar and unwelcome sound echoed through the air. It was the sound of the muffler-free, environment-hating gas guzzler of one Harold McKee, owner and sole reporter for the local paper, the *Crooked Creek Peek*—circulation three hundred.

"Goddammit," I breathed.

"How does he even find out about this stuff?" Skip asked.

"He lives across the street from me," I said for the sixth or seventh time.

"So he's stalking you? That's creepy, sir," he barked.

"It's not stalking if you can look out your living room window and see it." I wondered what the academy was teaching these days to crank out someone as dumb as Skip. He was well-meaning and honest, but not a smart man. I put a hand on Skip's shoulder. "Stall him for me, son. I'll finish the pictures and evidence collection. Remember: this is a crime scene—he has no journalistic right to enter this house, and you arrest him if he tries."

"Yes, sir."

I walked back inside and stood in the small foyer, sweeping my gaze over the living room where the body lay.

"What kind of monster would do this?" I said aloud to myself. "Who would even think of doing this, let alone go through with it?" I had no answers at the moment.

I looked over the room, sweeping my gaze left to right.

"Where are the clues? Surely there's something left behind that's incriminating." I looked at the bookshelf, then the piano, then the couch. I didn't see any of the typical telltale signs of a struggle, although my knowledge of the telltale signs of a struggle came entirely from episodes of *Perry Mason* and *Murder, She Wrote*. "What am I missing right now?" I pleaded with myself.

In that moment, I wished with all my might to be a better cop, a better detective, and to find the clues that had surely been left behind. But I was looking at the crime scene like any layperson would. It was maybe the first time I had felt unprepared to do my job.

But I knew one thing I needed to do for certain. I took out my handkerchief, picked up Mrs. Hillary's phone, and called my boss, the mayor of Crooked Creek, the right-honorable asswipe Sean Burke.

He answered on the third ring, as he always did. "What?" Mayor Burke had a way of always sounding annoyed. I'm sure even his orgasms sounded annoyed, if he ever had them.

"Mister Mayor, sir," I said respectfully. "It's the sheriff here. I've got one hell of a fucking corpse on my hands."

Three minutes later, after another lecture about my unprofessional phone demeanor, Burke agreed to get Derrick Dobbins, the medical examiner, to Crooked Creek by morning for a full autopsy. He also planned to call the county sheriff, Craig McNewel.

"County's got no jurisdiction in city limits," I whined.

"He's got ten times the experience you have, and another pair of eyes won't hurt," the mayor shot back. It was a conversation we'd had several times, or any time he felt I was in over my head. It didn't help that he had backed my opponent for sheriff.

Mayor Burke was on his tenth four-year term. Early on, the township didn't have term limits in place, so he just kept running and, because nothing much ever changes in corn country, he kept winning. When the hippies in the late sixties managed to get term limits on the books, well, Burke ran and won the legally allowed two more times. Then, on his way out, he persuaded the board of aldermen to strip the mayor's office of power, giving the authority to a newly created city manager position. The city manager would be chosen by the board of aldermen, not by the general electorate, whose votes would continue to fill a mayoral office that no longer held any real power.

Then the board appointed Burke city manager. It was the best end-around I'd ever heard of, outside of some Barry Sanders highlights.

Everyone in town knew what had occurred, and no one really cared. They kept calling Burke "Mayor," even though that wasn't technically his title anymore. And the actual mayor, voted for but powerless, was largely anonymous to the general public, as he only showed up for ribbon cuttings and other ceremonial, meaningless events.

Burke had been "mayor" of this town longer than I had even been alive.

His phone sign-off tonight was "Goddammit." And then he hung up. Like it was my fault I had a weird murder in my town.

Harold McKee appeared just outside the front door, with Skip making an X of his arms and legs in the doorway as a kind of human blockade. I was beginning to lose faith in deputy Holmes's ability to keep the press at bay.

Harold published the local rag—the *Crooked Creek Peek*—using the copy machine at the library. He stuffed the weekly "paper" into every mailbox he could, and while many locals read and discussed it, the *Peek* had no true subscribership as far as anyone knew.

"What are you hiding, Sheriff? What's the big secret?" Harold said the same things every time I saw him, always seeking evidence of a conspiracy of some kind. Only this time I finally had something I didn't want him to see or photograph. But it was already too late.

"Holy . . ." Harold trailed off as he popped his head under Skip's arm and took in the visuals of the living room, the dead body, and the threaded lily stem. As he raised his camera up to take a photograph, Deputy Holmes earned his first gold star *and* his first demerit by kicking the news photographer squarely in the crotch—leading to a lawsuit that, last I heard, the city of Crooked Creek was still fighting in appellate courts.

"Cuff him and put him in the back of your squad car," I ordered Deputy Holmes. "We'll charge him with interfering with an investigation."

"He's gonna fight it in court, Sheriff," Skip reminded me. We'd arrested Harold a half dozen times over the years, usually for trespassing or otherwise being a nuisance to us and his fellow citizens in the pursuit of some kind of juicy police gossip or hot news story. He always sued us afterward, and he always won in court, because the city judge was a ninety-year-old by-the-book rule keeper who thought freedom of the press was the most precious of rights, and because the county judge was an illiterate boob.

"Skip, please!" I shouted. I didn't care if the charges stuck. I just wanted that paparazzo out of there for a few minutes.

"You got it, sir," he relented.

Needless to say, Harold and his journalistic curiosity were now out of commission long enough for me to do a comprehensive search of the scene.

Skip and I covered the body with a blanket that we found in a nearby closet, both for basic human-decency reasons and in the hope that that would keep her identity private if any other amateur news photographers dropped by. Then there were next of kin to notify, a job I would normally give to whichever underling was standing next to me. But tonight it was only Skip and me. And I figured he'd probably already been through enough. So I made another call, this time to Mrs. Hillary's son, Chris. He lived in California, so thankfully he was still awake.

"What do I need to do?" he asked, after I'd given him the news.

"Well," I replied, "I would contact a funeral home here in Crooked Creek—there are two of them—and make funeral arrangements." I paused. "Unless you want to have her interred out there in California or somewhere else, in which case you will still need to call the Jerusalem County morgue tomorrow to make arrangements." I paused again. "I'm terribly sorry, sir."

For a while I heard nothing but breathing, as he processed all the new information, and then finally he sighed. "Okay," he said. And then he hung up.

I hadn't told the son everything. I hadn't told him about the lily, or the way it had been incorporated into the scene. As I hung up, I realized he would eventually find out anyway. I hoped he would believe I had done him a kindness by not overwhelming him right after the bad news. I hoped he wouldn't be upset at the momentary omission.

The county had only one hospital, about fifteen miles away in Del Plains. But we had an ambulance here locally in town, at the fire department. It wasn't required by law, as it was in some states, but we paid extra to train all of Crooked Creek's firemen—both paid and volunteer—to serve as EMTs as well.

The ambulance arrived, and I saw Terry and John climb out and start wheeling in a gurney. Terry was the fire chief and happened to be on duty tonight. John, Terry's son, was a new addition to the crew. I noticed John was carrying a body bag.

"Terry, John," I acknowledged as they entered the home.

They both nodded in return. Our firefighters rarely had to fight actual fires, and even most of their EMT calls ended happily. This was a somber night for them, with only the flat, dull drive to Del Plains ahead of them, and that wouldn't cheer anyone up.

"You get all the pictures you need?" Terry asked.

"Yeah. And I've taped the outline of the body. Just try not to touch anything else," I replied.

I watched them load Tina Hillary's lifeless body into the cold, black bag and zip her up. I'd seen her just last week at church. She'd been so spritely and full of vinegar. I took a quick moment to say a prayer for her, wishing her soul safe passage to Heaven. Then I turned off the lights, locked all the doors, and strung police tape across the threshold.

I made a mental note to order more yellow crime-scene tape, since the roll was getting low after cordoning off this house. It was the same roll we'd been using ever since I'd taken the job eight years ago.

I gave Skip instructions on how to handle Harold back at the lockup tonight, and tomorrow when he would inevitably want to have his receptionist girlfriend, Lydia, post bail. Deputy Kent would be showing up in the morning and would need a debrief. Skip seemed to have a handle on it, so I said good night and drove home.

At home I poured a glass of scotch, put some food out for my cat, Zacchaeus, who didn't appear to notice that I had been gone for hours, and sat down in the living room, staring at my own reflection in the television set. I didn't like what I saw.

"What. The hell. Are you going to do?" I asked myself out loud.

I downed the scotch and threw the glass full of ice at the wall above the TV. It shattered, obviously, and now I wasn't sure what was glass and what was ice.

"Crap!" I yelled into the air, before deciding to just forget everything and fall asleep drunk right there on the couch. Whatever didn't melt while I slept would be glass, and I'd sweep it up in the morning.

I was asleep in two minutes.

My name is Father Solomon Lancaster. I'm a prophet of the messiah, preacher of the Word of God, priest at Jerusalem Independent Catholic Church, and sheriff of Crooked Creek township.

And I'm in way over my head.

CHAPTER 2

CONFESSION

"Forgive me, Father, for I have sinned," she began.

"It's okay," I said softly, interrupting her immediately. "We all have." I smiled warmly as I spoke, hoping she could hear that in my voice as I strove to make this a safe place for her.

She was seventeen-year-old Katie McGuire, head cheerleader at the high school, daughter of a church board member, and girlfriend to one Matthew Wright—the captain of the basketball team. Matthew's family didn't attend Jerusalem Independent Catholic; rather, they belonged to Crooked Creek Baptist, another church in town.

There were only three churches in the township. Ours—Jerusalem Catholic, as everyone called it—was the largest by far, bringing in nearly four hundred people every Mass. Crooked Creek Baptist ran about two hundred for each Sunday service. And the third church in town was Anderson Wesleyan, a tiny holiness church with about fifty regular members.

The rest of Crooked Creek's people were either lapsed, heathen, or undecided. You might think it's impressive to have nearly a third of the city's population among the religious, but religion was common in farm country. Your crops are dependent on good farming, the weather, and God; every farmer knows this. It's just that some worship him, while others blame him.

I should tell you up front that the Catholic Church, as a worldwide organization, denounces our congregation. They consider us heretics. This took place before I came to serve as priest here, but because I accepted the position, the ban now applies to me as an individual as well, and lasts my entire lifetime and even to the first generation of any kids I might one day have—despite our faith not allowing priests to marry.

Why the original ban, you ask? Because we have a dangerous biblical interpretation? Because we ignore tradition in favor of modern trappings of worship?

No. Well, kind of. But no.

It's because we didn't give them enough money. We didn't pay enough dues to the mothership in the Vatican and were stripped of our affiliation status.

Yes, the local church leaders were also accused of violating Vatican protocol for an exorcism back in 1975, but nothing was ever proven. It was just a lot of hearsay and rumors. Yes, we did a few things differently, but nothing that opposed the Bible or Catholic teachings. The mother church just didn't like us.

The name of our community—Jerusalem Catholic—was also a point of contention, no matter how many times we explained that the name was due to our Indiana county and *not* the historical holy city.

It ultimately didn't matter. Our Catholic community in Jerusalem County was fiercely loyal to the point of being almost rabid. The United States Marines have a code: unit, corps, God, country. Jerusalem Catholic members' code would be: local church, local town, basketball, God. The basketball might seem strange, as it's not really a Catholic thing, but, if so, you just don't know Indiana well enough yet. Don't worry . . . you will.

Katie's sins were pretty harmless. Some jealousy of another girl. Some bitterness with her parents over their not wanting her to follow Matthew to whatever college offered him the best scholarship. Some fighting with her sister.

I felt sorry for Katie, I truly did. About a year ago her best friend, Deena Jaines, had disappeared. One day here, then gone forever. We'd scoured the county for leads but had never found her. Some folks still believed she'd simply up and run away. Katie never believed that, and she'd had a bit of pain in her smile ever since.

"Is there anything else you want to confess?" I usually asked this of everyone, just to make sure a person had one final chance to get everything off his or her chest.

Katie was a straight arrow, so I was surprised to hear such a long pause before she answered. Finally, she responded. "Just ... one more thing, Father."

"Sure," I said softly.

Nearly a minute passed, during which she murmured several times and seemed to be crying a bit. There were sniffles.

One of my best qualities as a priest—and as a public servant—was that I was exceedingly patient. I could wait out almost anyone.

Eventually she summoned the courage and blurted out: "I slept with Matthew." Then she sobbed.

While this was considered a sin, this did not surprise me. Teenagers are hormonal beasts, and we basically tell them to bottle it all up and then point them at each other for youth-group mixers and state-fair jamborees. It was only my pursuit of the priesthood that had kept me pure during the late teenage and college years. God gave me the strength to endure that time in my life.

And now I had porn to get me through.

But Katie wasn't a priest. Or a nun. She was a scared kid.

Through her deep breaths and sobs, I learned that the sexual contact had occurred more than a month ago, but that she'd recently missed her period. Matthew had offered to pay for a quiet abortion—something she would have to leave the state to get done, if only to keep people around here from finding out.

Matthew was worried about his scholarship chances being dinged if he were to be outed as a teenage father. Katie just seemed to love Matthew. And even though her love was immature and unformed, it was powerful.

That poor kid. I felt so bad for her. She really did want to do the right thing. She knew deep down that she couldn't abort the child and live with herself. But she feared her boyfriend would leave her if she defied his wishes.

Most of my confessors were people being jealous of their neighbor's garden or folks feeling guilty about their contributions to the parish. But Katie's was one of the heaviest confessions I'd heard in my fifteen or so years as a priest.

I didn't do "Our Fathers" and "Hail Marys." I suppose that's one of the things the Vatican thought we were doing wrong. But I didn't see how reciting read or memorized words counted as an act of contrition. I usually recommended Bible study, good deeds, or community service. I often asked the penitents how they thought they could best atone for their confessed sins. I thought an honest, intentional act of contrition better demonstrated a sincere desire for forgiveness than parroting back some words you'd said so many times in your life that they barely had any meaning. I wanted to create long-lasting change for good in the hearts of my flock. Or at least frequent short-lasting change for good.

"Katie." I tried to sound fatherly but gentle. "I am not your physician or your psychologist. I'm not your parent, and I'm not you. I cannot advise you beyond anything except your spiritual health. So today you have confessed to the point of a clean heart, and I have heard your earnest fealty." I paused for a breath. "What you decide to do about the situation is between you and God, and I cannot, in good conscience, tell you what you should do.

"For the sins confessed today, I would like you to volunteer in the church nursery for a minimum of four weeks to help you better understand the needs of a young child and the responsibility it requires. I'd also insist that you talk to your parents about this as soon as possible. This is a scary time, but you do not have to go through it alone. Your parents love you and only want the best for you, and if you make any decisions before including them, you will be making a huge mistake. Do you understand?"

"You're not going to tell my parents?" she asked meekly.

"It's not my job to tell your parents: it's yours. And everything said to me in confession by anyone is held private between myself, the confessor, and the Almighty God." I smiled. "Okay?"

Through the sniffles and chirpy cry noises, I heard a soft "Yes."

"Okay, then." I smiled. "In the name of the Father, the Son, and the Holy Spirit. Amen."

"Amen," she said, before standing to her feet and shuffling out of the confessional.

I waited another twenty minutes for any stragglers. Sometimes there were stragglers; sometimes life gets in the way and slows you down. But today there were none. Fifteen minutes after the end of my posted confessional hours for the day, I rose and exited.

I looked around the empty sanctuary, my eyes finally landing on the silhouette of Mayor Sean Burke leaning against the foyer doorway.

"Anything to confess?" I asked, still trying to crack this old bastard's hard exterior.

"We need to talk. I'll be in the car." He turned and left the building.

I sighed long and loud. I recognized that the sheriff job was oftentimes more important, at least in an earthly and legal sense. But I always viewed my priesthood as my real job, the one that was making the biggest impact in the world and in my community. It certainly paid better than the law-enforcement gig, not that I needed much money to get by nicely in a town this tiny. I just knew that the mayor and the county sheriff, even some of my own deputies . . . they didn't necessarily respect my church work. I was often reminded that it might ultimately interfere with my police work.

After checking all the doors and locking those that weren't already locked, I walked out front and climbed into the passenger seat of the mayor's Cadillac.

"Do you want me to put the top down?" he asked with a cocky grin.

"I really don't."

● ● ●

Nine minutes later, the mayor and I were in his office, along with all three of my deputies, the county sheriff, and the medical examiner, Dobbins, who was giving us his report.

"Ahem," he began. Dobbins was a two-pack-a-day smoker, so most of his sentences started with "Ahem" or some other throat-clearing mechanism. "Tina Hillary, aged eighty-four." He put a slide on the overhead projector; it showed the body on his examination table, covered in a sheet except for the left arm. The stem of the lily had served as thread, and it stretched the skin in each of the places where it entered or exited.

I had skipped breakfast before confession hours because I'd expected this briefing, and I was glad I had, now that we were getting into it.

"Cause of death, asphyxiation." Dobbins was a factual man. He was ugly in face and personality, and I hated being in his presence, but he was a knowledgeable and skilled medical examiner.

"Asphyxiation?" I asked. "Someone choked her to death?"

"Well." He chuckled the way extremely nerdy people sometimes do when about to reveal some science factoid that the rest of the room was ignorant of. "Yes and no. She was not physically choked, no. No one put their hands to her neck and suffocated her. Neither do I believe that anyone used a pillow to smother her. But the lungs were still incapacitated."

"How?" I was annoyed that I felt I had to lead the medical examiner through his prepared information. Despite my patience, I hated a slow trickle of information when a river was available.

"Asphyxiation," he continued condescendingly, "is merely the deprivation of oxygen to the lungs. It doesn't have to be a physical action outside or around the windpipe. In this case, I believe, it was an exaggerated allergen. Some kind of homemade poison or dust concoction. There's residue in her lungs that, under a microscope, resembles what I've seen in extreme pneumonia cases."

But Mrs. Hillary had been in good health and hadn't been diagnosed with pneumonia or any other disease, I thought to myself. She wasn't ready to run any marathons, and she had a bit of arthritis, but she was the healthiest eighty-four-year-old I'd ever known.

"But Mrs. Hillary had been in good health and hadn't been diagnosed with pneumonia or any other disease," Dobbins said, seconds after I'd thought it. "So, ultimately, no real conclusions are supported by the data beyond asphyxiation."

"So we know she choked, but we don't know how or on what?" I was summarizing for my own benefit, not dumbing it down. I'd gone to community college just long enough to learn about how important it is to paraphrase back to a speaker what you heard them say.

"That's correct," he replied.

"Shit," Skip breathed, unprofessionally, earning a glare from Mayor Burke.

Dobbins continued. "Though we will know more for sure. I've sent some samples off to the lab at Purdue, and they have equipment that is way more powerful than ours. Should hear back from them in about a week and a half . . . maybe two."

I sighed deeply. I hated the idea of an unsolved crime in my town, let alone an unsolved murder. The citizens were already buzzing just three days after the death, and they were only going to get more restless until the culprit was caught.

The room went quiet for a bit.

The mayor spoke first. "What do you think?" He was speaking to—and looking at—the county sheriff, Craig McNewel. I had total jurisdictional authority here, but he was still asking his old golfing buddy instead of me.

Craig McNewel had been county sheriff for thirty years, so his relationship with the Crooked Creek longtime mayor went back a few decades. But before moving here to Indiana, McNewel had been a state trooper in Massachusetts. And despite his many years in Jerusalem

County, his accent was as Boston as ever. I secretly suspected he was faking it—or at least exaggerating it—as some sort of method of intimidation. Maybe he thought it gave him an air of authority.

McNewel drew in a deep breath and then said, "I can't remember seeing anything quite like that flower sewn up her arm. I really don't know what to make of it."

Such wisdom, I thought sarcastically to myself.

"So you think I need to call in the FBI or some outside help?" the mayor asked.

Objection, your honor, I thought: *leading the witness.*

"Given that this is ultimately my jurisdiction and therefore my call, can I just weigh in here a moment?" I had their attention. "Now, the flower thing is weird. That's new and definitely strange. But I haven't even been allowed to properly investigate this murder, and you're already talking about bringing in the FBI? Why, sir?"

"I understand you feel like your toes are being stepped on a mite here, but I'm concerned . . ." Burke went around his waist, tucking in his shirt, which came slightly untucked every time he stood up or sat down. "I'm concerned that this might be the work of a serial killer or something more sinister than a regular crime of passion."

Just like a politician to go straight from "a weird murder" to "a serial killer." I was aghast. I'm sure it was obvious.

"A serial killer?" I spat. "I'm sorry, sir, but the qualifications to consider a suspect a serial killer haven't even begun to be met!"

"Sewing a flower into her arm?" he bellowed back. "That's beyond a regular killin'!"

All around the world, in places where regular folk live, there are officials who balk at science and evidence and make decisions based more on what will get or keep them in office than on what's best for the greater good. The mayor knew the citizens were already buzzing about a serial killer. And he wanted a show of force. The FBI slipping into town overnight with bodies, vehicles, and helicopters . . . that would make a lot of people feel safer. Or so he thought. I figured it could just as easily cause a panic.

The elected officials of the city council were no doubt pressuring him, as they themselves were also being pressured by constituents.

"I agree, your honor," I said, hands up, palms out in defensive position. "The sewing of the lily into the arm and the placement of the flower in the hand suggest that this was not an ordinary crime-of-passion murder, for sure. It indicates premeditation, it indicates wrath, but it does *not* indicate a serial criminal nature. I promise you, sir; I did my master's thesis about this very subject."

This wasn't true, because I didn't have a master's degree. But my résumé said I did . . . and my résumé even said it was in the study of the repeating nature of serial killers. I tried not to use this ammunition often, because eventually I figured the mayor or some other enemy would check it out. But it was enough for now to buy me a few more days to investigate before the feds got called in and I got relegated to a bench player or spectator.

"You cannot declare a serial killer," I paused, breathing in and out again, "unless two or more crime scenes share similar evidence, be it fingerprints, style of killing, murder weapon, etc. We don't have any of that! We just have one weird murder!"

The room went quiet for a moment. I thought I had made some good points, but even my own deputies were staring at their files or looking out the window aimlessly. Well, except Skip, who gave me a thumbs-up so obvious that it could have been seen from space.

"Fine," Mayor Burke finally said. "Conduct your investigation. I will not call in any assistance . . . for now. But I expect to be impressed at our next briefing, Sheriff."

● ● ●

The ride back to the office was insufferable if only because all three deputies and I were in the same company SUV. I'd declined a ride back to the church from the mayor because his Cadillac smelled like shoe polish.

Big mistake.

"I thought the receptionist was hot."

"Which one? The girl who buzzed us in?"

"Wait, wait, wait! What about the girl who brought us the waters?"

"Oh, yeah, she looked like a model!"

"That was the same girl."

"Hey, Sheriff, do you think we need to go back to the crime scene?"

"I'd fuck that receptionist in a heartbeat."

"Aren't you married?"

"So?"

"Ha, ha, ha! My dick never gets hard anymore."

"That's a self-burn, bro, not a burn on me. Maybe you've had enough to drink, buddy."

I tried to put it all out of my mind and focus on two things: the road in front of me, and how to solve this fucking murder.

If the FBI were to be called in, I'd not only lose control of the investigation, I'd also lose the next election for sheriff.

The only way to earn the trust of the mayor, the county sheriff, or anyone really . . . I needed to solve this murder quickly and do it on my own without outside help.

But I knew, on some level, that that wasn't going to happen.

CHAPTER 3

INTERVIEWS

By the time we got back to the office, it was after lunchtime, and our reinforcements had arrived. The mayor had called the governor, who had leaned on nearby cities and counties, asking them to send any available officers to help in our investigation.

Someone, probably Maggie, had ordered some sandwiches from the Stoplight Diner—a pretty average diner located at the only intersection in town that had a stoplight. Vicki Clemmons ran the place, and the restaurant served everything from breakfast to burgers to spuds and salads—typical deli/diner fare. Enough on the menu that they weren't able to make any one dish very well, but they could make a bunch of dishes quite averagely.

Crooked Creek had only three restaurants. The Stoplight Diner was arguably the most popular, but we also had Umberto's Italian—a pizza and baked-pasta joint owned by a guy named Bill Boxwell, the least Italian guy you ever met. He was from India, but his American accent sounded sort of Canadian.

Finally, there was M Spot's Chicken. M Spot's had no seating and did only takeout business, but it had been an institution in town for decades. They specialized in fried chicken, pork tenderloins, lake perch, and roast beef Manhattans . . . all the Indiana staples.

At the office, everyone was eating quickly, while still trying to make proper introductions. Handshakes were more important in this part of the world than not speaking with a mouthful. After a half hour, I called it and asked everyone to move into the briefing room. I gathered my notes for about five seconds that felt like five hundred, and then walked to the front of the room.

I stood at the podium, with my own three deputies before me, along with four loaned officers—each of whom looked as thrilled to be here as marshmallows at a fire convention. But they were bodies. And I needed bodies more than I needed minds, at least for now. I almost preferred them to be mindless or stupid; I was used to Skip, so I'd be able to control them more if they weren't too bright.

"Listen up, everyone," I began. "Let's get started so we can get done with this and get out there doing police work. First of all, a heartfelt thanks to our four new officers loaned from nearby precincts. We have Officer Cindy Baxter from next-door Foster County. We have Deputy Greg Grayson from the Perrington Police Department, Officer Brad Banks from Del Plains City Police, and . . ."—I looked at my piece of paper for reference again—"Detective Wayne Neil from Huntersville County."

Other than Cindy, they all looked the same to me; average-height white guys with brown hair. My brain took to calling them Huey, Dewey, and Louie, though it took considerable effort not to say those denotations out loud. I'm not even sure I knew which one was Huey. The point is that they all brought similarly bland personalities and ended up serving similarly bland roles here in our investigation.

I gestured to the back row. "Let's give them a warm welcome. They'll all be staying at Betty Q's, so be sure to make them comfortable in town during this investigation."

Betty Q's was the only bed and breakfast in town. It was run by Betty and Bart Quest and was really the only place in Crooked Creek for your out-of-town guests to stay if you didn't have room for them in your own house. The next best option was a ten-room motel over in Markleville, about eight miles west.

"For now, I think each Crooked Creek officer should pair up with a loaned officer, and our emphasis is on interviewing neighbors, friends, and family. If you see someone speeding on your way to an interview, let it go. If you see someone stabbing an old lady on your way to your interview . . . I hope you know to stop the goddamn car and make an arrest."

The group chuckled a bit.

A hand shot up in the front row, and I knew before turning my head that it was Skip Holmes.

"Skip," I said, somewhat reluctantly.

"What about something between speeding and stabbing? Like . . . what about a purse snatchin'? Or a carjackin'?"

"What?"

"It's a sliding scale, boss. I'm just trying to figure out the line between do and don't stop to arrest."

"How many carjackings have we had since you joined the force?"

"None, sir."

"Just lean toward don't, and if you aren't sure . . . call me on the radio."

"Excellent, sir, thank you very much for the clarification."

I wished for a gag.

Another hand went up in the back row. It was Cindy Baxter, the only female loaned officer. I pointed to her.

"For these interviews, are we concentrating on what people saw in the days leading up to the murder, or just general overall knowledge about the victim? I just want to know what you want us to be inquiring about."

"Thanks, Cindy," I replied. "The answer is 'both.'" I smiled politely. "Ask about general knowledge about the victim. Ask about previous encounters. Ask about anything suspicious in recent days. Ask about anything. Anything at all." I looked around the room and tried my best locker-room speech. "We have a community that is frightened. We have an unusual murder. It's up to us to use our heads and solve this quickly in order to restore peace to the Crooked Creek community."

● ● ●

"So, how'd you get into law enforcement?" I asked as I drove out toward the Hillary place.

Cindy Baxter of Foster County had been paired up with me for the investigation, mostly because . . . well . . . I guess it was assumed that I, as a priest, was the most likely to treat her with respect and equality. Which was true. Skip was too dumb to make a move, but my other deputies were known horndogs, despite both being married.

"My daddy was a cop," she replied. "Up in Michigan—Flint. Never got higher than patrolman, but he put the bug in me for sure. Waking up every day, protecting people, putting your life on the line for little-to-no respect, just because it was the right thing to do . . . I wanted to be a cop almost as early as I learned to say 'da-da.'"

"I'm sure he's very proud of you today," I said on reflex.

"He was very proud of me. He died on duty about eight years ago. Stopped a drunk driver only to be struck by a speeding car," she said. It was detached, as though she'd memorized it or said it so many times that it had become robotic.

"I walked right into that. I am so sorry, Cindy," I said sincerely. One of my biggest faults was rushing into good news as though no bad news lay around any of the nearby corners. It was a very specific variant of foot-in-mouth disease.

"You're fine, sir," she said genuinely. "It was a long time ago. I'm used to talking about it. My husband is a therapist, and he's been really helpful while I work through all that stuff."

"That's excellent. I'm so glad you have such a positive partner." As a priest, I was often the closest most of my parishioners ever got to mental health treatment or therapy. I was a spiritual leader and a psychologist for many. At least a sounding board for some.

"He's the best. He—his name is Todd." She smiled, like a newlywed. "Todd is the best. I'm lucky to have found him. He's not super-excited about this detail, mind you, but he's also too far away in Indy to do anything about it."

"Indy?" I said, surprised. Indianapolis was the capital of the state, for certain, but few in our little town had ever even been there.

"Oh, yeah," she realized. "My husband's practice is in Indianapolis. Not much of a market for psychologists here in the middle of farm country. But in the big city, he's got plenty of clients. He's got relatives in Foster County, and he didn't want me to serve on the force in Indianapolis. Very protective. We only moved here a couple years ago when he finished his PhD."

"Does that mean you two are apart for long stretches?" I was definitely making small talk while we drove, but I also figured it couldn't hurt to learn a bit about the officer who would be my partner for the next week or two, if not for longer.

"Four days at a time." She nodded. "In Indy Monday through Thursday, then back home in Milkwood until Sunday night." Milkwood, the largest city in Foster County, had about four thousand residents.

"Well, I'm sorry that you will miss time with him while we're on this investigation," I said, meaning it.

"I'll miss him too, sir," she said, not sounding finished.

"But?"

She smiled slightly. "First real police work of my entire law-enforcement career, sir. Excited to be of use."

"Excited to have you."

●●●

Tina Hillary's nearest neighbor lived in a house a thousand yards away, across Main Street. His name was Greg Brandon. He owned and farmed about fifteen acres of land, was in his midsixties, and was a widower. He was also a notorious crank-ass, which admittedly could be said of 25 percent of our local population.

"I ain't seen nothing, Sheriff," he repeated over and over. Not like a guilty person lying to cover their tracks, but more like a man who was so worried about his crops that he didn't want to waste time talking need-lessly to police.

"You never saw anything strange over there? Hell, Greg, your kitchen window looks directly over the Hillary homestead." In a small town, every-one was always on a first-name basis, even during a murder investigation.

"Sheriff, I go to bed at six p.m. SIX. P. M. So that I can be up at three a.m. in time to do everything I gotta do just to make sure this fuckin' corn don't get screwed up, just so I can sell enough of it to *maybe* pay off my mortgage this year." He fumed and took a few deep breaths. He'd earned our silence for now. "Now what time you say this murder occurred?"

"We think around eleven p.m.," I said sheepishly.

"I was asleep. I don't know what to tell you. Except that if you'd ever farmed a day in your life, you'd know you were wasting my time before you even rang the dang doorbell." And with that, Mr. Brandon slammed the door.

We turned to walk back to my SUV.

"Friendly folk around here," Cindy remarked.

"Oh, right," I scoffed. "Because Foster County's full of saints and angels."

"Fair enough, sir," she laughed.

We both chuckled as we walked back to the car. Rural farm commu-nities in Indiana were pretty similar; they all had their Greg Brandons.

● ● ●

"Her light was on."

The next closest neighbor to our victim was Jennifer Olney, a widow-turned-farmer who lived back on the same side of Main Street, just about a third of a mile farther out of town. The land between the homes was flat and treeless, and the two ladies frequently spoke by phone—typically to complain about the farming conditions or the tendency of the local post to be delivered late more often than on time.

The post office in Crooked Creek employed fewer people than my office: three, to be exact. Two for deliveries, and one for counter service and sorting. If even one of them got sick or showed up late for work, the entire town's mail delivery was thrown off by hours, sometimes days.

"And that was unusual?" I asked.

"Not for her light to be on," Mrs. Olney continued, "but for it to be on that late. She wasn't a night owl, that one. Lights out by eight p.m., pretty regular. We're both old-lady farmers, you know," she said, smiling. "I even called her to check on her, but no one picked up. I called twice, actually."

I could see in my peripheral vision that Cindy's eyes lit up, and she looked instinctively at me to gauge my reaction. But as a priest, hearing confessions for years, I'd long since perfected the poker face.

"How many times do you think you let it ring before you hung up?" I asked, trying my best to stay calm in the face of possible new evidence.

This question seemed to stump her for a few seconds. She picked up one of her cats and sat down on the arm of the couch to ponder. "I think maybe . . ." The cat jumped down. "Maybe five times? Six?"

"You don't remember for sure?" I double-checked.

"I don't really remember, Sheriff. I'm sorry, sir."

Cindy handed the woman a tissue.

"Let's just pull back a bit," I suggested. "Let's talk about Tina Hillary in general. You two were neighbors. What do you know about her? What did she like? Dislike? Did she ever complain about anyone, or did you ever hear anyone complain about her?"

"Complain?" She seemed shocked. "About Tina? No one who knew Tina would ever have complained about her. That woman was a gift. A saint!"

"She never made any enemies? Never had anyone angry at her?"

Cindy's hand was writing rapidly, taking notes on everything she could, both for the case and for her training as a police officer. She also had a tape recorder running.

"For what? Switching to soybeans instead of corn after her husband died, despite the pressure from the corn cabal? For attending city council meetings and railing against Crooked Creek growth at every turn, trying to keep the town small and free of big money? For burying her husband in the back yard without a permit despite rebukes from local and state officials?" Jennifer Olney's point was well and fully made. Plenty of people might have been angry at our victim.

"Were you angry with her? Did you ever have any grievance? About the soybeans or otherwise?" Cindy asked, as any good police officer would—unless they had read the room correctly.

"The hell you say?" You could tell Mrs. Olney was legitimately upset.

"Oh, boy," I breathed, barely audible, knowing what was in store for Cindy.

"Listen here, young lady. You may know how to be a cop, but you don't know shit about farming life in Indiana. Here, if you farm, your neighbors are your kin. Your lifeblood. Sharing information about fertilizer, weather, pesticides . . . it's fucking crucial! You idiots think we're all enemies because we all farm, but we're like the original gangsters, man . . . farming only lives at all because it lives through each of us. We compete complete . . . we all fail. We share information and work together. We all thrive. We learned that shit long before you assholes invented the Better Business Bureau." With that, Mrs. Olney shut the door, with emphasis.

"Well, now we've both had a door slammed in our face today," I said with a smile, hoping to make Cindy feel better.

"And still no closer to solving the case," she sighed aloud.

"Don't be so sure," I offered. "Now we know the two nearest neighbors saw and heard nothing, and one of them was in fairly frequent contact with our victim. Which means that whoever did this went about it in sneaky fashion. No big sights or sounds."

"So we're looking for a ninja," she replied, opening the passenger door to my police truck and climbing inside.

I climbed in a second later, shutting my door and starting the engine before responding.

"No, Officer," I said. "We are merely looking for someone who knew about the neighbors, their views, and their schedules. We're looking at a murder committed by either a burglar prepared for every scenario at all times who was suddenly surprised by an old woman . . . or we're looking at something that was premeditated."

CHAPTER 4

TENDERLOIN

AFTER DRIVING THROUGH M SPOT's for some pork tenderloin sandwiches and coleslaw, Cindy and I found ourselves back at police headquarters, sharing one of the tables in the main meeting room.

"This is pork?" she asked, for the third time.

"It's a pork chop . . . hammered and slammed flat, breaded like a chicken breast, and quick-fried. Look, you're losing a lot of your Indiana street cred here. It's leaking profusely."

She laughed. "I'll be honest. I moved here from New England and mostly ate what my husband ate in Indianapolis before we bought the place in Foster County." She looked the monster sandwich over. "I've never even heard of this thing, but let's go."

Now, I'll be honest. To an outsider, particularly an adult, a traditional pork tenderloin sandwich probably doesn't taste like much at all. It was created as a low-cost way to imitate a chicken fried steak or even a fried chicken sandwich. It never really caught on outside of Indiana, Illinois, and Iowa, but within that area it was quite a popular dish and still is to this day. I'd been as confused as Cindy on my first encounter with the sandwich.

"New England," I mused while she chewed. "I didn't think you had much Indiana in your voice." I took a rather large bite of my own sandwich—not hitting any bun—and we chewed together in silence for a few seconds.

Skip Holmes returned just then with his case partner, Officer Brad Banks from Del Plains. Brad, who I called Huey, had been on the force for a handful of years. He seemed competent without appearing exceptional.

Skip was mid-story when the door opened. ". . . and you have never seen a slipperier pig," he said. "I swear to God!"

The frustration was visible on Banks's face. I knew that look. Anyone who had spent a single shift with Skip would know this look.

Both were carrying their own M Spot's to-go bags.

"So, what do you think?" I managed to get out before Cindy took a second bite.

"It's very interesting," she said. "I don't think I've ever had anything like it." And yet, with that, she took another bite straightaway, a big one.

"If this case goes on for more than a few weeks, you'll be living and dying by these things," I predicted.

Deputy Travis Kent returned just then with Deputy Greg Grayson, our loaner from the Perrington Police Department. Grayson, who in my mind was Dewey, had a mustache that was too large, and he walked like he'd just gotten off of a horse. They tossed a pizza box from Umberto's on the table and sat down next to Skip and Banks.

Travis was my most reliable deputy. He had experience, he took the job seriously, and he was in it for the long haul, looking to make sheriff one day on his own. His only flaw was his love of chasing tail, which meant he had something in common with roughly 75 percent of the police officers in the state, perhaps in the country. Cops love the ladies who love the badge.

As I watched Travis and the others eat and laugh, I wondered what they'd learned. I thought about the interviews they'd conducted and what leads they might have turned up. My imagination ran wild, even while my brain knew there was likely no new pertinent information whatsoever.

Maggie manned the reception desk, eating leftovers she'd brought from home. Maggie always ate leftovers or home-prepared meals for lunch. "Too much sodium," she would always say when asked why she didn't visit local restaurants. I'd heard about health nuts and had seen some characters in TV shows and movies that only ate plants and avoided grease and fat. Maggie was the closest thing our town had to a health nut.

Finally, Deputy Gene returned with his loaner officer partner, Detective Wayne Neil from Huntersville County. Wayne was my Louie, and the only thing that distinguished him from the other loaner officers was the fact that his police cap was two sizes too big.

Deputy Gene—we called him Deputy Gene, but Gene was his first name; his last name was Harris—had served in law enforcement in the township of Crooked Creek for forty-three years.

He'd never aspired to be sheriff and never sought a role higher than deputy. He was known to be kind and fair, but he was a firm follower of the law. And he knew literally everyone in town. Sometimes he'd stop by the local pickup game and shoot hoops with the kids—something he'd been doing for decades—though he missed a lot more than he made these last few years, not that the kids would admit to it.

Everyone loved Gene.

I'd paired Deputy Gene with Detective Neil out of respect. Detective Neil was the most experienced officer we'd been loaned, and he'd worked and solved murder cases on his own already. Pairing him with our most experienced and knowledgeable officer seemed like a way to show that I understood his level of expertise and how lucky we were to have him, even if I couldn't remember his name or tell him apart from the other male newcomers.

Neil sat down next to the others and grabbed a slice of pizza, while Gene approached our table and sat down next to Cindy.

"Some pretty big sandwiches there," he said, nodding at our food. Gene was notorious for being a scavenger. Some thought he was cheap, but I think he just liked free food, and the variety that came from snagging other people's leftovers.

No one had ever seen him reach into a trash can or dumpster for food, but the workplace had a suspicious lack of food garbage.

It got to be such common knowledge that we would often drop our leftovers on Gene's desk as we walked by, whether he was there at the time or not. And sure enough, without fail, you'd get your dish washed and returned within twenty-four hours, along with a thank-you note.

I wasn't really hungry today, to be honest. Maybe it was the gruesome nature of the murder case. Maybe I was just stressed out. I'd only eaten half my sandwich, so I slid it over to Gene with a smile.

Cindy was six bites into her tenderloin, clearly loving it more than she had expected to. "Deputy Gene here," I told her as she chewed, "his last name is Harris, but sometimes around here we call him Hoover. Deputy Gene Hoover. Because he vacuums up leftovers in the blink of an eye."

Cindy smiled, putting a hand up to her mouth to prevent a little crumb from escaping.

"You're laughing," I said as I stood up, "but he's already done." I pointed at Gene's empty sandwich wrapper, and Cindy gaped in awe. She looked up at me, and I nodded.

"You still working on that?" Gene asked her.

She turned the sandwich away from him, turned her back, and took another large bite.

I laughed as I walked to the corner to address the room.

"Ten more minutes," I shouted, quieting everyone down. "Ten more minutes, and we'll meet over here in the conference room and break down all that we've learned today. I hope you all recorded what you were able to and took good notes. We're going to need to let information drive this case." I paused, realizing I was already going into debrief mode. "Anyway, ten more minutes, and we'll see everyone inside."

I looked back at the table to see Gene finishing Cindy's pork tenderloin sandwich. I panned over and saw her smiling and holding up a $5 bill.

Shit, Gene, I thought, *the whole sandwich is only $3.95 at M Spot's!*

● ● ●

The briefing started out with Cindy and me covering our standoffish encounters with both of the victim's closest neighbors. Cindy seemed shy or preoccupied, so I did most of the talking. I was a priest. I preached every week. I was used to doing most of the talking. In fact, I loved it, and I was sad we didn't have more solid information to share so I could talk even longer.

Skip Holmes and Brad Banks presented their findings next. Skip had taken an excessive amount of notes, as usual. They'd also recorded their interviews.

And look, every interview in this case was important, but I had definitely sent Skip to interview the witnesses I considered to be the least important. They'd been sent to interview church members and Sunday School friends of Tina Hillary's, for background and color information.

Mrs. Hillary attended my church, as it happened—though the odds were still one in three. I knew sooner or later I would have to submit to questioning myself, but I would cross that bridge when I came to it. For now, I wasn't a priest and potential witness, I was only the sheriff. Besides, Tina had never come to confession, had never held a position in the church, and had never invited me over for dinner. Our interactions had been limited.

The church family had a lot to say, and the pair of officers had managed to complete only five interviews before heading back to the station for lunch. They talked to the organist, Fred Freel, a ninety-year-old man who'd been at the church longer than almost anyone. They talked to Mrs. Joiner, the Senior Sunday School teacher; Herbert, the janitor; Patricia, the church secretary; and Benny, the choir director.

Their conclusions after five interviews? That Tina Hillary was beloved by everyone, and no one could think of any reason someone might want to kill her. She'd even recently donated a healthy sum to the church children's department to fund a few years of Bible School.

She seemed like a saint.

Kent and Grayson would have gone next, if they'd accomplished anything more than a flat tire. No interviews. They'd been sent to talk to select neighbors south of town; a long-shot attempt that someone caught a glimpse of something. Instead, they'd hit a nail somewhere near the cemetery and spent the morning waiting on a tow truck.

Crooked Creek had only two tow trucks, and there'd been a wreck just north of town on State Road 17 involving multiple cars. So Kent and Grayson waited for three hours, smoking cigarettes and passing the time with chitchat. It wasn't their fault, really, but I couldn't help but think of the wasted payroll hours, paid for by the citizens.

Anyway . . . Deputy Gene and Detective Neil finished up the post-lunch debrief. They'd been sent to interview the Rook club. Mrs. Hillary went once a week to a traveling game of Rook—a card game similar to euchre and popular among religious people in the Midwest as an alterna-tive to using "face cards." Participants at the game Mrs. Hillary attended consisted of our victim, Mrs. Vickery, Mrs. Ruth, and Mrs. Oaks. They'd been playing together for nearly eight years.

None of them seemed like suspects, though Gene did note that Mrs. Oaks had been standoffish "at best." But even so, all three had plenty of good things to say about Tina Hillary. She was known to be philan-thropic with her money, even though she didn't have much. She was also apparently a wicked Rook player, who followed the rules to the letter and suffered no fools—this appeared to be the center of the trouble between her and Mrs. Oaks: Mrs. Oaks had, on a few occasions, been accused of cheating—everyone said so—each time, accused by our victim.

Detective Neil added that all the ladies seemed defensive and closed-off, and that Gene had eaten leftover bits from at least two interviewees' plates.

Just as I was about to summarize and then send the troops off for an afternoon of more interviewing, a call came in to Maggie from the county 911 dispatch.

"Sheriff!" she shouted, having no trouble overpowering the din of the conference room. "911!"

"Everybody sit down and shut the hell up!" It was Skip, my dumbest deputy, who was also reliable for a few important things, like respecting the rules of the police office, written and unwritten. His voice bellowed twice as loud as you'd think a skinny man could muster. And everyone shut up and sat the hell down.

"Go, Mags," I barked. I feared the worst. I feared it was another murder, and not just another murder, but another one with a flower sewn into the victim. I held my breath for what seemed like minutes. Finally Maggie answered.

"Naked man on the run with a shovel, sir. Fifth and Eubanks," she reported.

I sighed audibly. "Okay, that sounds like Buzz Martinson," I announced.

Buzz Martinson was easily the best athlete ever to come out of Crooked Creek. In high school, he was a pitching ace in baseball season and a dead-aim placekicker for the football team in the autumn months. He made all-state in both sports all four of his high school years.

No local kid had ever held such promise or achieved so much at such a young age. He was as famous in our tiny town as Larry Bird was in French Lick.

At least, he had been.

There wasn't anything selfish about Buzz. On the baseball diamond, he spread the work around as best he could as a pitcher. As a batter, he made most pitchers look stupid, spraying the ball around the field almost at will.

Until the accident.

Buzz had been in a car with his older sister Greta and his best friend and baseball teammate, Sean. Some people think they had the radio up too loud. Some people think the train's horn wasn't used. Others still think the intersection's bells signaling an oncoming train weren't loud enough. Regardless, the train hit the car, dragged it for half a mile, and killed two of the three occupants.

Only Buzz, the driver, survived. He'd been thrown through the windshield on impact because he hadn't been wearing a seat belt. And he'd slowly gone mad with guilt ever since. That's not fair—he probably had complex mental-health issues related to the post-traumatic stress disorder from the crash itself. And then he went off to war. He'd had more than his share of troubles in this life, and it sometimes manifested in strange public behaviors, often involving nudity.

When he stayed on his meds, Buzz was a solid citizen of Crooked Creek. He bagged groceries at the market and even came to church regularly. But when he went off the meds, he was unpredictable. He'd certainly seen the inside of our local jail cells before.

"I'll take this one," I announced. "Everyone else get back out to the rest of your interviews. We'll meet back here at five for a recap. Oh! And the ladies of my church are doing a potluck here for dinner for all of us, so . . . go work up an appetite."

"Sir," Cindy asked. "You want me to stick with you, or group up with someone else?"

I stopped to think about it. I didn't want her to have to deal with Martinson's nudity and probable erratic behavior. But I also didn't think she could handle our afternoon interviews on her own without me. I wasn't even sure she could find the locations of the next interviews—not because she was a woman, but because she was completely new to our town and largely new to Indiana as a whole.

"Come with me," I finally breathed. "Just . . . know that we are going to pick up a naked man, and you might see some stuff."

She laughed as she walked toward the passenger door of my company SUV. "I've seen naked men before, sir," she assured me. "I'm rarely distracted or impressed by the nudity itself."

And that prompted relative silence for the drive up to the phoned-in last sighting of the naked shovel man. We drove to Fifth and Eubanks, where we spotted something in the middle of the road.

It was a passed-out Buzz Martinson, his shovel, and a sleepy raccoon . . . all gathered in a precious little ball directly in the middle of the intersection.

I put the vehicle in PARK and sighed again. "Reach in that glove box," I said. "Grab two pairs of gloves." I paused and said a quiet prayer. "Let's grab the raccoon first," I managed to say without laughing.

CHAPTER 5

THE HOMILY

"GOOD-BYE IS ALWAYS TOUGH," I said to open my first sermon since the passing of Tina Hillary, congregant of this very church.

We'd already done the formal funeral service and burial out at the gravesite, but both of those were sparsely attended midweek affairs. Weekend Mass was always well attended, and I knew many members would have Tina on their minds. It seemed right to preach about the issues at hand.

"When you know a good-bye is coming, you can plan for it. You can steel your emotions. You can take time to do or say things you always wanted to. But not all good-byes are planned."

I heard some sniffling as I looked out over the congregation. The church was packed today. Fun fact everyone probably knows: church services are usually most packed at holidays and after the death of a prominent citizen. Something about the death of someone in your own close-knit community causes one to remember their own mortality.

In the very back row on the left, I spotted several officers: Skip, Cindy, Kent, Gene. It was a day off from the investigation, and no one was required to attend church, so it was nice to see them here.

"Some good-byes sneak up on you. Assault you. Some feel like a knife in the back." I coughed a bit, mostly clearing my throat. "The Bible teaches us to be ready every day. Even the mundane days where it seems as if nothing could possibly happen. But those are the very days when things like this happen, and if we aren't prepared . . . we lose it all."

The congregation cried and sniffled in appropriate proportions. I was getting through to them. Which is all any preacher hopes to do.

"No one knows the day or the hour," I paraphrased from scripture. "Your own day or hour is unknown. And so we act accordingly. Keep your heart pure and loyal to God every day, because you do not know when your time will come.

"Tina Hillary knew this," I continued, knowing that dropping her name would evoke even more emotions in my congregation. "She lived every day the way she thought Christ wanted her to."

A murmur of agreement pulsed through the crowd.

"Last month, she paid the rent for two in-need families, through our church's Poverty Recovery mission." More nods and murmurs in the congregation. "Two weeks ago, she dropped a check in the mail to this church in the amount of ten times her regular monthly tithing donation. When I asked her about it, she said she felt like some families were going to struggle with their giving in the coming months, and she wanted to make space for them to feel okay about it.

"You need look no further for an example of Biblical living than Tina. She set the bar high." I paused. "Let us all strive to be just a little bit more like Jesus tomorrow. Now let's pray."

● ● ●

I pulled into Betty Q's parking lot, shut off the engine, and sighed. Another Sunday afternoon, another meal playing the role of priest.

A priest or pastor is a leader of a community and sometimes gets celebrated. Everyone wants to get to know the priest better. Everyone wants to get on his good side.

And everyone wants to have him over for Sunday dinner.

I'd been here about ten years, and I was still working through a back-logged list of parishioners who had invited me over for Sunday dinner. Some Sundays I took off and kept to myself, of course, to recharge or reboot. But not many. I considered it a part of my Fatherly duties to visit with the families in my care and break bread with them. Some Sundays there were special circumstances that caused a potential lunch host to be bumped ahead on the list. Like today.

Betty Q figured that since she was housing and hosting our four out-of-town officers assisting in the murder investigation, she ought to have me over as well, to fully get God's blessing on her side.

And look, I don't want to complain, because free food is great. It's free. But in rural Indiana in a town this small, how many of these housewives do you think are truly good cooks? Whatever percentage you guessed . . . it's lower than that.

Thankfully, Betty Q was an incredible cook—which accounted for her extremely high score with the local Better Business Bureau. Her food was rated higher than any of the three official restaurants in town.

I got out and was about to shut the car door when I saw Mayor Burke's Cadillac pull in next to my squad car. "Dammit," I muttered under my breath at the realization that Betty had invited the mayor as well as me.

I shut my door, looked up, and smiled as he got out of his car.

"Oh, shove it, Solomon." He slammed his door. "I don't want to be here any more than you want me to. But the woman makes a beef and noodles that's fit for God in Heaven himself." He walked past me and banged on the screen door, even though there was an obvious doorbell.

What a dickhead.

● ● ●

Betty Q's Bed & Breakfast had six available rooms for guests. It was built in an early 1900s farmhouse that had been renovated back in the early seventies. Betty and Bart had sold off most of the farmland to pay for the renovations, leaving only a few acres to pasture and garden food for their guests.

Our four guest police officers each had their own room, of course—paid for in advance by the week by my police force. The fifth room was, somewhat ironically, being occupied by Chris Hillary, Tina's son, and his wife, Fran. They'd flown into Indianapolis and driven up for the funeral. I even saw them in church this morning. The sixth and final room was being used by an out-of-towner Betty Q called Merritt. He'd been staying with them for a few weeks, working odd construction jobs until he could get his own apartment in town. His chair remained empty at lunch, which I was told was normal on a Sunday.

"Oh, baby," Detective Neil let out as Betty started around the table, dropping buttery mounds of mashed potatoes into the center of everyone's bowl.

Deputy Grayson was practically salivating. "My momma ain't made this since Daddy had his heart attack ten years ago, and my wife can't make it for shit."

Beef and noodles is a surprisingly simple and shockingly starchy meal. It's seasoned ground beef—or roast if you want—with wide egg noodles atop mashed potatoes. And it's every bit as delicious as it is rich and heavy. I usually carved out time for a nap whenever I had the dish, as I had for later this afternoon.

"I'm curious about how the investigation is going," Chris Hillary said suddenly. It didn't even take five minutes. Not everyone had even been served their food. I mean, I knew the son of the victim was going to ask about the case. I just didn't expect it to happen so fast. Perhaps I should have.

Mayor Burke immediately took a bite of his mashed potato bed, not even waiting for his beef and noodles. He was just filling his mouth so he wouldn't have to talk. I smiled a bit when I saw him go red from the sheer heat of the potatoes.

"Um." I really wasn't sure how to proceed, so I took a moment to think through the situation. "I'm happy to update you on the case after lunch, Mr. Hillary. I just think that, in light of our situation and our hosts—"

"There are only cops here, and the mayor and me and my wife!" he interrupted.

His wife, Fran, looked at her lap with intense focus, determined *not* to meet any gaze around the table.

"Indeed," I allowed. "But also Betty Q and Bart."

Just then, Betty Q was sloshing a juicy ladleful of beef and noodles into my bowl, covering the potatoes and sending steam up toward my face. It smelled heavenly. "Oh, sonny," she said with cheer, "I don't mind. Y'all talk about the case all you like. I learned long ago to tune out my customers' conversations, anyway. It's just not polite to eavesdrop."

And that was a knockout blow for my argument, and the case would now be discussed. Over lunch. I made a note to do what I could to steer things toward the mundane details and not the graphic ones that might cause one or more of us to revisit this lunch later.

"This wasn't the ordinary murder you led me to believe," Chris said, speaking directly to me.

"I did leave out some details on our initial phone call, yes," I admitted. "But only out of concern for your emotional well-being."

"Emotional well-being?!" he spat. "I got on a plane thinking Momma had had a heart attack maybe. I landed only to find out some freak sewed her up with a flower!"

"Excellent mealtime conversation," Cindy breathed, just loud enough to be heard.

Betty had made it around to Cindy and ladled a steaming portion of beef and noodles over her potatoes.

"Why don't we try to keep it to mealtime-worthy topics for now, and if you want to discuss particulars, we can do that after the meal," I said.

"Fine," he agreed flatly. "I just don't understand why you had to lie to me."

"It seemed obscene to go into those details seconds after you'd learned of her death. If I erred in judgment, I do apologize. I promise I was only thinking of your mindset as you traveled across the country."

There was a silence that I took to mean either forgiveness or at least acceptance of my answer on the part of Mr. Hillary. For a moment, there were only the sounds of silverware and chewing.

"This is delicious, Mrs. Q," Detective Neil said, mouth still full.

"Mmmhmm," Grayson agreed.

I decided to take a bite. The beauty of the mashed potatoes in this dish was their ability to help you contain noodles on your fork that would otherwise be flopping around all willy-nilly in a pasta-only dish like spaghetti. It was incredible. Earthy beefy sauce, slippery noodles, and buttery potatoes combined to make a single bite of utter joy. I got to enjoy it all of one second.

"So, are there any suspects?"

I sighed internally, swallowed quickly, and reached for my iced tea for a quick washdown before finally responding. "No. Not at this time."

"No? That's all you got? No?"

"It's a murder investigation, sir. We have no witnesses, no motive, no leads. It's going to be a process." I took another bite, hoping it would slow him down.

"Maybe we need some more resources," barked Mayor Burke. I could hear the grin in his voice. "Maybe we don't have enough experience with this kind of thing."

"I like the sound of that," Chris agreed quickly.

The other cops at the table—all on loan from nearby departments—murmured a bit.

"Or maybe it's only been five days," I reminded everyone. "I know we solved that gas station robbery last spring really quickly, but the perpetrator did pass out in the parking lot with his pants down, so . . . we had a little easier go on that investigation. Unfortunately, our suspect in this case did not pass out at the scene of the crime, nor leave any obvious clues, so we are going to have to work to find them."

Suddenly Fran, Chris's wife, stood up from the table and walked out of the dining room.

"See," the younger Hillary said, gesturing after her but speaking to me. "You've upset my wife." He then stood and followed after her.

If Deputy Gene were here, he'd have just slid their plates over to his own setting and finished their meals for them.

"I apologize, Betty," I said as she came back in from the kitchen.

"For what?" she asked. Then she winked and asked, "Anyone need more sweet tea?"

CHAPTER 6

AN OLD PRIEST

THE TENSION AND FRUSTRATION around lunch had left me unable to finish my meal. So I skipped the planned nap and took a drive out to call on Wendall Warren, my mentor.

Wendall had been priest of Jerusalem Independent Catholic Church prior to my arrival. He'd retired at sixty-eight years old and moved one county over to a little town called Fullerton. He said he felt it was important to get away from the church and allow me to fully lead the parish, but that he had too much Indiana in him to move too far away. Fullerton had a small Catholic church, and he was happy to be near and far from Crooked Creek all at once.

He'd hand-selected me from all the applicants and had been an official mentor to me for my first few years. Now it was unofficial, which only meant the Church had stopped paying him; I was still seeking his advice whenever I hit a rock.

It was a hot summer day, so I drove with the windows down. I wouldn't be able to hear the radio much with all that wind, but I rarely listened to the radio in the car anyway. I didn't want to miss something from the police radio or some other sound in the community that could signal trouble.

Field after field, mostly corn, some soybeans, every mile looked the same as the last. It was the thing that drove a lot of people crazy about Indiana: the never-ending flatness. The repetitive scenery went by as if it were being reused, like the background in old cartoons whenever characters ran.

I loved it. I loved the simplicity of it. I loved how the nearest big city felt thousands of miles away.

I'd heard a story at a sheriff's conference a few years back about a guy who robbed a bank in Turnble, a town even smaller than Crooked Creek up in northwest Indiana, in the dead of winter. He made off with a few thousand dollars in cash from the drawers, and raced into the vast and empty farm country. Endless enormous snow-covered white squares as far as the eye could see. After five hours, he was so lost that he called 911 so he wouldn't freeze to death. I wasn't sure I believed the story, but there was no doubting that people could get lost on the country roads of the Hoosier State if they didn't know where they were going.

Twenty miles later, I was pulling up Wendall's driveway, with his dog, Bones, running to greet me. I use the word *running* loosely. Bones was fifteen years old and moved as if he were twenty-five. Wendall often joked about which of them was going to hang on longer.

I parked my SUV in the dirt driveway behind Wendall's beat-up old Ford truck. (Now, there's something I was pretty sure was going to die soon.) As I came around the back of the car and to the front sidewalk, Bones finally arrived, tail wagging. He was half blind but still knew me whenever I showed up, I suppose by smell.

"Bones," I heard from behind the screen door. "Bones, you let him by, now. Come on, boy."

I walked up the two steps to the concrete front porch and smiled at my friend behind the screen.

"Father," he said warmly.

I smiled. "Father."

He waved his hand dismissively. "How many times do I have to tell you I'm not a formal priest anymore?"

"We are never out of his service," I replied. We opened most of our conversations this way.

"Oh, I don't have time for all this; I've got arthritis. You get in here; and Bones, you come too!" He opened the door and hugged me as I came through. I could feel how much skinnier he'd become since my last visit in the embrace. It made me sad momentarily.

Bones went immediately to his spot on the large living room couch. Wendall had told me he spent most of his days on this couch, flipping channels, reading the paper, sometimes calling someone on the phone.

Near the couch, perpendicular to it, was the recliner that I always sat in when we would visit together. I didn't know how many visitors Wendall got in the average week, but I assumed it was a few. He'd been beloved in the church and still was to this day. But no matter how many visitors, he always made me feel like the only—or most important—one.

"So, what's new with you, Father Lancaster?" he sighed as he eased back into the couch.

I sat in the recliner as usual and countered: "You know darn well what's new with me, old man. Why do you always act like Crooked Creek news doesn't reach your ears before I'm able to drive here?"

"I like to give you an opportunity to tell me what you'd like to talk about, rather than just immediately asking about the latest town gossip." At least he was being honest.

"Well, that's very generous of you," I said sarcastically.

"Go on, son. What's bothering you most?" he asked, with love in his voice.

I sat for a moment, cycling through the last week's events. "I've got this freakish murder, no leads, a parishioner dead. I've never been less sure where one of my jobs ends and the other begins."

He struck a match and lit his pipe. Lots of priests smoked a pipe now and then, because it was the only form of smoking people of faith considered dignified. So they didn't look down on it or consider it a nasty habit. A priest who smoked cigarettes . . . well . . . he had to hide it.

"She really had a flower sewn into her arm?" he asked, not quite sure where the line between fact and gossip was drawn on this one.

I merely nodded grimly.

"You saw this?"

"I'm the sheriff."

"Right," he said, as though he'd forgotten. "I've never heard of anything like that."

"Father," I said to him, still using the title out of respect, "what's the weirdest death you can remember ever taking place in these parts?"

He'd been priest at the parish for almost thirty years, so I knew he had tons of experiences that I hadn't had.

"Nothing like this," he said almost immediately. He puffed on his pipe while he thought some more. Bones inched over, and Wendall started rubbing him out of habit. "I had a guy get chewed up by his tractor once, but two witnesses saw him fall on his own. He was drunk, of course."

I felt like I'd heard the story on that one before.

"Once," he half-chuckled, "we had a guy pull his pants down to pee outside the bar, but he peed on an electric fence and fried himself naked in the snow." He paused another moment to reflect. "But nothing like this, kid. Nothing like this."

"I have no leads. I have no witnesses. I have no evidence." I was talking to myself as much as I was talking with Wendall, though I think that was always the case when I came here. "How can a town this small have such a bizarre killing?"

"You're worried about your reputation as sheriff if you can't solve it?" he probed.

"Eh. Maybe."

"You're worried you have a conflict of interest as a local priest?"

"Sort of."

He lit his pipe again and sucked in some more smoke before parsing it out in tiny waves. "Or maybe it's something deeper," he finally pondered aloud.

"Like what?" I was honestly curious to hear his thoughts. He'd always been good at narrowing a discussion and targeting my underlying issues.

"Perhaps you don't feel like you deserve either of the jobs you have." He said it so calm and flat that it was impossible to be offended, and yet it still kind of hurt.

"And what if I don't?" I replied earnestly.

Another few puffs, and then: "Deserving or not, these are both jobs you have, and you owe it to the congregants and citizens to do the best you can at both of them. God doesn't ask us to be well trained or ready. He just asks us to act."

"So you're not going to tell me what to do?"

"Do I ever?"

"No." I smiled.

Typically, I would talk with Wendall and then have some kind of clarity or epiphany hours later, and this time would be no different. He wasn't there to give me the answers; he was there to be my mentor and counsel and guide me. My success as a priest and a sheriff could not be pinned on him; it was on me.

"Okay, then," he smiled. "Now, what about a confession?"

Even priests needed confession, and I usually turned to Wendall. "You know," I dodged, "I can come visit you just as your friend. I'm not always here because I need confession."

"Ah," he chided like a schoolteacher. "I am your friend and your priest, and one cannot be separated from the other. I would not be doing my duty to God if I didn't hear your confession."

I thought some measure of his self-worth was tied up in still being able to offer his priestly services now and then. He'd done it for so long; maybe he didn't know how to stop. "Sure, okay," I said. "Let me get the screen."

For in-home confessions, which were not as rare as you might think, some priests kept a simple room divider to serve as a confessional screen. I placed it between us so we were out of each other's field of view.

"Bless me, Father, for I have sinned. It has been. . . ." I paused, trying to remember.

"Nine weeks," Wendall offered wryly.

"It has been nine weeks since my last confession. Wow, has it really been that long?"

"Don't lose focus. I know your sins are always mundane, but they are still sins and must be confessed to keep you reconciled with God and the Church."

"Right." I scanned my memory for things to confess. In truth, I lived much too boring a life to do a lot of sinning. "I saw a very pretty woman in the grocery store the other day."

"Seeing a pretty woman is not a sin."

"She was really pretty, though."

"Did you lust for her? In your heart?"

"I don't think so."

"If you don't think so, then you didn't. It's no sin to be attracted to a beautiful woman. You don't think Jesus ever found a woman attractive?"

"Sure, I mean, objectively. But not . . . sexually."

"Jesus was human in every way we are. He was tempted by every single temptation you have or will ever face. He wasn't half human and half God; he was all of both! Of course he found women sexually attractive. It's not even a question."

I pondered that one silently for a moment.

"What else?" he groused.

I wondered if he'd been this rushed in confession when he'd been a practicing priest, or if his age and deteriorating health were causing him to lose patience.

"I coveted my neighbor's garage."

"You coveted . . . a garage?"

"He never has to warm up his car or scrape snow off the windshield. Ever. No worries about rain on the vehicle or the groceries inside. A garage is a luxury."

"I've heard enough," he sighed. "Say a few 'Hail Marys' on your drive home and call it even. I miss the days of hearing some really fascinating sins."

●●●

I got home by 3:30. I didn't technically have any church responsibilities for the rest of the day. Jerusalem Independent held Sunday evening services only once a month, on the first of the month, and we were halfway through this August.

I decided to take a nap after all, knowing it guaranteed a late night of nachos and caffeine-free cola.

Zacchaeus, my cat, jumped up on the bed and curled up inside the bend of my knees—his favorite spot. We both slept for three blissful uninterrupted hours.

●●●

By 6:30, I was awake and on the couch, watching the latest episode of *Pinkerton P.I.* It was an average detective show, focusing on the Pinkerton cops trying to stop train robberies and other threats to the railroad. It starred a guy whose name always escaped me but whose face was quite familiar. He'd been in movies, I think. I love crime shows like *Murder, She Wrote* and the old-school *Perry Mason*, so *Pinkerton P.I.* was right up my alley. I tried not to miss an episode.

I had a VCR, given to me by a church member the year before, but I was too afraid of it to try to use it. Too many buttons. I did my best to catch the show live. The VCR sat under the TV, but it wasn't hooked up to anything; it was just for show in case a church member stopped by.

This week, the *Pinkerton P.I.* case was a murder in a railway town. Two witnesses blamed a local cowboy, while two other witnesses blamed an outlaw from a nearby free-grazing outfit. I enjoyed watching the crimes get solved in the days before forensics and autopsies. It felt simpler, though I suppose, if I'm honest, Wild West justice was probably often misapplied, and innocent folks got punished for no reason.

Eh, who cares? I thought.

I had a steaming plate of Indiana nachos before me and plenty of television to entertain me for a bit.

Let's talk about Indiana nachos for a moment, though. Indiana nachos in the 1980s . . . well, they meant the best. They had good intentions. They were ignorant but wholesome. No one was trying to stomp on authentic Mexican flavors. Hell, we had to drive an hour and a half from Crooked Creek to Ft. Wayne if we wanted to eat at a Mexican restaurant. And wasn't nobody from here driving *that far* just to have Mexican food.

And, of course, Ft. Wayne's Mexican food was a far cry from the real thing, since Mexico was a couple days' drive from Indiana anyway. The point is that Indiana nachos weren't Mexican food in the slightest, but they were as close as rural farmland Indiana could come.

So . . . recipe for Indiana nachos: Single-layer some generic round tortilla chips on a microwavable plate—bonus points if the chips are stale. Open a can of refried beans and drip-drop some of that shit onto the chips. Finally, cover generously in shredded cheese—the milder the cheddar, the better. Nuke in the microwave for one minute, and enjoy.

Most eighties Indiana kids thought this was authentic Mexican food because their parents didn't know any better and because it tastes awesome. I like to toss a few shakes of tabasco on mine.

Inevitably, halfway through a plate of Indiana nachos, the rest needs re-microwaving. And it was during this half-plate-of-nacho microwaving that I received a police dispatch call from Maggie.

"Shit," I said instead of "Hello" as I lifted the receiver to my face.

"Hello?" Skip said cautiously. He probably expected me to be asleep. It was 11:30 p.m., and he wasn't wrong; I should have been in bed for sure.

"Skip?"

"Sheriff, sir? Is that you?"

"Just . . . spill it, Skip. I'm in the middle of a meal."

"You may want to put that meal up, Sheriff. I got some real . . . unsettling news for you."

"Hang on!" I walked a few steps to the trash can and dumped my entire plate of food in. I tossed the dishes in the sink and moved to my recliner. "Okay," I said as I breathed in deep. "Hit me."

"Sir. We got another body. Another weird set of circumstances."

I panicked for a moment. Then I gathered myself and went into sheriff mode.

"Another lily sewn up the arm of the victim?" I ventured.

"Naw," Skip replied. "This is something else entirely, sir."

CHAPTER 7

THE NEXT BODY

"WELL, SHIT," I thought out loud.

Seventeen-year-old Katie McGuire lay mostly naked across a narrow section of Crooked Creek like a bridge. And I mean the actual creek; yes, there is an actual Crooked Creek, upon which the township is named. That shouldn't surprise you if you've been paying attention so far.

Floodlights illuminated the area, powered by the cigarette lighters in the two cruisers parked ten yards away. A few flashlights were in use as well, so there was no question that we had another murder on our hands.

A crude patch of mud and leaves covered her groin; I couldn't be sure if we had a modest killer or if one of my men who first discovered the scene had covered her up. Her crotch turned out to be moot.

Her hands, however, had been removed postmortem and replaced by daffodils.

This time there was no sewing. And there were a number of other differences between this and the death of Mrs. Hillary. The body was outdoors instead of inside, to begin with.

"Nobody found her. . . ." I trailed off. "Nobody found any body parts nearby that might have been removed?"

"No," they answered in unison.

"You've taken all the pictures?" I asked, turning away.

"Yes, sir," Skip replied.

"Body and surrounding area?"

"Yes, sir."

"Footprint molds and photos? Tire prints same?"

Gene replied quickly. "Already done, sir."

"Then cover her up, for God's sake," I managed to get out before vomiting into the brush. My mind continued working even as I heaved.

But the flowers . . . the flowers told a different story. There almost certainly was a connection between the two deaths; anyone would think so.

I was more certain than ever that I was in over my head. But I wasn't ready to relent and give over to Mayor Burke.

"You need to leave this crime scene alone until the FBI can get here," he bellowed, oblivious to the rules of procedure and full of his own self.

"Sir," I barked, "if you want to call in the FBI, you need permission from the city council, then the governor, and that's going to take at least twelve to twenty-four hours. Until that time, I plan to investigate this murder the way I would any other death or crime in my city. Now please back away from the creek so you don't contaminate the crime scene with your footprints any more than you already have."

He literally growled a bit deep in his throat, then turned and stomped away, his shoes squelching in the mud as he went.

I whipped back around to see the body now covered in a blue tarp. "Who found her?" I barked.

"Treemont kid, out looking for his lost dog," Skip responded.

Treemont was the next town over, maybe two miles total—close enough for someone looking for a lost dog, for sure.

"Which one of you was first on scene?"

Skip pointed across the creek to Deputy Gene, who took a huge bite of a cruller.

"Who covered her . . . who covered up her parts?" I asked awkwardly.

"Kid says he found her that way," Gene replied.

Skip weighed in. "Hey, Sheriff, doesn't she date that football player?"

"Yeah," I agreed, leaning down a bit to examine the body as I held up part of the tarp.

"Reckon we'll have to talk to him about this. No?"

"Yeah."

"You want I should give his family a call?"

I knew he was inexperienced, but sometimes it was hard to keep my cool about his ignorance.

"You don't give a warning call to the family of potential murder suspects," I advised. "Just gives them time to escape. Any sign of Harold McKee?" I asked, changing the subject.

"Not yet, sir."

"Well," I sighed, bending down to my knees over the body, "let's get this scene processed quickly before he shows up."

Harold always showed up, because he had a police scanner. And the last thing anyone needed was him slapping a picture of this poor girl's body on the cover of his so-called newspaper.

I reached down and used an ink pen from my pocket to reposition the victim's arm, when something fell out into the shallow waters below. It was an earring. "Gene," I asked, "can you bring me an evidence bag?"

● ● ●

"We need the FBI now!" Mayor Sean Burke bellowed while pacing around the front of the conference room. "This is a serial killer!" His excellency was on quite the rampage. His face was even redder than normal.

"I think we need help," I agreed. "I think there's a connection between the two murders, yes." I paused to prep for the backlash. "But I'm not ready to call this a serial killer case, sir."

"Of course not," he spat back, "because you don't want to give up control."

We were at an official performance review of me, called in emergency fashion by Mayor Burke, which meant that it was being logged by a court reporter. I needed to choose my words carefully, if possible, since they would be on the permanent record.

"I am happy to yield control to more experienced investigators. And I welcome the help of the FBI. I will step back if our advisers suggest I do so. I merely question the label of 'serial killer' at this point in the game, sir. I fear it will only cause further unrest among the citizens—and it's my job to protect them. There is no known motive, the method of death is different, the victims have nothing in common outside of the presence of flowers. . . . Katie McGuire's killer could be just a copycat, sir. We released details about flowers being at Mrs. Hillary's murder site, but we never said what kind."

"This board has heard your position, a few times now," Alderman Nancy Green replied. "We will take it under advisement when we make our final vote."

And that was that.

They would dismiss all spectators and argue in private, then ultimately agree with Mayor Burke that we needed to call in the FBI, I assumed.

I sometimes wondered why I bothered going through the motions when I knew the outcome was inevitable regardless. But I figured the historical record needed someone that, at least, challenged the entrenched power establishment.

It was probably a futile line to draw, but I drew it anyway.

●●●

I stood in the hallway looking out at the parking lot, a cup of vending-machine coffee in my hands.

"Rough day?" It was Cindy; I could tell before I even turned around.

I spun around and smiled. "It's the warrior of Foster County! To what do I owe the pleasure of your visit?"

"Eh." She waved her hand dismissively. "I was in the area and heard the news."

"Listen," I said in a "change the subject" kind of tone, "you learn anything at Betty Q's about this out-of-towner staying there? Merritt?"

She sighed, in the way someone hoping for a more personal conversation might sigh when confronted with business talk. "I've seen him twice at breakfast," she allowed. "Never spoken to him. He's in and out, that one. I think he's working on the new firehouse project, putting in twelve-hour days and then some."

Crooked Creek was near the midway point of building a new firehouse. It wasn't a second firehouse. Our only current firehouse wasn't even up to code—though the mayor had long kept giving them a pass. The new firehouse was intended to replace the old one, and it was twice as big—meaning we would have room for two trucks instead of just one. It was a project I'd supported during my campaign for sheriff.

"He's been vetted?" I asked softly.

"We aren't allowed to look too deep, sir, but we did plug his name into the database. Didn't find a thing."

"Could be an alias."

She nodded. "What about Matthew Wright?"

"Yeah," I agreed. "We're bringing him in for questioning. My deputies are on the way out there to collect him now."

Matthew was Katie's boyfriend and a logical choice for questioning in a death like this. I also had the privilege of knowing that Katie had been pregnant with Matthew's child—a fact I could not reveal to my fellow officers if I wanted to uphold my oath of confidentiality as a priest.

I began to worry that sooner or later, my obligations as a priest would be undone or superseded by my obligations as a sheriff. It was a conflict of interest I had always hoped to avoid. Foolish.

CHAPTER 8

MATTHEW WRIGHT

"Matthew, can you tell us where you were last night at ten p.m.?" I started soft.

We hadn't arrested him; we'd merely asked him to come to the station for questioning. But he already had a lawyer: Perry Parnell. Perry Parnell was the local ambulance-chaser. He made his money on plea bargains and settlements. He was here to make sure Matthew never faced official charges.

"Objection," Parnell stated flatly.

"This isn't a deposition," I stated.

"Right," he apologized. "I knew that."

He didn't know that. He'd just learned that . . . because Perry Parnell took most of his knowledge of the law from television shows. I had suspicions that he'd forged his way through the bar exam, such was his lack of understanding of the law and legal procedures.

Matthew's father, Jackson Wright, was a truck driver, and he was out on the road currently. He wasn't expected back for several days. Matthew's mother, Jenny, was wary of the police and had called Parnell immediately. Still, she chose to sit outside the interrogation room, which I found a rather striking and peculiar decision.

I repeated the question: "Matthew, can you tell us where you were last night around ten p.m.?"

Matthew shrugged.

"You don't know where you were, or you aren't sure you can tell me?" I was plenty used to dealing with teenagers.

Matthew smiled at my clarification. Then he sighed. "I guess I was at home."

"Can anyone verify that you were, in fact, at home at ten p.m. last night?"

"Well," he said, kind of snotty, "not my dad, 'cause he's out on the road, and I ain't seen him in a while. And not my mom, 'cause she started drinking about three o'clock and was passed out by seven." He paused obnoxiously. "The dog could verify it, but he don't speak English."

The priest in me tried to look past the brash and taunting tone of voice to see the pain inside him that caused it. I often found my faith to be a helpful way to empathize with the folks I encountered as a sheriff.

Clearly, Matthew was an angry young man, murderer or not. His posture, tone of voice, facial expressions . . . everything about him suggested a troubled teenager struggling to find a way to express his frustration. Pain could be disguised behind cockiness. Then again, so could guilt.

"You know why you are here, son?"

"Yeah," he started angrily, before shifting quickly to sorrow. "Katie's dead." He sobbed for several seconds. It seemed genuine enough, but I also knew that Matthew had starred in a number of his school's drama productions over the years. I'd seen him personally in *The Diary of Anne Frank*, and he'd moved many in the audience to tears.

"How were things between you? Were you two fighting about anything recently?"

"Why? What makes you ask?" He seemed defensive. Of course, I knew the reason why—her pregnancy—but I couldn't reveal that. I had to get him to admit it. It wasn't hard.

"You don't seem like a killer to me, Matthew," I said honestly. "But you're clearly hiding something from us. Why don't you come clean and make yourself feel better?"

"You don't have to answer that," Parnell barked, not knowing anything else to say.

"I'd give good money if you'd shut up," I said calmly to the detainee's attorney. "The boy has a chance to clear his name."

"You're just trying to set him up!" he barked back at me.

"I'm trying to eliminate suspects in order to find a killer, but your client is making it pretty darn hard to eliminate him as a suspect!"

"My client," Perry bellowed—he was good at bellowing—"is about to stand up and walk out of here if you don't present some kind of concrete evidence."

"Stop posturing, you—"

"We will walk!" he shouted.

In a tiny, momentary breath between shouts, Matthew Wright spat out a whisper of truth he could no longer suppress. A secret so toxic that it was slicing him to bits from within to keep it quiet.

"She was pregnant."

The room, and probably the entire township, stood still for a solid seven seconds. Then thirty seconds of everyone in the room speaking over one another until I finally quelled the outbursts.

"Katie was pregnant?" I asked, clarifying for the record.

"Yeah," Matthew responded immediately. "And it was mine. No reason to lie about that."

Perry Parnell just shook his head and counted the dollars he was going to lose if his client kept speaking openly. I could see his eyes doing the math.

"And had you two talked about whether or not you wanted to keep the baby or maybe have an . . . abortion?"

It's always wise to pause before saying a naughty word in Indiana. It gives sensitive ears time to tune out.

Suddenly the teenager started bawling into his palms. "We were going to keep it," he managed to blurt out between sobs.

He cried for another two minutes, and I let him. I couldn't be sure if he was crying over the loss of his girlfriend, or their child, or both. I thought it was even possible that he was mourning his upcoming senior year of high school basketball, wondering if he'd be shunned by the community; of course, if they'd chosen to keep and raise the child, there would have been no way he could be able to be part of the team's busy schedule. Now he'd have time for sports, but maybe not the mindset.

Finally, I broke the silence. "When was the last time you saw Katie?"

Parnell leaned in and whispered loudly, "You don't have to answer that."

"Last night. About eight o'clock," Matthew answered flatly.

If it was an attempt to make me see him as an ally in finding Katie's killer . . . well . . . it sort of worked. At least for now.

"Where were you?" I probed deeper.

"In my car, sir," he responded. "I dropped her off at home. We . . . did a little necking, sir. Then she went inside."

"Had she told her parents about the pregnancy?" I was no cop, to be sure, but after I was elected sheriff I did a lot of reading about being a cop. About interrogation, even. And one tactic of questioning was to ask a question related to the main topic but tangential to it. It was supposed to throw the detainee off balance.

Matthew just shrugged. "I don't know," he finally said.

"Son, you realize that the more people who knew about the pregnancy, the more potential murder suspects we have; no?" I paused before continuing. "And that right now you are the only suspect we have?"

Parnell poked him with an ink pen.

"Her parents are pretty religious," Matthew finally replied. "I suppose they might be inclined to . . . I don't know . . . tell her what to do maybe? They're really into their reputation and stuff."

"You think they wanted her to terminate the pregnancy?"

Again, the boy just shrugged.

I took a solid minute to consider things. I stared him down the whole time, though he was facing the floor.

"I get the sense that you want to do the right thing," I said softly, "but someone has—"

The door to the interrogation room opened suddenly. "This questioning session is over. You two"—the man pointed at myself and Deputy Gene—"out." He flashed an FBI badge. "This investigation is ours now."

Matthew and his lawyer started to stand up.

"Sit the fuck back down," the FBI man barked.

Gene and I stood and walked outside into the hallway, our hands in the air. The door slammed shut behind us, and some other agents led us back to the main precinct lobby.

● ● ●

"The FBI is now in charge." Mayor Burke seemed very happy about it. I'll be honest; his glee at calling in reinforcements seemed directed specifically at me. "You will liaise with them and be helpful to them however they may need. Here's the board and governor's approval."

He slapped a couple pieces of paper into my chest, and I took them. "Thanks for, you know, letting me know about this ahead of time."

"You knew I was going to do it."

"What about the loaner officers?" I asked.

Burke thought for a second. "State's already paid us for them for three months. Let's keep 'em on. Town's gonna get jumpy, and we could use regular law-enforcement help outside the investigation of the murders." The only thing Burke enjoyed more than dunking on me was dunking on his fellow mayors and getting something for free. "It'll be a show of force. We'll double patrols to help people feel safe."

"Anything else?" I asked.

"Not for now, no."

I started walking away.

"Where are you going?" Burke called after me.

"To the interrogation viewing room, to meet the FBI officers I'll be assisting and to listen in on the questioning." I turned to leave and then whirled back around for one more thought. "The FBI may be in charge of this investigation, but you cannot take me off of it."

Burke looked at Deputy Gene for support, but Gene just raised his eyebrows, smiled, and walked away. Gene probably knew the law better than anyone else in the whole of Jerusalem County.

I waited. I knew I was right and that I could still be part of the investigation. I just wanted to hear that dickhead say it. Instead, he stomped
off in frustration, barking at one of his aides to hurry up. He gave me one
last glare as he left the station through the glass front doors.

I made eye contact with Cindy across the main room as I walked back
down toward the interrogation room. Her face conveyed concern. Mine
probably conveyed indigestion, but I promise I was going for "I've been
demoted on the investigation, and the mayor is an ass, and I'd tell you
more, but I have to go back in and reclaim some sense of my authority
right now."

●●●

The FBI interrogators were militant. I didn't see how they ever got anything done using that tactic. *You're interviewing someone you think might
be a serial killer . . . but you think you can scare them into talking?* It's nuts.

"How long have you been pressing her to get rid of the baby?" one
of them barked.

The interrogation viewing room wasn't like the one on TV shows,
with a fancy two-way mirror and a speaker switch. In our precinct, the
security camera feeds ran to my office. We had three cameras, black and
white, none of them recording to any kind of tape; one out front, one out
back, and one in the only interrogation/questioning room we had in the
building.

So the FBI officers—nine of them—were all crammed into my office,
watching the questioning on a small television screen. They all turned to
look as I walked in.

"Hey. Sheriff Lancaster." I pointed to the nameplate on the open
door. "My office," I said sheepishly. "Just want to listen in and help the
investigation."

Eight of them basically ignored me and went right back to the tiny
TV screen. The ninth man, a handsome young man with dark brown hair,

looked at me a moment or two longer, smiling. Then he crossed himself, letting me know both that he was Catholic and that he knew I was a priest. I smiled back, closed the door quietly, and stood leaning against it.

A few seconds went by before the agent seated at my desk turned to me. He looked to be in his fifties, and he spoke in the tone of a person in charge. "Is this thing recording?"

"Oh, no, sir," I replied. "Just a live feed."

"Branson, go get a VCR that can record for this kind of system. You may have to drive to Ft. Wayne or Indy." A young man in front stood up off the floor and started my way.

"Is anyone writing this down?" the boss barked at his own men. Then he turned back to me. "Why isn't there a tape recorder in there?"

"Oh," I said. "We ran out of batteries for ours."

"But you have one?!" He seemed an impatient man.

"We do."

"Branson!"

Branson had just reached my position and put his hand out for the door handle. He froze and turned around.

"Get some batteries too!"

"What kind, sir—"

"All kinds! Get some of each. Go!"

I suddenly had the strangest notion that I was in Hell and might remain there for several weeks.

CHAPTER 9

THE BODY AND THE BLOOD

COMMUNION—OR THE EUCHARIST, as it was officially called—was one of my favorite parts of the Mass. It was a time to learn which of my parishioners were honest with themselves. You see, in order to take Communion during Mass, you are supposed to be in "a state of grace," which is a fancy way of saying that you can't recall any major sins you've committed since your last Communion.

I've often wondered if the rule was designed to get more people right with God before Communion, or just to get more people confessing. Regardless, I knew a lot about these people. Many of them had given confession in the last several weeks. Many had not.

And as sheriff, I knew even more than I did as priest.

For instance, Billy Meade, a local bank teller, had never missed a Communion in the last five years. This despite having been arrested three times for public intoxication and once for solicitation of sex—from a street-sign pole. And I hadn't heard confession from him once since arriving here.

Then there was Fred Sandsman, the owner of the only car dealership in town, Sandsman Chevy, and the only Crooked Creek resident with a cocaine addiction. Still, without coming to confession in years, he continued to take Communion every Mass. He knew I knew. He just didn't care, because he knew I couldn't say anything about anything other than public details.

It was hard for me, at first, to realize how much hypocrisy there was inside my own parish. I'd spent many a visit out to Wendall's talking about this very issue as I grappled with it for months, if not years. Eventually he'd taught me to focus not on these obvious sinners taking advantage of the Eucharist, but rather on the good ones—those in the parish I knew to be walking the walk and living with the Lord. Those were the successes of my ministry, he argued. Every church had fakers. What mattered more was how many fervent believers and followers you'd cultivated as shepherd.

I hoped he was right.

• • •

After the cathedral had cleared out and I'd gone back to the sacristy to change clothes, I walked the short hallway to the fellowship hall—an addition I'd spearheaded eight years ago and which had been a great success. The church used the facility for games, youth nights, potluck dinners, adult athletic leagues, and in many other ways that had increased our ability to minister to this community.

Right now, though, the fellowship hall was on loan to the murder investigation. The influx of FBI officers into Crooked Creek had quickly made our tiny police station outdated and useless. I'd volunteered the extra space at the church, and that offer had been quickly accepted.

The fellowship hall had been built to be multipurpose. So on the far end, it had a stage and two closed side rooms on either side of the stage, just like the main sanctuary. This was in case we ever needed to hold regular or overflow Mass in this building.

On the near end, the part you pass through first, was a full kitchen. Above the far end over the pulpit was a basketball hoop, and several ping-pong tables were stored in one of the off-stage rooms. The main floor was rubberized concrete and could be set up with tables and chairs for a meal, or pews or chair rows for a service, or cleared entirely for athletics or youth-group sleepovers. We were quite ahead of our time on this particular flooring decision, as soon churches and grocery stores and even private residences started sporting the rubberized concrete.

Upon arrival, I saw that the FBI had quickly reworked the entire space.

The two off-stage rooms were now interrogation rooms. Of course, now we had no cameras, but a tape recorder was placed in each room—the church had an endless supply of blank tapes, which we'd bought in bulk years ago and used to record and mail out sermons to members stuck at home or unable to attend.

The main fellowship-hall floor was divided into three spaces: One was large enough to hold all the FBI and local officers at the same time . . . for updates on the case and mass meetings. The other two spaces were each half that size; one was being used for clerical purposes—phone bank, copiers, fax machine, etc.—and the other was being used as a sort of holding cell or intake valve—a lobby, if you will.

The kitchen was being used as a kitchen. Cops are hungry, and so are FBI agents, and even suspects. The kitchen was a combination of mass-cooked meals and refrigerated home-brought lunches. Anyone on lunch break was basically hanging out in the kitchen or at one of the three large picnic tables set just outside the fellowship hall.

We'd equipped the fellowship hall kitchen to be able to cook for and serve an entire congregation of eaters, so there was more than enough space for the thirty-five or so officers. We had our own five, myself included; then the four loaners, which made nine. Then the twenty-six FBI officers.

If the murders had happened during the school year, I have no idea what we would have done to house all those FBI agents. But since school was out for the summer, we stuck the agents in the middle-school gymnasium—don't worry, we scoured the town for mattresses, rollaways, and sleeping bags. Only a few FBI agents had to sleep on the floor.

The head FBI man in charge was Regional Director Logan Rathburn; he'd been the one to greet me inside my own office back at the station. He was based out of Indianapolis, as it turned out, but oversaw an area covering Indiana, Ohio, Illinois, and Michigan. He was fifty-five years old and was a cranky no-nonsense son of a bitch. I liked him a lot.

He'd brought with him a few of his own lieutenants, as well as twenty or so of the state's finest field agents.

Before I could even acclimate to the bustling surroundings, Director Rathburn approached and grabbed my hand, shaking it violently. "Father Lancaster, so glad you're here. We could really use your help!"

I felt a momentary delight in feeling needed by the FBI. "Of course!" I replied. I barely noticed he'd addressed me as Father and not Sheriff.

"We're having trouble with some of the street names in this town, and our officers keep getting lost." He sat me down at a nearby desk with a local map of Crooked Creek. "You have five different roads called Crooked Creek!"

I sighed heavily, hopefully at least one second shy of being obvious about my disdain. I'd been interrogating a witness one day earlier; now I was being asked about road names. It was a stark change in just twenty-four hours. But I was still more interested in the case being solved than in my being the one to solve it. "Can I get a coffee?" I asked.

As an FBI agent with more law-enforcement training than I'd ever received ran off to get me coffee, I held court with the ranking agents for a lesson in local geography.

"First off, the streets don't actually have the same name. There's Crooked Creek Drive, which is in the Fairfield subdivision here. Then there's Crooked Creek Street, which runs along the creek, give or take a half mile, through the whole county. That's here." I pointed with my pen, just as the coffee arrived. "Thank you," I said before continuing. "There are two Crooked Creek Roads, but they are clearly labeled East and West on all maps and road signs. Finally, Crooked Creek Lane is the entrance to the funeral home, and it's ceremonial only—there's not really a street there, it's just a driveway."

A murmur began until an agent interrupted it with a new question. "What's the difference between Crooked Creek and Crooked Stream?"

"Crooked Stream is just a small tributary off the main creek. It mostly runs through the Millers' farm and dead-ends."

"I told you so," the agent said, slapping the shoulder of the man next to him.

As the agents in attendance turned the map around the table and tried to get their bearings, Rathburn pulled me aside. "Say, you know these parts so well. You wouldn't mind going with my men today, would you?"

I had to smile at that. I'd lost jurisdiction in this case, and the FBI who took it over needed my help in order to navigate the local landscape. Almost as though I should just be in charge of the case. "Sure," I chuckled. "Where are they off to?"

"We want to interview this Buzz Martinson character," he said, reading from a legal pad. "What do you know about him?"

I smiled. "Plenty, sir."

"Good. I know it might be hard to have the FBI come in and take over a case, but we will truly need your local knowledge here." He spoke like a golfer hoping to get an advantage at a course he was playing for the first time.

"Of course." I paused. "Y'all aren't really considering Buzz as a suspect, are you?" I'd known the young man to be erratic, unpredictable, and even violent at times. But he was no killer in my eyes.

"We're looking at all angles. For now, everyone's a suspect." I was being asked to aid the investigation but being fed the same bullshit they were giving the Harold McKees of the world. Surely I was qualified for more detail than the *Crooked Creek Peek*!

"I see."

"Just make sure my officers don't get lost, okay? Every minute is valuable." With that he walked away, having dropped the hammer on me. I was still not a part of this case. I was merely a tour guide.

Seemed fine to me for now. At least this way I couldn't be held responsible for fucking up the investigation.

CHAPTER 10

BUZZ

Buzz Martinson lived alone, as hard as that is to believe, given his condition. His daddy had run off when the child was six, but his momma, Lydia, had soldiered on, raising him alone. She never missed one of his games. Sadly, she also never missed a drink. She'd veered off the road several years ago, smashing into a giant oak tree, leaving Buzz to fend for himself against his demons.

Buzz still lived in the family trailer out on County Road 13—aptly named, given the luck poor Buzz had endured throughout his life.

The FBI sent out six officers, plus me, in two vehicles, which I found to be excessive. They were all geared up with bulletproof vests and automatic assault rifles and fancy sunglasses.

In my years as sheriff, I'd arrested Buzz no fewer than twelve times. The charges ranged from speeding to drunk driving to public indecency to petty theft and property damage. But this was not a serial killer. The fact that it was going to take six FBI agents to determine this, instead of just trusting me, was an indictment on the use of federal tax dollars. Then again, these people didn't know me from Adam. Maybe I wouldn't trust me either in the same circumstance.

After rapping on the door several times, and my reminding the agents that the trailer sat on eleven acres of wooded land, we spread out to look for Buzz in the back and side yards.

"I think we should all meet back here in ten minutes," I offered.

"Why?" Lt. Irwin asked. Lt. Ted Irwin was the apparent second in command for the FBI, under only Regional Director Rathburn from what I could tell.

"It's . . . it's eleven acres, Lieutenant. It would literally take all seven of us hours to search this property, and we don't even know he's home."

"Tell you what," he snapped back. And this was the problem. The lieutenant knew he had authority on the scene, and he wasn't a big fan of local law enforcement. "You go around the house and see if any doors are unlocked . . . and we'll search the woods, and we'll be back whenever we're done." He motioned to his men, and they all spread out in different directions.

Lt. Irwin gave me a sarcastic head nod, then turned and disappeared into the woods.

"Fucking FBI," I breathed to myself before turning back to the front porch. I prayed aloud as I walked. "Father, help me find him before any of these wartime dickheads do." And I meant it.

I'd climbed three of the five steps to the front door, when it opened. And closed.

I looked down to see Harrison, Buzz's pet raccoon, dart between my legs and down the stairs.

Let's follow the raccoon, my brain strangely suggested. And my body went with it.

Harrison, named after Harrison Ford, Buzz's favorite actor, rounded the corner of the trailer and disappeared from my view.

"I'm gonna have to run," I muttered as I started what could generously be compared to a slow jog. I wasn't in the best of shape, and it was the eighties so no one else was, either—leave me alone.

By the time I reached the corner and turned, Harrison was nowhere in sight. I jogged another twelve feet to the next corner and peeked into the back yard . . . but no sign of him. But a small shed stood about thirty yards away. I figured the raccoon was either under the trailer—and I was not going to follow him there, by any stretch—out in the woods somewhere, or in that shed.

"Buzz!" I said loudly as I crossed the lawn toward the shed.

I got to about five feet from the shed and heard the faintest of sounds. I stopped to listen more closely. Music!

I stepped to the partially open doorway, slid the aluminum door open, and startled the hell out of Buzz Martinson. He stumbled and fell, landing on his back, electric sander in hand, as he shouted, "Harrison pickle jar Christ!"

Younger generations in Crooked Creek couldn't remember Buzz's athletic greatness and only knew the bullet points of his story; they called him Pickle Jar. He couldn't understand that it was an insult, and it had become a regular part of his vocabulary.

I put my hands up in a defensive position and shouted, "Buzz, can you turn that thing off?"

He did.

"Man," he growled while rising to his feet, "Harrison is supposed to warn me when I got visitors."

"I think he was trying to, buddy," I said, chuckling. "I'm just faster than he is. He seems a little chunky."

"I only feed him two cans of Chef Boyardee a day, plus treats."

Harrison waddled away back toward the trailer.

I clicked the button on my radio. "I found him. Main house." I turned back to Buzz. "You know them killings?"

He nodded and seemed sad.

"The FBI wants to ask you a few questions—make sure we can rule you out as a suspect."

His eyes got wide.

"You aren't a suspect, Buzz," I said immediately, and it seemed to help. "Just need to ask a few questions, and then we'll move on to someone else, okay?"

He shrugged, which, in my history with Buzz, meant that he agreed.

● ● ●

Inside the trailer, three agents and myself were crammed onto the couch. The smell was … difficult. The three other FBI agents who'd opted to wait outside had definitely chosen wisely.

Buzz insisted on making us coffee; but, as we watched, it was easy to see that he had no clue how to make coffee. He put the grounds into mugs, then put all four mugs in the oven, which he had not turned on. At that point, he returned to the living room and sat in the recliner.

"Shouldn't be but a few minutes," he said, nodding back at the kitchen, referring to the coffee no one wanted to drink.

"We'll probably be done before then," I said for the third time. "Listen, Buzz, did you know Katie?"

He immediately stiffened and lowered his gaze to the floor. He nodded.

"You've heard that she died, I take it?"

Again he nodded.

"Do you remember where you were that night? What you were doing?" I was casual in tone.

He shook his head side-to-side.

"You don't remember where you were three nights ago?" Lt. Irwin barked, growing impatient.

I leaned over to whisper to the lieutenant. "Sir, as I mentioned, his memory is shot to shit. He sometimes can't remember his most recent meal."

"Well, that seems convenient," he barked back out loud.

I decided to try a different approach, even if it shamed me to do so. "Buzz . . . who are your best friends?"

He smiled broadly, as my own face turned to a frown. "Oh, the bees, and the ants, and the mice and the birds!" He was bubbly as a cheerleader. "Harrison, of course, but also the trees and the grass and the leaves and the deer and the tiny, tiny microscopic thingy-dos!"

He continued rambling as I turned to Lt. Irwin and bluntly asked, "Does this seem like a well-planned serial killer to you?"

Irwin sighed heavily. "No."

"Do you wanna arrest him for the illegal raccoon pet?"

"No." He sighed again. "Let's go, agents," he ordered, before I could poke at him any further.

And with that, Buzz Martinson was no longer a suspect.

● ● ●

Later that evening, I was watching the news from one of the Indianapolis stations, eating a casserole donated by Mrs. Hillsock. Mrs. Hillsock was a generous soul, a long-standing member of the parish, and a truly awful cook. But bachelor priests couldn't be choosy, so I slogged through the broccoli, shrimp, and gravy casserole because, while bland as hell, it was better than anything I could have made.

The news seemed focused on international tension and the possibility of war, which seemed far from Crooked Creek. No mention of our double murder, though it was only a matter of time before the news of the twin killings went statewide, or even national. There were just too many similarities between the two deaths.

Zacchaeus jumped up onto my lap, demanding attention. I mindlessly scratched him while still waiting for the news to mention our local serial killer.

● ● ●

I woke up five hours later, Zacchaeus on my lap, my disgusting dinner now completely gone, courtesy of the fat cat before me. Just as well . . . I wasn't going to eat any more of it.

I lifted the feline and set him on the cushion next to me. He grumbled.

I left the dishes and lights and even the TV to deal with tomorrow and stumbled off to my bedroom to dream of a time when I wasn't working a series of local murders.

CHAPTER 11

CURFEW

KATIE'S FUNERAL WAS EVEN MORE HEAVILY ATTENDED than Mrs. Hillary's had been, mostly because so many of her fellow students and age-group peers had come.

We had to set up folding chairs for overflow seating behind the back pews, and even out in the foyer.

This annoyed the FBI agents in the fellowship hall, who had to stand while doing their job throughout the entire memorial proceedings. I said a prayer for patience that I might not punch out any selfish FBI agents.

"Our community is in crisis," I opened my homily. I'd always used community and world events in my sermons and messages to the congregation. And every single person in the room was wondering if we had a serial killer in our little town. There was no ministry to the townspeople in ignoring the facts. Indeed, you can only minister to those whose reality you accept as being real—even if only to them.

"Two deaths inside of a week. Senseless deaths. Lives taken before they were ready to go." I paused to look around the sanctuary. "Everyone in this room knew Katie McGuire. We knew her to be bubbly, lively, free-spirited, and full of love. We knew her to be charitable with her time—she was a volunteer with half a dozen organizations just here in Crooked Creek."

It was common for a priest to deliver the entire message stoically from behind the pulpit. I was too much of a pacer for that. I removed the microphone from the holder at the pulpit and began to pace the stage as I continued talking.

"Why would God take someone so young and full of promise? Well," I paused for effect, "he didn't. Just because God doesn't always interfere in our humanity doesn't mean he doesn't love us or that we deserve what happens."

I walked back and forth on the stage, making eye contact with as many in the congregation as possible as I continued. I wanted everyone thinking I was speaking directly to them.

"I know we want God to intercede in our lives and make things better; and sometimes, indeed, he does. But not all the time. Not even rarely." I stopped and turned back toward the choir. "Are we being tested?" I asked. I slowly turned back out to face the main audience. "Are we on trial?"

I worked my way back to the pulpit before leaning in to the microphone dramatically just as I set it back in the holder . . .

"Always!"

●●●

Everyone's death is different. Sometimes there's a funeral service. Sometimes it's a memorial service. Sometimes it's in a church, while other times it's at a funeral home, or even at a gravesite.

Some folks are open-casket, forcing their loved ones to take one last look at their creepy, smelly dead bodies. Others are closed-casket folks with good souls who protect their loved ones from creepy funeral visuals. Still others are cremated, which can save a lot of money if you use the right place. Tip: never use amateur crematoria.

Where Tina Hillary's service had been relegated to the church, and only a handful of family members went to the graveside event, Katie's family had invited anyone who cared to come to take part in the graveside memorial. Nearly two hundred showed, despite a light rain.

At this service, I was merely a spectator, other than a final prayer. I watched as her friends and family members embraced and cried and shared memories. I cried as they cried. I laughed as they laughed. And those emotions were real; I wasn't a robot on autopilot. I'd cared about Katie, especially in light of her final confession.

Katie's father was particularly emotional, and who could blame him? He gave a long eulogy, followed by another presentation from his wife. Then they yielded to Katie's friends from school and sports, and nearly an hour of heartfelt eulogies followed. No one seemed ready to leave. I guess leaving would mean she was really gone forever.

The notable absence, of course, was Matthew Wright, her boyfriend. Matthew was still a person of interest in the murder case, and his lawyers had no doubt persuaded him to skip the funeral—if only to avoid any press inquiries.

But there had been no press. Harold McKee had been there, of course, but he hardly counted as press in my book.

Two mysterious deaths in the rural bowels of Indiana; no one outside the area would really care, at least for now.

The truth was that no one outside of Crooked Creek would miss Katie McGuire, or even remember her. And that was the real tragedy.

● ● ●

Later that evening, the FBI implemented a city-wide curfew of 9:00 p.m. The only exceptions were emergencies and people driving to or from work.

This would be enforced by, drumroll please, my local officers and the other county loaners. This meant that the FBI would continue to work the case during the day and sleep at night, while my crew was left to monitor the roads for curfew-breakers—most of whom were likely to be teenage skateboarders or out-of-towners passing through.

Cindy and I ended up paired again, at this point mostly out of habit. We'd grown accustomed to each other's company. We took position on the north end of town, parking in the Crooked Creek Baptist Church lot. Gene and Skip were down south of town near the dry cleaners.

My other deputy, Travis Kent, and the other three loaner officers, the three nephew ducks, were all in bed. I was going to need to have people on duty during the daytime to keep abreast of the murder investigations, and it didn't take all eight of us to monitor a curfew in a town this small. So we would alternate nights.

County Sheriff Craig McNewel had been acting like an FBI agent ever since they'd arrived and would be of no help to me or my other local officers.

"This is so pointless," I said, being more honest than I intended.

"What is?"

"This curfew." I sighed. "Anyone even remotely familiar with this area would be able to move about freely even with us watching the main roads."

"Maybe it's more about perception than reality?"

"It is definitely that. It's a show for the residents, with little chance of actually catching a killer."

I wiped my brow.

The sun was down, the windows were down, but both of us were sweating our asses off. Typical Indiana summer heat.

"So, what's the life of a priest like?" Cindy tore open a bag of chips we'd picked up at the gas station and popped one into her mouth.

"That's a pretty open-ended question," I replied.

"Day to day? What's your life like? I figure you basically are praying all the time you're not in church or on duty as sheriff. No?" She smiled.

"Okay, let's see . . . I have a cat. I watch too much TV. I stay up late most nights, often fall asleep in my chair, and drink too much whiskey."

A car drove by, but I recognized it.

"Clive Dewerson, overnight stocker at the grocery."

"What's his name?"

"Clive Dewerson," I replied.

"No, the cat."

"How do you know it's a he?"

"Hunch." She chomped on another chip.

"Good hunch. His name is Zacchaeus."

"Oh, from the Bible!"

"Right." It was my turn to smile.

"And is he a wee little man?"

"No, he's humongous. He climbs on my lap after I fall asleep in the chair and eats my leftovers. So I always wake up to a slumbering cat and a clean plate."

She laughed. "Sounds like you are a pretty hands-off cat owner."

"I feed him. I pet him now and then. What else is there to do?"

A semi truck passed, heading into town. Its trailer was painted with the Hughes Grocery logo, which meant it was bound for the next town south of us, Lambert. We both saw the branding and ignored the truck.

"I know dogs, not cats."

"You have a dog?" I asked, suddenly animated. I'd always wanted a dog.

"Had. He passed last year of old age. German shepherd named Hank." There was unmistakable love in her voice.

"Sounds like a good pet."

"He was. Had him since high school. Never really took to my husband, though."

"How's he taking all this? Your being gone so long on loan out here?"

"He's fine," she said, a little too quickly. "He's spending so much time in Indy, working so many cases, I do think he hasn't missed me much at all."

There was a long pause before I finally broke the silence.

"Every time I wonder what it would be like to be married, someone comes along and makes me stop wondering."

She laughed out loud at that. "Well, glad to be of help."

"I'm sorry," I said, still chuckling. "I really do admire married folk. It takes more than single people realize to make a marriage work."

"You can say that again."

Before I had a chance to take the easy joke and repeat myself, a cyclist rode by, headed out of town, alerting us with the streetlights bouncing off his wheel reflectors.

Cindy and I looked at each other.

"No clue," I said, turning the engine on as I spoke.

In no time we caught up to the cyclist, who happened to be none other than Buzz Martinson . . . naked.

I put the car in PARK and turned to Cindy before opening my door. "Don't ever run for sheriff of a small town."

CHAPTER 12

VICTIM THREE

WHILE MOST OF THE TOWN was sleeping that night, and while four of us officers of the law were keeping watch, another killing had taken place. Well, another killing had been discovered; it was yet to be determined just when the killing itself had taken place.

By the time I made it in to the office, around 10 a.m. and after two hours' sleep and a cold shower, the FBI agents were about to leave for the scene of the new murder.

"Great job by your surveillance team last night," Mayor Burke barked in my ear as soon as I walked into the room. "Really prevented crime last night!"

He knew, and everybody in the room knew, that four officers could not adequately protect any town against crime overnight. Even if I'd deployed all four of the other officers I'd put on alternate night watch, we wouldn't have caught this killer. The fact was, we were dealing with a killer unlike one we'd ever encountered, and he knew these parts well, and he was more than one step ahead of us.

I stopped short, held my hand to Burke's chest to stop him as well, and leaned in to whisper: "You are an elected official, sir. And if this murder spree goes on long enough, folks will blame more than just the local sheriff or the FBI; they'll blame you. So . . . consider being part of the solution here, instead of making every piece of information some kind of ammunition against me."

With that, I left the foyer and walked outside, leaving what I hoped was a stunned mayor behind.

I hopped back in my truck and motioned for Kent and the two fresh loaner officers to follow: Grayson and Banks—Dewey and Louie, I think. Cindy had shown up on little sleep, as I had, and she tagged along with the group.

●●●

"Fuck me." It was Cindy, summing up the scene for the rest of us while simultaneously endearing herself to the boys a little more through casual swearing.

I merely sighed, looked down a moment, and took a few deep breaths. These crime scenes were getting harder for me to take.

We were inside the home of Vernon Yarbrough. Vernon was a local farmer—like nearly half the town. He was unique in that he was single: no wife or kids. No farmhands. He farmed his land 100 percent by himself, and everyone respected him for it.

He was handsome, in a rugged way, only forty years old. And he lay in his bed, robed and clean . . . his eyes gouged out and replaced by black-eyed Susans.

As a victim, Vernon ran counter to serial-killer thinking, at least according to the few serial-killer experts that existed.

First of all, men were typically not known to be common victims of serial killers. Second, this made the killer's pattern even more random and harder to track or predict. He'd killed an elderly woman, a teen girl, and now a middle-aged man. What common denominator could these three victims possibly have?

It made no sense.

Personally, I had never met Vernon Yarbrough. He did not attend my church, and he was not known as a social person. I saw him at the grocery store or the hardware store once or twice. That was it. I knew of him, but I didn't know him.

I had my gloves on, but I wasn't there to collect evidence or work the case. Officially, the FBI termed me and all my deputies as "observers."

We were allowed on scene and could still collect evidence. Cindy took notes, while Kent, Grayson, and Banks mostly just stood around slack-jawed, watching the FBI agents work the scene.

I suddenly snapped into law-enforcement mode. "You three," I barked at the immobile deputies, "get outside and start covering the property." The FBI was in charge, but the agents were not infinite in number. There was plenty of police work to be done outside the home, and I hated nothing more than an idle officer of the law. "Footprints, fabric, dropped items . . . go!" I figured there would be none of those things to be found, but it wouldn't be police work if we didn't look.

● ● ●

We found nothing. Nothing that looked like evidence, at least. No stray clothing. No out-of-place hairs. No sign of a struggle. And the FBI came up as empty as my officers did.

Burke railed against all the officers gathered in the meeting room. Then, signaling his intention to call the governor and ask for the National Guard, he stormed out.

As soon as he was out of the room, Regional Director Logan Rathburn took the podium. "Okay," he said, glancing after Mayor Burke, "we all know the National Guard isn't coming out here for three dead bodies. And even if they did, it would be to police the streets, not to investigate murders. These crimes are ours to solve, gentlemen." He seemed to spot Cindy and added, "And lady." He nodded toward her. "Nothing changes. Get out there and run down everyone this latest victim had contact with and did business with. Let's start knocking on doors!"

Everyone ambled out, and Lt. Irwin started barking orders to various groups of FBI agents.

"Sheriff!" I heard Rathburn call. I turned to face him. "You got a minute?"

"I got all the time you need, sir." I smiled.

As most of my own officers headed out with the FBI agents to chase leads, I walked into my own office, which Rathburn was temporarily occupying, and sat in one of the guest chairs. The regional director slouched into my chair behind the desk as though he'd been doing it all his life.

"Sheriff," he began, "who do you think is doing these killings?"

I scoffed aloud, but I think I covered it with a sudden cough. "Excuse me, sir. Seasonal allergies."

"You've lived here a long time, right?" he probed.

"Yes, sir, ten years or so. Still never get used to the allergies."

Robotically, reluctantly, he slid the box of tissues on the desk over to my side.

"Thank you," I said as I grabbed one and blew my nose.

"Do you think anyone in town is capable of this kind of thing?"

"No, sir, I don't. I can't say that I've personally met every single citizen of Crooked Creek, but I've met most of 'em, and I'm aware of the rest. I can't fathom it, sir."

"Not even this Buzz character?"

I was fortunate to be getting a glimpse into the FBI's thinking, though it was depressing to learn that they really had no thinking as of yet, beyond the obvious.

"If you're asking if Buzz is capable of murder," I suggested, "then I'd have to say he probably is. But three murders of like circumstances such as these? I just don't find him capable of it, respectfully."

"Any drifters?"

I nearly laughed in his face and felt the urge to make a joke about the musical group before I realized he was serious. "No drifters, sir. Got one guy staying at the B&B working local construction jobs for the last couple months. No drifters."

He sighed long and hard and then leaned forward. Remember: this is my desk he's using to intimidate me. "You hear a lot of confessions, don't you?"

Here it comes. I'd been waiting my entire law-enforcement career—which hadn't been very long—for someone to try and leverage my role as priest in a procedural investigation.

"Sir?" I left it wide open, so Rathburn could spell it out himself.

"If you heard the confession of a serial killer . . . like . . . I don't know how it works, you see? But would . . . would you have to report that to me?"

Now it was my turn to sigh. I realized the entire meeting had been about buttering me up to see if I could be a source of new leads in the murders.

"No, sir," I replied. "Catholic law forbids me from revealing the contents of someone's confession."

"What about Indiana law?" he countered, a bit too cocky.

"Even more archaic, sir," I replied.

He stood up, slamming my beloved office chair into the filing cabinets behind him, pacing back and forth behind the desk.

"So you're saying," he fire-breathed, "that you might already know who the killer is due to confession, and you wouldn't tell us?" The regional director was beginning to remind me a lot of my own mayor.

"I'm only saying that I am not permitted to share the contents of confession with you."

"That sounds like a 'Yes' to me," he barked.

"I said a lot more words than that, sir," I countered.

"If push comes to shove, and I think you have answers, I'm going to force you to testify to a grand jury."

"You do what you have to do, sir. Just know that I'm here to help you, and I want to find this killer as much as you do."

There was no court anywhere in the state that would force me to disclose confessed information from one of my congregants. And I was pretty sure he knew it as well as I did.

● ● ●

"Bless me, Father, for I have sinned. It's been prolly about two or three weeks since my last confession."

It was Bradley Norris. He owned the Norris & Sons funeral home and cemetery on the south side of town. He'd inherited it from his father, because none of his other brothers—the named "sons"—wanted anything to do with Crooked Creek, Indiana.

"I have . . ." He sniffled and then began to cry as he spoke. "I have delighted in the deaths of others, Father, because it has been good personally for my business."

You had to know Bradley Norris to know that this was typical. He took every death in town personally and regretted making money on people's sorrow—even though his profession was necessary and his services worth paying for.

"I think it's okay to be happy for your business without being happy that people are dying," I offered, before I really rolled it around in my head for a moment.

"I don't see how it is, Father," he countered. "One thing leads directly to the other."

"Maybe you're not cut out for the funeral business, Bradley? Maybe you're meant for something else?"

"Then who would run the funeral-home business?" It sounded as though he'd never even considered any alternative to running the funeral home.

"What about Mark?" Mark was an employee there who did most of the embalming and body-prep work before viewings at the funeral home.

"Mark is an artist," he allowed, "but too gruff with people to run a funeral home. Too blunt."

"You could sell it," I offered, feeling as if that were an obvious solution. "It's one of only two funeral homes in the county, Bradley. You could earn enough to start a new business, here or somewhere else."

"That seems like such a big change."

"Let's set that aside for now. You can ponder that idea for a few days. For now . . . do you have any other sins to confess?"

He paused. "I took the Lord's name in vain several times." He paused again. "There's a cashier at the feed store, Father—she's young and pretty. I thought about her a few times; it felt bad after."

I smiled, remembering how mundane my own sins were to Wendall. I was also pretty sure I knew which cashier he meant, but this was neither the time nor the place.

Bradley continued: "I got two dollars extra change from the cashier at the bank, and even though I didn't realize it until I got home, I didn't go back to report it. That's stealing, I think."

He went silent then for a good twenty seconds.

"All right," I finally said, "Here's what I'd like you to do. Say ten 'Hail Marys' about the 'Lord's name in vain' thing, just for repetition. Then, regarding the cute cashier, I want you to buy your wife flowers and take her out to dinner. And as for the two-dollar bank error, I want you to take two dollars of your own money and give it away to someone else unsuspectingly." My turn to pause. "You got all that?"

"Yes, Father," he replied. He stood to leave.

"And think about selling that funeral home, sir, for your own happiness," I said.

And then he left.

I was probably pushing too hard on the business sale, but the work seemed to make him so sad. How can you run a business when you feel guilty about every single transaction?

Then I realized exactly how many enterprises traded on guilt.

● ● ●

There's nothing stranger than watching a national nightly news anchor mention your town, particularly when your town is as small as Crooked Creek. But three murders in three weeks, all with similar circumstances, were bound to draw at least a little national news interest.

Most of the FBI officers were in the converted event hall, along with a few of my local and rented Indiana officers. Back in my private church office, I watched a small television along with Cindy, Gene, and Skip.

"Do you think they'll say your name, Sheriff?" Skip exhaled.

I hope not.

"Shut up, and we'll see," Gene replied.

The entire news report was a blip: thirty seconds or less. Just a mention that three similar murders had occurred in Crooked Creek, Indiana, and the FBI was involved. That was it.

At first, I was offended. Disappointed. How dare they dismiss it so easily?

On second thought, I realized, we just made the national news! This would put our town on the map!

Third thought: We are going to get all kinds of tourists, amateur sleuths, media members. . . .

Fourth thought: Fuck.

● ● ●

"You want MORE loaner officers?!" No one could bellow quite like Mayor Burke. His voice was uniquely designed to bounce off any and every surface and to increase in volume while doing so.

"We don't have to pay for them, sir; the state will do that. And I can use the extra officers to patrol, as well as chase down leads."

"Why can't the FBI do all that?"

"The FBI, sir, has repeatedly said they have sent all the agents they intend to send, and it's not enough. We're still having murders."

"You're not even correctly using the loaner officers you've been given. I won't ask for more."

"Fair enough, sir. The request is in writing. You'll have to sign it to complete your refusal. Once I have your signed refusal in hand, I will be filing a lawsuit on behalf of the townspeople of Crooked Creek against your office for not taking full advantage of state resources to solve a multiple homicide. Good day."

● ● ●

Six more loaner officers from surrounding counties were ordered the next morning by the governor's office.

CHAPTER 13

COUNSELING

I KNOCKED ON THE DOOR several times. I even momentarily got worried that something was wrong. But finally Wendall opened the door, pulling it back as he reversed in his wheelchair.

I paused briefly to process the wheelchair. My mentor's health had been waning of late, so the wheelchair should not have surprised me. But it did. And it double-punched me with sadness. Wendall's age was catching up with him.

As he struggled to work the wheelchair backward to allow me to enter, I asked about Bones, who hadn't come to greet me.

"Oh, he's over here next to the couch." Wendall finally had the wood door pulled back all the way and motioned me to come through the screen door. "Yeah, neither of us is getting around too well these days, I guess."

I opened the screen door and walked through the threshold. I took two paces to allow the door to be closed, knelt down, and called to Bones. "Here, boy!"

Bones stood on his front two paws, but his entire back half remained on the floor.

I glanced at Wendall, who was working the deadbolt, then back at the dog, who clearly wanted to come to me but either could not or would not.

"Hey, boy!" I amended my greeting, walked up to Bones, and scratched his head.

"You want some coffee?" Wendall called, already rolling toward the kitchen slowly.

"I mean. Sure, I guess. Do you want some help making it?" I was trying to be helpful.

"I can make my own dang coffee, Solomon," he barked. He almost never used my first name, so it usually meant I'd crossed a line.

Given the new wheelchair, I figured pretty fast that my mentor was still dealing with prickly feelings regarding his new confinement. "Good, Father," I replied softly, settling myself into my usual position in the reclinable chair.

"Two sugars and two creams, right?" he called over his shoulder.

"Right." I liked my coffee black, and he'd gotten it right for years without even needing to ask for clarification.

Bones crawled over to my position, using only his front paws. It was somehow simultaneously adorable and pitiful. I began scratching behind his ears. I heard the banging and clanging of kitchen noise but resisted the urge to call out offering help.

Looking around the room, I saw some new indications of Wendall's deteriorating health. The dog dish by the door was empty, for instance, but several inches away there were three piles of emptied canned dog food on the floor, half eaten.

The blinds were all open, and it was summer, so the light and heat coming in were intense. Yet the two window air conditioners were turned off.

The TV was on, but it was tuned to static, the volume off.

Finally he returned from the kitchen and handed me a mug, rolling to the other end of the coffee table before stopping. "How is it?"

I hadn't even looked at the contents of the mug, but suddenly I grew worried. I looked down to a swirling sea of charcoal liquid and hundreds of floating solids. I guessed it was instant coffee gone wrong, but I couldn't be sure. Still, I didn't want to hurt his feelings, so I pretended to sip.

"Good, thank you," I said, sincerely enough for acting class.

"I hear you have some more murders," he said bluntly.

"Yes, Father. A total of three now. All different, but all with flowers placed into or onto the bodies."

"And how is that impacting your ministry?" he replied. Wendall was always asking about my ministry, which was just his language for asking about my own purity of soul. My own mission.

"Negatively, sir," I admitted. I had always been honest with my mentor, and this was no time to stop that particular streak.

"And how is your ministry impacting your ability to do your job as sheriff?" He was a verbal boxer, even in his deteriorating state.

"Negatively, sir." I smiled.

He reached down to pet Bones, not realizing the dog was still next to my chair. He sat up and kept talking. "What else is new?"

"There's a female officer assigned to help us out, from another county." I stopped there.

He jumped on it. "Are you sure this shouldn't wait until the confession portion of our visit?" He was grinning ear to ear.

"No, you old pervert." I laughed. "It's not like that." I paused a moment. "But the friendship has grown quickly, and with ease. I can see why people get married when I spend time with her." I meant it, though I was admitting it to myself at the same moment that I was admitting it to my friend.

"Friendship is important," he agreed solemnly. "Not many priests have friends."

"We're still no closer to solving these murders," I sighed.

"It's not on you anymore," he reminded me. "The FBI was called in. No?"

"Yes."

"So it's up to them now. You can help, and I'm sure you *are* helping a lot, but it's not on you anymore, son."

"I know that," I replied. "It's just . . . knowing that and *feeling* that are different."

"You see yourself as shepherd of the flock of the citizenry?"

"I do, yeah." He was insightful as ever.

"That's not the sheriff's role, though," he replied. "You're confusing your two professions. I bet you find your priest-self more litigious lately. No? Checking people on the rules of the church?"

I hadn't been getting on anyone else at the church regarding the rules, but I had been giving myself a harder time lately, meaning Wendall was right again.

I nodded.

"I told you when you decided to run for sheriff that the two jobs would eventually clash."

"I know. You told me every time I saw you for, like, two years."

"Well, I was right. Wasn't I?"

I breathed out slowly. "It seems you were, indeed," I admitted.

"Be a cop when you're a cop, and be a priest when you're a priest," he opined.

"I wish it were that simple," I replied.

"Let's do confession," he said, as though he hadn't heard me.

I stood and grabbed the confessional screen from its position leaning against the wall. Dust flew out with every move I made. "Father," I coughed, "this thing is so dusty! How long has it been since *your* last confession?!" I laughed as I coughed some more.

"Okay," he chuckled before firing back. "My confession screen is as dusty and out-of-use as your arrest powers."

I ignored him, set up the screen, and sat back down into the recliner. Bones started licking the fingers of my outstretched left hand.

"Bless me, Father, for I have sinned. It has been two weeks since my last confession." The opening was always the easy part for any Catholic, because it was always true. Getting into the specifics of the sins . . . that's where the lies started to come, and they were harder to pull off for those who felt like lying. I felt like telling the truth. "The woman officer we mentioned earlier—Cindy—I am attracted to her, Father."

"Have you acted on this attraction?"

"No, Father."

"Does she feel the same way?"

"I think so, but I have so little experience. And she's married."

He was silent for half a minute or more; it was interminable. Finally he spoke again. "Feelings are only feelings, son. Humans all experience unexpected feelings. It's how we react to those feelings that matters. And you have not reacted in any sinful way so far. Try to limit your one-on-one contact with the woman and continue praying about the issue."

I nodded. "Yes, Father."

"Any other sins to confess?"

"I am gaining weight, Father. I'm eating more than normal, probably out of stress."

"Well, that doesn't sound sinful."

"I'm worried about gluttony, Father," I reminded him.

"You have miles to go before you approach gluttony."

It seemed like he was taking it easy on me, which I would have appreciated in times now gone by. But today it made me think he was dismissing me for his own selfish reasons.

"Thank you, Father," I offered. "Those are all the sins I have to confess."

A minute went by. I thought I heard faint snoring. Suddenly he lurched to life, shouting, "Thirteen 'Hail Marys' and thirteen 'Our Fathers'!"

Stunned, I merely whispered, "Of course, Father."

"Confession session over," he bellowed, knocking the confessional screen to the floor with the sweeping of his right arm.

I was in shock. I decided to wait a few moments to let things breathe. I could hear the dog panting and Wendall taking deep breaths as well.

Finally, I spoke. "Thank you, Father, for hearing my confession." I decided to pretend as though nothing strange had occurred whatsoever. Because that was easier than talking about it. "I should be going now."

I stood and walked toward the front door. I heard the squeaking of his wheelchair behind me. As I reached the threshold, I turned.

"I'll be back soon," I promised as I walked outside. The screen door slammed shut behind me.

"Solomon," he said softly, just before closing the main door.

"Solomon?" I asked. "You're using my first name all of a sudden? Do I have to get used to this now?"

"Only for a short time," he replied, smiling weakly.

"Okay."

"Next time you come see me," he started, before taking a deep breath, "will you take me back out to my daddy's farm one more time?"

One more time? This was the talk of a man who thought his time was near. And I wasn't ready for that. But I quickly reminded myself that this wasn't about me. "Sure thing, Father," I responded. "I'll call the Maples to make sure it's cleared."

Back in the early days, Wendall's grandfather had owned about four hundred acres of farmland over in Jerusalem County. Over time, it had been sold off in pieces for smaller, more modern farms. Ken and Presley Maple had inherited the largest piece from Ken's folks—about seventy-four acres.

Over the years, Wendall and I had visited the Maples' farm a few times. He had the best smiles and expressions of joy whenever we were there.

I just liked to get permission first, since it was technically private property.

CHAPTER 14

INTERROGATIONS

THE FBI BEGAN HAULING IN TOWNSPEOPLE for questioning without any real cause. Of course, these folks were all welcome to say "No" when asked to come down to the station to answer some questions, but this was a small town. People were polite and naïve. The agents were hoping to catch the killer off guard.

First up, the so-called "stranger" staying at the bed and breakfast, Merritt Wilson. This guy was Joe Cool. I'd studied enough body-language stuff to know he was not the least bit concerned about this interrogation, which meant he was most likely super-innocent. Either that, or he was an incredible actor. And we couldn't rule out that our suspect might be an incredible actor, in front of both police and victims.

I was still confined to the video screens, allowed to watch but not allowed to participate.

"What are you doing in Crooked Creek?" one of the agents asked. I think he was called Leon.

"Yeah, what are you doing here?" the other parroted. I think he was called Haynes.

Merritt finished the drag on his cigarette, slowly breathed it out, and calmly replied, "Work."

"What kind of work?" Leon continued immediately.

Their interrogation technique seemed grounded in speed. Speed of questions following a subject's reply. It wasn't anything I'd ever seen before, and it seemed hilariously useless. Unless the subject was lying.

"Construction, mostly," Merritt replied before taking another leisurely drag. "Hammered some frames. Hung some drywall. Dug a few graves. Whatever keeps me afloat, sir."

"What brought you into this area?" another FBI agent asked, with plenty of disdain.

Merritt shrugged. "Guy that was giving me a ride dropped me off here. Said it was thirty more miles to another town, and I was tired as hell."

The detectives, big-city guys both, were perplexed by the nomadic working lifestyle. It seemed more *Of Mice and Men* to them than modern reality.

"So you just move from town to town?" Banks said.

"Until the people turn mean or the work dries up, yes, sir." Merritt was not only the most at-ease murder suspect I'd ever seen questioned, but he was also the most polite.

Another fifteen minutes, and the FBI had had enough of Merritt and sent him on his way.

●●●

"Where were you on the night of the murder?" Leon shouted at Matthew Wright, Katie's boyfriend.

"Which murder?" the boy replied honestly.

The FBI agents, apparently not prepared for that type of response, conferred among themselves.

"The murder of your girlfriend, Katie," Leon finally said aloud.

●●●

"Have you ever killed anyone?" Leon asked in a friendly manner.

Buzz Martinson just swayed in the chair, smiling.

"You ever see this person?" He held up images of the victims, one by one. Buzz never once turned to look at them.

"Buzz, can you hear me?"

Buzz nodded emphatically without speaking. Then he took off his shirt.

"There!" Buzz yelled, slamming his T-shirt onto the table. "That is my testimony!"

I smiled to myself at the big-city boys trying to handle my country citizens.

● ● ●

"How did you commit the murders without anyone hearing you?" The FBI interrogation manual seemed to consist only of making wild accusations and then trying to interpret the suspects' reactions.

The subject here was Millard Clifford. He was a local lawyer who focused mostly on divorce law and general legal-document preparation. No one with any sense thought that Millard was the killer, but the FBI agents went about attacking every interviewee as some form of policy.

I knew Millard to be a man who gave generously to local charity drives. He'd apparently helped draw up a will for Vernon Yarbrough. That was his only connection, but the FBI was so desperate for clues that the agents were grilling every witness as accomplices.

I'd had enough. I turned, picked up my phone, and made a quick call.

The public defender for Jerusalem County was a nebbish little man named Stewart Snell. He had a whole county to cover, so he was a busy man, but he was still a government employee. I called and leaned on him hard to come to Crooked Creek and represent Millard Clifford and others who the FBI was unfairly targeting.

"There's a lot of innocent people here right now being grilled like guilty meat. I need you here yesterday," I urged quietly.

"Sheriff, I've got a lot on my plate. Don't you have any lawyers in Crooked Creek?"

"One of them's one of the suspects!" I barked back.

"I'm sorry, Solomon," he said earnestly. "Best I can do is tomorrow."

"Tomorrow's going to be too late," I snapped. "Tomorrow won't be in time unless some . . ." A sudden thought occurred. "Never mind. Tomorrow's just fine. Be here first thing in the morning, Stewart."

I hung up and walked out of the office just as Cindy walked in with several bags of lunch. I pulled her aside immediately. "Announce chow, get everyone into the main room for lunch, and then . . . I need a distraction." My voice was soft and urgent.

"What kind of distraction?" she asked quietly.

"The kind that allows me to grab the bow and arrow in my office and slip out the front door to my truck unnoticed."

She glanced inside my office to see the bow on the wall—actually, I had three bows on the wall. I was an avid bow hunter. She then glanced around the police station and back at me. "Okay." And off she went.

I slipped back inside the office and pretended to look at the books on the bookshelf. The glass windows of my office overlooked the entire police station, so I had to be sure heads were turned away before I grabbed the bow and made my move.

Cindy, to her credit, might as well have gone to acting school. She basically turned lunch into an auction. She'd picked up food from all three local restaurants, and she made the officers and agents bid on them—with proceeds going to the families of the victims. The tenderloin sandwiches from M Spot's went first and were the most hotly contested.

As they outbid each other for food, I slipped out the front door with one of my compound bows and a quiver of five razor-tipped arrows. I ultimately decided to leave my vehicle in the parking lot and ran into the field across the street. There was a bunching of brush and trees at the corner, and the corn was tall enough in the field to provide cover.

I knelt, visually traced the electrical wire from its pole to the police station, then back up to the pole. I quickly checked for wind and then fired. The power line to the police station was now severed.

Because the connecting pole was on my side of the road, I was able to shimmy up, easily pull the arrow out, and climb down without anyone noticing. This was a small town, and only two houses were even in viewing distance of the station; both were obscured by the brush I'd knelt behind.

Meanwhile, the power outage in the station caused pandemonium, as I'd hoped.

Interrogations were halted and everyone poured out of the building, seeking daylight and cooler air. After all, it was the middle of the summer, and I'd just killed the few air conditioners and fans that the police station had.

They considered moving operations to the overflow office in my church's recreation hall, only to find that the power was out there as well. I'd chosen my arrow's target carefully, as the church drew power from the same line the police station did; they were only two blocks away from each other.

Everything in Crooked Creek was only two blocks away.

An hour later, Regional Director Rathburn called it a day.

This bought me the time I needed for the public defender to arrive prior to any more reckless FBI accusatory interrogations the next day. Everyone assumed the transformer had blown, and I kept it that way by paying the electric company repair guys to haul it away before it could be inspected. By sometime the next day, power would be restored and the public defender would arrive and the FBI would have to start playing this investigation straight.

I decided to celebrate with a steak dinner at the only place where one could order a steak dinner in this town: the Stoplight Diner. The steak wouldn't be good, nor would the accompaniments, but even a bad steak was better than no steak at all, or so I told myself.

I sat at the counter and pored over my murder-scene notes while waiting for my food. By the time Vicki brought my meal to me, I'd already had a minor breakthrough.

"Vicki," I said playfully, "what do you see in this photograph?"

She leaned in. "A car."

"Be more specific; look closer," I urged.

"A Ford," she offered.

"Indeed," I agreed. "Thank you, ma'am."

What Vicki didn't recognize in the moment, and what most folks outside town didn't even know, was that Crooked Creek was a General Motors town. Granted, the auto-parts plant was a good twenty-minute drive away and was technically in the city limits of the next town over, Mount Orchid. But Mount Orchid had only three hundred residents, and more than 50 percent of the plant's workers lived here.

In Crooked Creek, you either farmed or you worked for GM.

And no one in town drove a Ford.

CHAPTER 15

ANOTHER CONFESSION

THE MURDERS WERE TAKING UP A LOT OF MY TIME. Even so, I still kept regular confession hours. I did have an associate priest, Father Daniel Barrett, but he was not ready for confession duties. He was still learning basic liturgical practices and phrases. He was a good kid, but he was fresh out of seminary and greener than the summer grass.

During posted confession hours that next morning, I heard the confessor door open and close, and a female voice said, "Forgive me, Father, for I have sinned."

I knew instantly that it was Cindy. Cindy wasn't Catholic, so my guard went up. I waited for her to continue the traditional confessional sentence structure.

I heard the shuffling of papers. "It has been . . . my entire life since my last confession."

At this point, I realized she wasn't really trying to hide her identity.

"That's okay. God hears confessions of all kinds," I replied.

"Glad to hear it," she said, settling into position.

"First time with the kneeler?" I asked playfully.

"Yes, Father." Another pause. "I'm not Catholic." She chuckled.

"You don't say," I replied sarcastically. I was willing to play the game as long as she was. In fact, it was expected of me, as a priest, to behave as though I didn't recognize the voices of my confessors.

"But I do have something to confess. Something I hope you will be legally bound to keep between yourself and me, Father."

"Of course."

"No, I mean it. I need a promise."

"You have it."

"Can you say it?"

"I promise."

A humongous pause followed. Finally she spoke again.

"I've fallen in love with a new co-worker, and I'm not sure how to proceed." She took a deep breath. "I'm married." There was a pause. "And the person I've fallen for is not my husband," she further qualified.

Even as I hoped she was talking about me, I shoved my emotions aside and did my job as a priest. "Well, feelings alone aren't much. But acting on feelings like this would be sinful."

"I'm afraid I might act on my feelings, Father."

I was used to being tested during confession, having to subdue my own personal thoughts or emotions in order to behave the way a priest was supposed to behave. But this was the most difficult suppression of real emotions I'd ever experienced. If I'm honest, this revelation excited me beyond measure.

"Then I recommend you spend some serious time in prayer. 'Hail Marys' and 'Our Fathers' won't help. You need to list all your lustful feelings to God and explain to him how you will account for them and atone for them. Your penance from me: Re-read the story of David and Bathsheba. In addition, donate a few dollars or an hour of your time to the women's shelter nearest you."

It was sound advice and along the lines of what I would have told any random female confessing the same sins. But it was rushed, and I'm sure she could tell. Because I needed her to leave quickly before I betrayed my oaths.

"Thank you, Father," she said.

And then she was gone.

Thankfully, there were no other waiting confessors, because I cried to myself for ten minutes.

I think people think it's easy . . . to be a priest . . . to put God above human emotions like love or lust. But it's really fucking difficult, man. You have no idea.

And it seemed pretty clear that Cindy was trying to signal me about her affections as much as she was looking for redemption for those feelings. Or perhaps she had been seeking reciprocation.

I'd obviously already noticed her good qualities. But I wasn't allowed to go beyond that and consider her a potential romantic partner.

But I did.

● ● ●

Later that afternoon, power was finally restored, and the interrogations of random Crooked Creek citizens continued. But this time Stewart Snell, the county public defender, was present, and I felt a lot better about how things would go when each witness had representation.

Still, I stayed in my office watching the video feeds throughout the day. I was afraid to bump into Cindy and have some kind of awkward conversation. I was also—and perhaps more importantly—intensely interested in the suspect interrogations. Even if I couldn't ask any questions, I could still learn by watching.

Thankfully, Stewart was able to get many so-called witnesses excused, since the FBI was using the term so loosely in order to question as many people as possible. They might as well have called everyone in the phone book to come in and give statements.

Of course, no one was required by law to answer any questions unless or until they were charged with a crime, which Stewart told every single incoming subject. Yet many still chose to answer questions, in the hopes they might help the police solve these heinous crimes. But Stewart's presence did the one thing I hoped it would: it stopped the aggressive and accusatory questioning techniques by the FBI. They would no longer be able to scare people as a means of fact-gathering. At least for now. After two hours of watching, I felt comfortable leaving the observation room and letting Stewart serve as protector of the innocent on his own for a while.

I went straight to the break room for coffee—and, of course, Cindy was there, along with Gene and two FBI agents. I hitched my step as I entered, but I don't think anyone noticed.

"Hey, Father," Cindy said cheerfully, "how are things going in the interrogation room?" She didn't seem to be acting weird in the least.

"Fine," I replied evenly. "Now that we have a public defender in the room, I feel a lot better." I poured coffee into my cup.

"Awesome," she replied.

I stirred my coffee and turned to face the table, leaning on the counter. Cindy and the FBI agents continued their discussion, which turned out to be about baseball, while Gene shoveled potato salad into his mouth with a giant serving fork.

Was I wrong about Cindy being the mysterious confessor? Or was she just a better actor than I ever imagined? It's strange how, the further you get from a weird event, the less sure you become of the things that initially were certain facts. Ultimately it didn't matter. We were here to solve murders, and that came first.

"All right, I'm back out on patrol. Cindy, you with me?"

"Yep. Give me three minutes," she replied before stuffing the remainder of a sandwich in her mouth.

"I'll be outside in the SUV." *I guess we're going to act as if that confession session never happened,* I thought to myself as I walked outside. *Honestly,* I figured, *it could be worse.*

I climbed into the vehicle and flipped on the radio. The main popular-music station was playing romance songs, something I didn't need at the moment. I tried the oldies channel; more love songs. Thinking music wasn't in the cards, I flipped to the nearest talk-radio station, which happened to be a sports channel out of Indianapolis.

"...we're supposed to just embrace this football team that very clearly slipped away from their previous city like a whore in the night?"

I turned the radio off. Sometimes silence was best.

Thankfully, Cindy came outside shortly thereafter and made her way toward my vehicle.

● ● ●

After a few minutes of driving quietly, I finally spoke up. "So, we are supposed to interview the Atkinsons, the Watkinses, and the Dicers. All county-line farm folk," I added for context. "I guess the idea is that someone on the run from the law might cross county lines and do so on private property."

"Sounds easy enough," Cindy replied. "Hey, you hear the one about the farmer who lost his hearing?"

I was so relieved to hear her telling a joke that I didn't think it through. "No," I answered honestly.

She then mouthed a few silent words—pretty sure it was "They can't tell what you're saying"—and then laughed at me.

"That gag probably works better if you're not driving," she admitted.

I started having serious doubts that the girl in confession had been Cindy. Regardless, I was happy to pretend as though that confession had never occurred—which is how I was supposed to behave anyway, as a priest.

"Do you know any of them?"

"I know them all," I replied. "The Atkinson and Watkins families both attend my church, and the Dicers are vehemently anti-church. All three families are farmers."

"Shocking," she deadpanned.

"Hey! If you're good at something, you keep doing that something. And Crooked Creek is good at farming." I smiled. "We are the fourth-highest-producing corn county in the state, actually."

She didn't believe me and just scoffed.

"I'm one hundred percent serious, Officer Baxter. Look it up."

"Well, it *is* everywhere here," she sighed, glancing out the window.

"You've spent too much time in Indianapolis," I said, trying to joke. "But this here is the true heart of Indiana."

Things went quiet and awkward just then, and I can only figure that mentioning Indianapolis reminded Cindy of her husband, and maybe she missed him. Or maybe she *had* been in the confession booth that morning and now felt guilty about it. Regardless, it was clear that I should not have mentioned Indy.

I tried to ease the tension by turning directly *into* it. "You probably miss your husband. I'm sorry I mentioned Indy."

"Oh, no." She waved her hand in the air. "You didn't do anything wrong." She didn't say anything about her husband.

I wasn't sure what to say, but as we rounded a curve, we came upon a bizarre sight. I was almost thankful for the distraction.

"What in the hell?" I murmured as we approached the roadblock.

"Is this some kind of regular thing?" Cindy asked.

In front of us, mostly blocking the road, was a series of nose-to-nose tractors, mowers, combines, and more. They were lined up the way I'd seen kids play with Hot Wheels. In front were the basic mowers. But each successive piece of equipment got larger and larger. It was as though they were being laid out for inspection.

I sighed long and loud, knowing full well where we were. We were at The Bend, the convergence of the county's two largest farms, the Kemps and the Andersons. This was our county's version of the Hatfields and McCoys. They'd been fighting over tiny bits of land since before this very road was even built.

They called it The Bend because, well, it had a prominent sharp curve and most roads in these parts were straight, to be honest. Sure, there were other roads with curves in them, but none as prominently traveled as this stretch.

"Sheriff Lancaster to base. Maggie, come in," I barked into the radio.

There was some static before she responded. "Maggie here, sir. Go ahead, over."

"Can you send Gene or Skip out here to The Bend, please? We have some kind of tractor-based dick-measuring contest going on in the middle of the goddamn road. I'm gonna go around and go do these interviews, 'cause I don't have time for this shit." I paused. "Over."

"Will do, Sheriff. Over."

I drove onto grass on the right side of the road, land I knew to legally belong to the county, though both these families claimed it as their own. When I got around all the farm equipment, I pulled back onto the road and flipped on my loudspeaker.

"Mr. Kemp. Mr. Anderson. You're both going to get a huge fine for this, cutting into both your bottom lines this fall!"

CHAPTER 16

FOXHOLES

The Watkinses' farm would be the first we would come to, followed by the Dicers' and then the Atkinsons'. If things went well, we'd be done with questioning and back in town for supper.

And even though it is not pertinent to anything, the Watkinses were great at sex, which is to say they were proficient at it. There were fourteen Watkins children, all between the ages of two and eighteen. And they needed every one of them, as the Watkinses' farm was the third largest in the county, requiring all those extra hands just to bring in the harvest and keep the enterprise afloat.

The ninth-eldest Watkins child answered the door. I believe he was seven, his name might have been ... Chad. Or Charles. They all had C names, which was hard enough, but they also all ran around shirtless all the time. It was impossible for someone like me to visually recognize any of these children.

"Hi there, young man," I said. "Is your mother or father home?"

He simply disappeared from behind the screen door without a word.

"Is that a 'No'?" Cindy asked.

"I don't think so."

Soon enough, an elder Watkins son appeared. This time I recognized him as the eldest son, Cyrus.

"Yeah?"

"Cyrus, hi," I said pleasantly. "Is your father or mother around?"

"Dad's out on the back field with a sick horse; Ma's on the toilet."

The Watkins clan didn't mince words. I knew that "the back field" in this instance meant the very farthest-away section of Watkins farmland.

They had more acres than you can fathom, and Papa Watkins was easily a half hour or more away on horse or ATV.

I didn't even want to ask for more information on Ma.

Cyrus would have to do.

"Look, Cyrus, you know we got these murders happening in Crooked Creek, right?" In the background, a child screamed.

Cyrus was nonplussed. "Yeah, heard about 'em."

"All we wanted to ask is that you guys maybe keep an eye out. You have so much land. This guy is clearly moving in and out of Crooked Creek via nontraditional methods."

"Nontraditional?"

"We don't think he's using a car, Cyrus. We think he's traveling between private farmlands."

"Well, I'll shoot any son of a bitch that tries to trespass on my land."

"That's not . . . that's not what I'm looking for here, Cyrus. In fact, I need you to *not* shoot people these days if you find 'em on your land. I need to bring them in for questioning. They could be serial killers; you see?! And Indiana law does *not* allow you to shoot trespassers, Cyrus, I do hope you also know that."

"If they're killers, you don't want us to kill 'em?"

"Exactly. I don't want you to kill them. We need to arrest them and bring them to justice."

"Daddy says 'Ain't no justice greater than a revolver.'"

"Well," I hedged, "as much as I'm sure your father believes that statement, it doesn't line up with the law. We have dozens of FBI agents in the city now investigating these murders. Let us do our jobs so we can catch them, okay?"

Cyrus looked me up and down, like I was a zoo animal, shrugged, and shut the door.

● ● ●

The Atkinsons were next. They had half the acreage of the Watkinses, but they were wealthier, due to inheritance as well as the Atkinsons splitting their land up into pieces in order to grow different crops. The Atkinsons primarily grew corn, as it was the proven money-maker in these parts. But soybeans were starting to make inroads, and the buzz was heavy that soybeans would be able to be used for dozens of products. They were also dabbling in large-scale tomato farming, as well as wheat and hay.

They had only two children, both teenage boys, who definitely worked the farm. But the Atkinsons also used hired farmhands, several of whom lived on the property in the barracks.

They also had, by my estimation, the longest driveway in the county. I turned onto the gravel drive that ran in between a wheat field and a horse pasture.

"So, tell me," Cindy asked after several moments of silence: "what makes a farm one that needs horses versus a farm that doesn't need horses?"

I glanced at her with mostly-mock scorn. "Don't ask that question out loud around here unless you want to be laughed at."

"Well, I don't know. How am I supposed to learn if I don't ask?" she laughed.

"A horse farm is one thing," I began. "That's generally a place where horses are bred, typically to be sold for racing or work or show. You'll find many more of those in southern Indiana and Kentucky than you will here in the middle of the state."

She just nodded.

"Then there's a farm farm. A regular farm. There are all kinds of farms. Some people farm vegetables. Some people farm cattle or pigs. Some farm salmon, grow orchards of apples and other fruits, or do a combination of any or all of the above. Where the horses come in is due mainly to the size of the farm and the overall means of the family."

I continued: "Let's say you have fifty acres. Then to get from the main barn back to the farthest point away on the property, it would take forever by tractor *and* cost a lot of precious gasoline. Horse gets you out there much faster and with less overall cost. And then it's just a slippery slope. Once you have horses, you need a barn. Once you have a barn, you will get mice, so you'll need cats. Most farmers also garden and eat as much of their own food as possible, so a few dairy cows and some chickens are pretty common. But then foxes might come for your chickens, so you'll need a dog or three, and they can also help with herding if you have goats or sheep."

"I thought being married to a therapist was complicated," she laughed.

"Oh," I said, trying to reassure her, "farming is pretty simple. It's just really hard work. And no one who benefits from that work ever realizes how hard it actually is." With that, we slowed to a stop and parked.

Mrs. Atkinson was out the door with a tray of lemonade before we made it to the front porch. I did not know how she did it, but she was a consummate hostess.

"Lemonade?" she called as she shuffled up to us, blocking our path. "Sheriff, so good to see you again! Can I offer you any lemonade?"

"Of course," I agreed, as I took a glass. I looked at Cindy intently. To refuse a glass of Mrs. Atkinson's lemonade not only was to refuse a glass of deliciousness but also was something she would be personally offended by—and we were here trying to get information out of her.

Cindy, while still new to town, picked up on my facial expression and took a glass of lemonade for herself. I watched her take a sip before drinking any myself, because I wanted to soak in her reaction and also just in case it was poisoned—which would only be the case if this family harbored our killer, and I thought those odds were small. She moaned and sighed as though she'd just eaten a four-Michelin-star meal.

I laughed and finally took a drink myself. No one would ever top this woman's lemonade. I prayed a quick prayer that she and her entire family would not only be cleared of implication in any murders, but also live long and happy lives, for the betterment of the lemonade-needing community around her.

"Mrs. Atkinson," I began, before she cut me off.

"Beatrice. You call me Beatrice or don't call me at all," she giggled.

"Beatrice," I began again, being much more informal than I was used to. "We are here to talk to you about the recent murders in Crooked Creek."

"I know why you're here," she barked. "Your secretary, Maggie, called me this morning to let me know you'd be coming by. Come on in before we get too serious. I've got sausage balls and deviled eggs!"

I sighed and smiled at Cindy, hoping she understood my expression to mean "Welcome to law enforcement in Indiana." We would have to have a meal in order to get any kind of good conversation out of these folks. Fortunately, Mrs. Atkinson was an incredible cook.

● ● ●

After a full spread of sausage balls, deviled eggs, ham, split-pea soup, potatoes, green beans, and rolls, we were all extremely full, including Mr. Atkinson and the two boys. The males had no interest in talking to us; they just ate their meals, said polite good-byes, and went back out to work the fields.

I kind of respected that, even though those types of people made my job more difficult, because they paid attention only to their own job and nothing that might help me in a murder investigation. And they were the very folks most likely to see any suspicious activity out in their land.

But I had played this game before.

"Beatrice," I began, "what an incredible meal. Thank you so much."

She nodded the way people do when they desire the compliment but are unsure how to properly accept it.

I continued: "Now, can you tell us if you or any of the menfolk in the household have seen any suspicious activity out here on your farm? We believe our killer might be traveling around Crooked Creek and the surrounding area via the countryside instead of roads."

"Well, Sheriff," she started, "we got our own horse trails and such, of course. We use 'em to get around to various fields and sections of the farm."

"Right," I agreed quickly, not wanting to waste time on an education I didn't need.

"The boys did find some hoofprints the other day. Kinda surprised us."

"Why?" I asked instinctively.

"Wasn't one of our horses, of course," she said flatly.

"You can tell one horse's hoofprint from another?" Cindy asked.

"Well, shucks," Beatrice laughed. "No, sweetheart. We're not that good. But listen, here's the thing . . . our horses? We shoe 'em all." She paused to let us roll that around our brains a moment. "Leaves an entirely different kind of print in the ground, especially in the mud."

"You can tell the difference between a shoed horse footprint and a non-shoed one?" Cindy clarified her bewilderment.

This time Beatrice didn't reply with words. She just looked at Cindy with a complex-but-clear facial expression that silently said "Honey, shut up." It was clear she wanted no more ignorant questions from this woman who had clearly never farmed a day in her life.

I sat back a bit to ponder the revelation. It felt important. I looked at Cindy, and she at me.

"Does this happen often?" I inquired. "Folks riding through your land on their own horses?"

"I mean, sure. Sometimes. But not often, no. And not during a time when a bunch of folks are getting killed. Besides, there ain't much you can tell from a hoofprint. It's not a fingerprint, where every horse is different. All I can really say for sure is that someone went riding through our land recently." She stood. "Now, can I offer either one of you a piece of rhubarb pie?"

* * *

A slice of rhubarb pie later, we were back on the road and headed toward the Dicer farm.

"Fucking rhubarb," I muttered, rubbing my stomach.

"It doesn't agree with you?" Cindy asked.

"It's basically celery's angry cousin. It's a plant stalk soaked in sugar long enough that it becomes edible and sweet. I hate it."

"I thought it was tasty."

"That was the sugar."

We drove on for a mile or so in silence before I recalled a moment.

"Do you remember when you asked if she could tell the difference between hooved horseprints and shoed horseprints?" I laughed as I finished speaking.

"Shut up," Cindy barked.

"That was freaking hilarious!" I cackled. "I've never seen someone get shut down with a facial expression before!"

"How is a person supposed to learn shit if they are ridiculed when they ask questions?!"

Between laughter, I managed to explain: "It's not the question you asked, but the person you chose to ask it to. It's like asking Babe Ruth if he can tell a curveball from a fastball."

"Who's Babe Ruth?"

● ● ●

The Dicer farm was soybean only. They'd been the first in the mid-state to go all in on soybeans, and by the looks of their property they were doing very well with it. Large trees lined the long paved driveway, and a giant parking circle sat outside the main house with a massive fountain in the middle.

The Dicers were not religious. Even more, they were very wary of religious folks. I was thankful I was wearing my sheriff's uniform today instead of my clerical collar. I was still recognized immediately.

"Sheriff Father," Bart Dicer, the family patriarch, snarked. "And a lovely new assistant!"

I wish words could do justice to Cindy's face at being called a "lovely new assistant." If expressions of confused offense could kill.

"I'm on the grapevine," Bart continued. "I know you're here to see if anyone's been trespassing on my land, and the answer is 'No.'"

I stammered aloud. "Mr. Dicer, you have eighty-seven acres of land."

"And?"

"How could you possibly know definitively that no one has trespassed in the last few days?"

He paused a moment and then retorted. "How could you possibly know that someone *has*?"

Confused, I tried again. "Sir, you are not accused of any crime. We just think a criminal might have passed through your property on the way to commit a crime."

"I don't know nothing!" he shouted. And then he slammed the door.

Cindy scoffed. "Seems like guilty behavior to me."

I smiled. "You just don't know the Dicers. They hate the law almost as much as they hate the church. It was a long shot to even drive out here."

"I'm so exhausted, but also really hungry," she declared, yawning.

"It's been a long day," I agreed. "Let's go grab some dinner."

● ● ●

The ringing phone woke me from a dead sleep.

At first, just my eyes opened. By the third ring, I was sitting up. By the fifth ring, I was picking up the receiver.

"Go," I said softly. It was the only form of "Hello, this is Sheriff Lancaster. Please state your problem" that I was capable of at this point in time.

I figured the person who was calling knew who they were calling and at what time, so they would have information ready to go. Either that or it was a prank call, which I'd effectively ended in this community a year ago with a showy arrest of the most notorious prank-caller in the tri-county area, Edmund Silver, aka Clarence Crabtree, aka Silky Steve.

The voice on the other end jabbered at me for about a total of forty-five seconds before stopping. I sighed long and loud.

"Okay, son. Keep looking. I'll be there in a few minutes." I hung up the phone and flopped back onto the bed, sighing again.

"You're missing," I said aloud.

"What?" Cindy sat up next to me, sheet in hand covering herself.

"You're a missing person, and I have to get out of bed now to go help look for you."

"Oh, no."

CHAPTER 17

SECRETS

"THE GUYS AT THE BED AND BREAKFAST noticed you never came back last night." I smiled. "Now they think you're a possible victim."

"Oh, my God. What are we gonna do?" she panicked. She hopped off the bed and scrambled around my bedroom, looking for all her belongings, all while trying to hold the sheet to her body. Within seconds, she tripped and fell. "Dammit!"

"It's probably worth pointing out that I am every bit as interested in keeping this thing a secret as you are," I said, smiling warmly. "Let's work together."

"Right." She pointed at me nervously. "Correct. Right. Okay, you figure out a plan while I take a shower."

I just laughed a bit. I mean, I probably should have been more concerned about our one-night stand being discovered, but I just wasn't. I knew I had sinned, but I also knew that I had been pushed to the brink, stress-wise. And I also knew that God forgives.

I made a few more phone calls while she cleaned up. When she stepped out of the bathroom wrapped in a towel, her hair wrapped in a hand towel, asking "Well?", I was ready.

"The story is this: your husband called you late last night and had a free evening. You met him in between Crooked Creek and Indy, just outside of Muncie, in a roadside motel. You forgot to tell anyone, and you took a cab to get there, a really expensive cab because it had to come *from* Muncie to get you, as Crooked Creek does not have taxicabs."

"And they'll believe this?" she scoffed.

"They already do," I replied. "The manhunt is over. They expect you back this afternoon."

"So who confirmed this?"

"I did, posing as your husband."

"When?"

"Just a minute ago, while you were in the bathroom."

"And just what am I supposed to do all day while they wait for me to return?"

I opened a cabinet near the TV. "I have an excellent library of VHS movies." I smiled. "Just wait a couple hours and walk over to either the church or the police station—you're only a few blocks from both—walk in, apologize, get razzed for having a sexy time with your husband . . . end of story." I stopped in my tracks. "Oh, my, I just realized it sounds as if I've done this kind of thing before!"

"You mean you haven't?" Cindy kissed my cheek. "Just go do what you gotta do, and I'll show up in a couple hours." She smiled weakly. "Thank you for thinking of a cover story for me."

"For us." I smiled as I opened the door to leave. "For both of us. I really can't stress enough how much I would prefer the town not find out I am having sex at all, let alone with you."

"Right," she agreed.

"Watch out for Zacchaeus, my cat. He bites."

"Oh, is he a wee little man?"

I just laughed. She had no idea.

I closed the door behind me and said a silent prayer for forgiveness, grace, and protection, knowing a more complete confession was yet to come.

I don't mean to sound cavalier about it: I had sinned—a mortal sin—and I would need to confess it. But it's not like it was my first time. Or last time. I'd long ago accepted my own humanity, a quality I now believe all priests and sheriffs should possess.

● ● ●

Today the FBI man in charge, Director Rathburn, had called in a specialist.

Martin Braugher, PhD, was a forensic psychologist, or so his business card claimed. I'd never heard of such a job, and, in fact, it turns out Dr. Braugher was one of the very first of his kind. You see, he was an expert on serial killers, as much as anyone in the world could claim to be.

"There isn't a ton of data to go by to date, but most serial killers I have studied are quite particular about their victims. The victims tend to have similarities in demographics like age and gender; some serial killers even prefer a certain hair color in their victims." Dr. Braugher was speaking to the higher-level FBI agents, Mayor Burke, and me. All the other agents and all my own deputies were out patrolling and continuing our interviews of the townspeople.

"Your suspect here," he continued, "is therefore unique. His victims cross boundaries of sex and age. In fact, on the flight here, I was analyzing the case files you sent me, and there does not appear to be a single shared characteristic or trait for any of our victims, minus that they all live here in this tiny town."

The room let out a collective sigh of disappointment. The case did feel impossible to solve.

"But," the good doctor added at the last minute, giving us all a glimmer of hope, "the choosing of the victims is only one element of serial-killer behavior that we have modeled. Our victim-choice matrix may not apply here, but plenty of our other analyses should be of practical use."

"Like what?" I asked. I didn't say it snotty or anything; I said it like a regular curious person. Mayor Burke still shot me a dirty look anyway. What a dickhead.

"Oh," Dr. Braugher continued, not seeming remotely offended by the question, "frequency of murders, proximity to victims, actual methodology of the killings and crime scenes, lots of stuff."

Burke beamed like the principal had just sided with him in the breakup of a lunchroom fight.

"That . . . sounds like really useful information," I admitted. And for good measure I added, "Glad you're here, Doc."

Out of the corner of my eye, I saw Cindy enter. She looked over toward the conference room, and we made eye contact briefly. She strolled casually to Maggie's desk and made small talk. I was filled with a warm affection as well as a cold feeling of guilt—you'd be surprised how easily the two sensations could coexist, and for how long.

"Now, your man has killed . . ." Braugher checked his notes ". . . three times in three weeks. Is that correct?"

"That's correct, Doctor," Rathburn replied.

I raised my hand, and Rathburn nodded.

"We have a few deaths from before this string of murders that we are going back and looking at again, sir. They were originally ruled deaths of natural causes, but given that our killer used poison in at least one of his killings . . ." I shrugged. "Maybe he didn't pick up the flower thing right away? Maybe his first kill or two were sloppier, less planned? It's a long shot, but we're running it down."

"Good thinking, Sheriff," Dr. Braugher said. I could almost feel Burke's asshole tightening at the sound of my receiving praise. "I would go even further back in your research. Check deaths over the last five years or so that had either no explanation or that seemed super-normal."

"Will do, Doc." I nodded. "But it wasn't my idea, sir; it was Agent Rathburn's."

"Well, then, good thinking, Agent Rathburn," Braugher said.

I pretended to make a note of things, when really I was just doodling a stick figure of me giving Mayor Burke the middle finger.

● ● ●

As everyone returned for lunch, the bed-and-breakfast gang of out-of-county officers were relieved to see Cindy, but wasted no time giving her grief about her late-night liaison. She blushed as they teased her, but you could tell there was love there . . . they weren't making fun to be mean, but out of camaraderie.

She looked at me and smiled, and I smiled back. The optimal outcome had been achieved.

I sighed in relief that our tryst had remained a secret, even as a small part of my brain was already plotting how to pull off the next one. This, by the way, is how sin operates. It gets its skinny, tiny claws into you in a way that feels harmless. But again, the guilt was immediate, but mostly drowned out by the euphoria.

This wasn't my first sexual relationship: far from it. I hadn't been a priest my whole life, after all. But, yes, even after the priesthood, there had been a couple of instances. I wasn't proud of it. But the sexual urge in humans was known to be stronger than even hunger.

And even the thought of another tryst with Cindy was technically a sin, at least if I allowed that thought to linger in my brain, which I did.

I sighed and added it to the mental list for the next time I saw Wendall.

And anyway, Skip showed up just then with a couple of boxes worth of tenderloin sandwiches, and Gene was on the loose so I had to race to get mine.

● ● ●

After lunch there was a mass briefing for all officers and agents. It was too large for any room in the station, so we moved everyone over one block to my church's recreation hall.

"We believe, based on the past evidence," Dr. Braugher spoke, "that another murder is due to take place within the next couple of days."

A hushed murmur rippled throughout the crowd. I guess they were surprised by what seemed to me to be fairly obvious news. We were in the fourth week; a fourth body was only natural. But somehow most of the officers seemed shocked and saddened by this "news."

I was certain the murder had already taken place, and we simply had yet to find the body, but not everyone agreed.

The bigger problem with a fourth body, according to the good doctor, was notoriety. One more murder, and we'd likely see the national media converge on our tiny city as the story blew up beyond central Indiana. Crooked Creek was certainly not ready for that.

And yet . . . something inside told me that this could be the very remedy I was seeking. The national media spotlight would make further murders exponentially more difficult, simply due to all the added eyeballs and the cameras. Any murders that occurred after the national spotlight was on us would only hasten the killer's capture.

CHAPTER 18

FOURTH VICTIM

THE KILLER'S FOURTH VICTIM was found early the next morning by the local veterinarian upon opening up his office for the day. The body was sprawled out on an exam table, clothed in full veterinarian garb, magnolias stapled all over his jacket.

It was Vernon Stamper, a local widower known to love pets and animals. He was, as it turned out, the single biggest donor to the facility, both in terms of cash donations and supplies. Whoever had killed him knew this and made a point of letting everyone know that he or she knew it.

The vet's office kept two adopted dogs on site as pets, and I imagined they had been howling all evening.

"Two Vernons killed back to back, Sheriff," Skip noted, wondering where to draw the line between suspicious and coincidental.

I didn't have the patience to deal with Skip today. "Skip, why don't you go outside and keep an eye out for Harold McKee. If he shows up, arrest him."

"For what, sir?"

"I honestly don't care, Skip," waving my hand to shoo him outside as if he were a mosquito.

"Is this déjà vu? Did we or did we not just have a Vernon?" Lt. Irwin asked, walking up to our position in front of the house. "Is this somehow a completely different Vernon?"

"Well, sir, it would have to be, considering the other body is down at the morgue," I replied dryly.

"How can there be two people named Vernon living in the same small town?"

"The odds against coincidental outcomes are not as long as you might think, Lieutenant. Why, I'd venture most of the towns you find here in central Indiana have a pair of similarly named citizens."

"Well, goddammit," he barked before stomping off.

The "two Vernons" thing had long been a local piece of common knowledge; long enough for most locals to be tired of its charm. Both men were born and bred in Crooked Creek, and both despised the fact that someone else in town had the same name. They avoided each other at all costs, and both claimed to be the "true" Vernon or the "original" Vernon. They even got asked to appear in the dunk tanks at the local street fair or Halloween festival so that everyone had a chance to "dunk the 'REAL' Vernon."

Almost none of the people who lived here even called the men Vernon anymore because the name was so loaded. Most had taken to using the men's last names, or just not speaking to them at all.

It wasn't surprising to have the FBI agents confused by it, but it was definitely old news for us. Hence the sarcasm: we were tired of explaining the Vernon thing to outsiders and newcomers. In all honesty, plenty of locals would actually be glad to learn they were both dead so the issue could finally be laid to rest once and for all—except it would continue after death, as both Vernon's gravestones became the site of a competitive mourning situation.

Thankfully, I was ripped out of that mental zone-out by another person passing by. "Someone is killing all our best citizens," the main veterinarian wailed as he was walked outside by EMTs. Being the one to have discovered the body, he was clearly traumatized.

He had a point. Everyone the killer had knocked off so far had, for the most part, been perfect citizens. Many were philanthropic. None of them had a bad word spoken of them after their death. For now it was an interesting data anomaly, but it was one I would have to keep an eye on, or at least potentially explain in the future.

Crooked Creek was full of good Samaritans, of course. We couldn't exactly go about stationing police outside the home of every good person in town.

I'd been sheriff long enough to know that the good people here out-weighed the bad by at least twenty to one, if not better. And even the bad people were, like, shoplifters and drunk drivers. Angry ex-boyfriends smashing mailboxes.

Murderers? It was truly hard to believe one could be living among us.

● ● ●

I arrived at the vet's office expecting more of a ruckus than I found. As usual of late, I was getting to see the crime scene well after all the FBI guys had gone through it. I was certain they had tainted the evidence, but since I couldn't prove it, I just tried to see what I could find on my own.

"Magnolias?" I asked aloud, to no one in particular. Cindy was here, as were Gene and Skip.

"That's a weird flower for these parts. No?" she asked.

"That's affirmative, sir," Gene replied almost immediately. "Magnolia is a tree and flower much more likely to grow and flourish in the South. Georgia, Alabama . . . Tennessee for sure. Maybe Kentucky. But certainly not native to these parts."

"I think at this point it's worth looking into how this guy is getting these flowers, no? Did he drive to Nashville for the magnolia blossom or what?" I was growing frustrated, and I'm sure it showed.

"Maybe he has a private greenhouse, or access to one?" another agent offered.

"There's so much private acreage in Crooked Creek, it could be any-where," another responded.

"How will we find it?" yet another asked.

"Um," Cindy began, not necessarily wanting to challenge a room full of uniformed men. "Flower shop?"

Instantly there was a three-second pause, followed by the kind of pandemonium you'd expect when an entire police force is schooled by a simple question.

Unfortunately, after calling every single flower shop within a hundred-mile radius, we still had nothing. We even cross-referenced, wondering if the killer could have bought one flower at each florist in the hope that we wouldn't search for him that way.

Nothing.

"Maybe he gathered the flowers long ago and just froze them all?"

Every single person in the room turned to look at Gene with new-found awe. He'd just said the smartest thing any of us had said regarding this issue, but because we all considered him the "aloof guy who eats all the time," we had forgotten his innate police nature.

I rubbed my face in exhaustion. "That makes an awful lot of sense, Gene," I replied. I took a deep breath and then followed with "Care to let us look at your freezer?" I smiled and then laughed, and slowly everyone else joined in. Gene was clearly not the killer, but he had just given us an important bit of direction. "Gene's right, folks. We don't need to look only for fresh flowers, or even shipped-in flowers. It's possible most of these were bought or harvested here in Indiana and frozen for a future use."

It wouldn't take long for our research to reveal that even frozen flowers were off the list. Frozen flowers might retain their color, but almost nothing else about the flower would be the same, from touch to smell.

No, we were definitely dealing with someone who had access to fresh flowers.

●●●

"He was so angry," Theresa Stamper said between sobs. "The bigger farms . . . they were taking advantage of him. Negotiating against him."

This was an altogether different sort of crime than the one I'd come asking about.

"You're saying the bigger farms here in town were working together to price your son's farm out of business?" Collusion was a serious crime, but it was one of the toughest to prove. There were rampant rumors across the Midwest, but no proof.

Theresa clammed up a bit at that direct question. A few deep breaths, and then she said, "I ain't saying nothing on the record."

I got her meaning. "Okay," I said. "What if we talk about your son's friends and hobbies?"

"I ain't saying nothing on the record!" she shouted again.

"Ma'am," I said softly, "your son was a victim. He is not a suspect of any crime. We are only trying to learn more about him so that we can help find out who killed him."

"Understand that," she barked. "Tryin' not to be another victim myself."

"Are you saying that you are afraid that if you talk to us and give us too much information, the people or person who killed your son will kill you as well?"

At this, she sighed loud and long and slowly closed the door in our faces.

I put my head in my hand for my own long sigh.

Cindy just blurted out what came to mind. "What the hell?"

Understanding rural Indiana citizens is mostly about accepting the weird.

● ● ●

Vernon's mother wasn't going to be of any further help. Vernon had no friends. He was basically a ghost, even though everyone knew him.

Basically a ghost, even though everyone knew him.

That described pretty much everyone in Crooked Creek, now that I thought about it.

"You don't believe that story, do you?" Cindy asked, still sounding agitated as we climbed into the car.

"Which one?" I deflected.

"That the bigger farms are picking off the smaller ones."

I paused.

"Wait," she said, shocked. "Do you?"

"I don't know," I finally said. "I don't think the larger farms are behind these killings, and I don't think they would murder anyone. . . ." I trailed off.

"So then what?" she challenged me to finish.

"I wouldn't be surprised if the big farms are actively trying to destroy the smaller ones . . . and I wouldn't be surprised if they were breaking the law to do so."

"But . . . murder?"

"You have my statement." I smiled.

Forty minutes later, we were in bed together, forgetting the local murders and focusing on a new connection.

● ● ●

"I'm going to Hell, you realize," Cindy said as my alarm continued blaring.

I reached over and slapped it off. "If it's any comfort," I sighed, "I feel like most humans will be there."

"Even you?" she said, her adorable morning face suddenly closing in as she pecked me on the cheek.

I sighed contentedly before reality set in, and I responded. "Yeah. Even me."

She shimmied into her pants. "Do you think God will judge me more harshly for leading you astray?"

I smiled at her, still not quite ready to get out of bed. "You think you're the first gal who's led me astray?"

She gasped in mock offense. "Now you're making me feel like a whore." She laughed.

"Sounds like we sinned no matter what," I added.

"Would you hear my confession?" she cooed as she slipped her bra on.

"Please don't turn a phrase I hear every day into something sexy," I asked flatly.

"Sorry," she said before walking into the bathroom. "So," she called back, "what's the agenda for today?"

"You're not gonna like it," I replied.

"Why? More crazy Indiana country folk to interview?"

"Worse," I said. "I need you to go to Indy."

I heard four distinct barefoot stomps before she came around the corner, toothbrush in her mouth, and a look I can only describe as confused anger.

CHAPTER 19

ANOTHER FUNERAL

I T   W A S   I M P O S S I B L E   T O   T R A C E   the flowers back to the killer if he had truly acquired them months prior and frozen them all. But it was worth a shot, as any lead was in a murder investigation. It was also a good excuse to get Cindy out of town and back to Indy with her husband—which, I admit, might have been motivated by my own guilt. But she also knew the area, and her husband knew it even better. And that could help speed things along.

I sent Gene and Skip along with her, just to ensure a complete and secure investigation. There were more than fifty florists in the greater Indianapolis area, so they would be gone at least a week. They'd be looking for anyone who bought fresh flowers in bulk, and in wide variety, and within a certain recent window.

Cindy had not been pleased. I quite expected our affair to be ended after this move, though that wasn't my motivation for sending her. She just knew Indianapolis better than any of my own deputies, even if only by virtue of her husband's knowledge. Indeed, there was no less interest on my part today than there had been the day before. I was a bit relieved, of course . . . relieved to not have to keep up the act for a few days, though I knew that relief came with guilt.

Thankfully, I was able to postpone the guilt a bit by focusing on Vernon Stamper's funeral. While he'd attended Mass only a few times over the years, his will had a specific request to have his funeral here at my church—a request I never denied.

You might wonder how a man of the cloth would be able to write a funeral homily while still distant enough from God because of my unconfessed mortal sins. But it's surprisingly easy. After you've done a dozen funerals, the homilies write themselves. The bits of scripture, the summary of good qualities, the promise of eternal life. Bing bang boom. I honestly wished it were more difficult, so I could feel as if I'd done something more substantial to honor the man.

I sat in my office in the back of the church, flipping through photo albums Vernon's family had given me. It was impossible to know a man completely from looking at pictures of him, but you get to know him better—or know him at all—by doing it.

Vernon had been a fiddle player in his youth, and many of the pictures were of performances, jamborees, and competitions he'd participated in over the course of his musical career. But like most kids raised around here, music and the arts . . . anything but farming, really . . . is just putting off the inevitable.

Everyone raised by a farmer becomes a farmer. Sure, there are exceptions—usually when the farmer has multiple kids—but while most kids around here played a sport or an instrument, none of them ever had any illusions of turning it into a career.

No one ever got out of Crooked Creek; and if they did, they were merely the exceptions that proved the rule. And many who left ended up right back there, damaged. Like Buzz Martinson, who left after family tragedy, went to Vietnam, and returned more troubled than before.

● ● ●

Throughout all these weeks of murders and investigations, I still heard confession every week for at least a few hours.

I should say that I *sat* to hear confession every week for at least a few hours. Some days, no one came to confess. The entire community was gripped with fear over these killings, and many regular routines had been altered or eliminated altogether.

Attendance at Mass was down significantly; why shouldn't confessions suffer the same fate?

I'd heard a few jokes about how, with everyone staying home for fear of the killer, there would likely be a baby boom in Crooked Creek in eight or nine months. I figured a confession boom was possible as well, as folks got back into their routines while still realizing and living with the sin in their hearts.

This day was a bustling day for sinners, as I heard two whole confessions.

First up was Edith Neidermeyer. Edith was sixty-eight years old and came to confession every single week. She was, quite typically, only coming for appearance's sake. She thought she could fool God by being a terrible person in her life but confessing it all every week.

Her sins were always the same: drinking, gambling, and "whoring" as she put it. Yes, Edith Neidermeyer was getting more action than any other soul in town, at least to hear her tell it. I wasn't sure I believed that all of her sins were true. Sometimes people make up sins to confess, either for performance's sake or because they just like having someone who listens to them.

As usual, I asked her for real-world penance: to give up drinking and gambling for at least one day and instead honor the Lord by using that time to call a friend and share the love of Jesus. As usual, she pretended to be contrite and said she'd do those things we both knew she wouldn't do, and then she left.

About ten minutes before the hour was up, I heard the church doors open and close, then soft footsteps nearby, and then someone entered the confessional. I waited patiently while the confessor built up the necessary courage. I was used to this.

"Forgive me, Father, for I have sinned," I heard the person say.

I didn't recognize the voice at all. I remained silent for now.

"It has been . . . years since my last confession. I'm a really bad Catholic, Father." Again I stayed quiet. The onus was on the confessor in these situations, and it was my job to serve as intermediary between the confessor and Christ, *not* to coax confessions out of reluctant church members. "I've done some bad stuff," the voice continued. "I mean, I don't think I've made a confession in twenty years, Father. Should I just . . . bullet point it or give you the broad strokes, or what?"

Finally I spoke. "Confess only that which your heart leads you to confess. Formatting and length of confession is not important; what's important is clearing your heart of sin."

"I don't know what I'm doing. I'm sorry. I'm just . . . I need some forgiveness."

It was at this point that I recognized the voice as that of loaner officer Greg Grayson, from the nearby Perrington Police Department. I'd been calling him Dewey in my head but so far had managed to call him Greg or Officer Grayson in person. We hadn't spent much time together, he and I, but I had known him to be a warm and friendly individual.

"Go on," I encouraged.

"Father, I have had sexual feelings for a fellow co-worker for weeks, and it's tearing me up inside." He was almost instantly in tears.

I merely breathed in and out and said nothing.

He continued. "While I have not acted on my feelings, I have had lustful thoughts for a fellow out-of-town officer, Father. I lose sleep at night thinking about her, and then I spend my days kicking myself for thinking about her."

He was talking about Cindy. She was quite literally the only female out-of-town officer currently on loan to this investigation.

"She's even married, Father," he said, "but I can't stop thinking about her."

I smiled, knowing he couldn't see it.

Then I set myself straight and spoke, remembering I had in my own heart this man's sin and more. "It doesn't sound as though you are ready to confess the sin, since you are not sure you can stop it from happening in the future." Fifty percent of being a member of the clergy is just about sounding smarter than you really are. I guessed this was also true for schoolteachers, corporate leaders, and parents.

"How do I stop, Sheriff—I mean, Father?"

I smiled again, realizing most people in my confessional knew exactly which human being they were confessing to, despite the theatrics of confession-booth secrecy.

"The human sexual impulse is natural," I began. "You are not necessarily sinning by having an urge for sex. But when that urge is allowed to grow and is directed at a specific real-life person . . . you have crossed over from urges into intentional thoughts. That's the line of sin."

"Yeah," he agreed.

"Are you married?" I asked.

"Yes."

"Do you think your recent bout of infatuation might just be related to you missing your wife? The intimacy and comfort of her?"

There was a very brief pause, followed by a long sigh.

"Perhaps you aren't infatuated with this co-worker as much as you just miss your wife," I offered.

A few seconds of silence passed before I finally heard some light laughter—or it could have been sobbing. Regardless, he said, "You're right. You're absolutely right. How did I miss that?"

He'd already called me "Sheriff" by accident, because he knew it was me, but I kept up the ruse when offering advice. "Maybe ask your local boss or sheriff for a couple days off so you can go back to your wife and visit her? I have a feeling that might be approved."

"Yes, Father."

"In the meantime, let's do some penance for the casual lust, shall we? How about you volunteer for two hours interning with a local divorce lawyer—there are only two, and I'll let you choose your favorite—so you can see the impact that adultery has on loving marriages and families."

"Yes, Father. Thank you, Sheriff."

And he was off.

Later that day, I was happy to sign a vacation notice for Greg, knowing he would return to us refreshed and renewed after his visit home.

● ● ●

My evenings were used to being filled with conversation and companionship from Cindy. But since I'd sent her away, my evenings were a lot more boring. I heated up a TV dinner and sat down on the couch to watch some TV. Zacchaeus was happy to have my full attention for the first time in ages, so he sat on my lap. I had to go out of my way not to spill any of my meal on his back, but I was smiling the whole time.

There was something comforting in the routine of a house cat. Eat, sleep, eat some more, and sleep some more. It was peace-giving. Familiar. Calming.

I woke up in the middle of the night in the same chair, Zacchaeus still on my lap, as though several hours had passed instantly. I stood and gently returned the cat to my place in the recliner, where my body had kept the seat warm, and stomped upstairs before falling onto my bed without setting the alarm.

CHAPTER 20

NATIONAL MEDIA

I AWOKE TO THE SOUNDS OF TRAFFIC.

Traffic?

This was uncommon in Crooked Creek. We maybe got a couple of semis per night, driving through the county from one small township to the next. What we called "Main Street" was technically a state highway, so some small amount of through traffic was to be expected.

Today it was dozens of semis, or perhaps even more. The noise was obtrusive and, whether or not it was intended, sent the message that this town was in for yet another round of major upheaval. It turned out to be the national media rolling into town. Seems we'd hit the magic number of murders to qualify as an important national story.

I microwaved yesterday's leftover coffee and stared out the kitchen window while drinking it, marveling at the sheer amount of money behind this kind of mobilization.

Things were different here now. For how long remained to be seen. Maybe there would be no going back to the days of quiet, simple Crooked Creek. Now we had cameras, microphones, and even a helicopter.

We weren't fucking around anymore.

I had thought Harold McKee was stubborn and without scruples. But I had never met a member of the national media before this moment, and I would quickly learn just how tame and amateur Harold actually was.

Crooked Creek was no longer an unknown sleepy town in Indiana . . . it was the focus of all the world's attention.

I had three microphones shoved in my face before I could even enter the police station. I knew well enough to say nothing, but this was still a new and unwelcome change. The roar of the press questions died with the closing of the precinct's front door, and relative silence returned.

"You know, can we subpoena for use of their helicopter since we don't have one of our own?" I barked at the mayor, even though I had no idea if he was even in the building.

He wasn't, as it turned out.

"What in all the hells?" I continued to no one in particular as I made a beeline for the coffee machine.

I knew my work would bring scrutiny. I'd even been ready for more cops. But I had not expected the press. Just goes to show that you can never plan enough.

"They're all already in there," Maggie said, pointing to the conference room.

"I'm not even late!" I barked back at her angrily, though none of my anger was her fault.

I opened the rear door and entered the conference room. The briefing wasn't being led by FBI Field Director Rathburn, nor by his right-hand man, Lt. Irwin. Instead, it was being led by Crooked Creek Mayor Burke.

I guzzled my coffee and shook my head silently in disbelief.

"I want each and every one of you to flat-out ignore these media hounds. Pretend they don't exist. Don't run over them with your car, of course," Burke chuckled, "but make believe you cannot see them. That is a department order."

A slight murmur went through the room before the mayor shouted it down.

"Only one of you will talk to the media. And since we don't have a media spokesman here in tiny little Crooked Creek, I'm gonna give that responsibility to . . ." Burke looked up, locking eyes with me, silently telling me exactly how much he owned me. "Sheriff Lancaster." He beamed. "Solomon, you can handle that, right?"

"The FBI doesn't have their own—" I was cut off instantly.

"The FBI is devoting its resources to solving the case," he shouted back at me.

"Very good, sir." I said flatly, eating roughly my thirtieth plate of crow since being elected sheriff. I'd rather swim across Lake Michigan than serve as media spokesman, but I'd be damned if I would tell Mayor Burke that, at least to his face.

There were easier ways to get out of this assignment than arguing with him.

● ● ●

"I will read a brief statement and then I'll take a few questions," I said. "Just a few," I reiterated, in case anyone doubted my resolve. "Don't push it."

I was standing outside the sheriff's office, roughly fifty yards or so away, in an empty lot between the station and the Crooked Creek Bank. About fifteen members of the press stood before me, microphones extended. I saw logos and emblems for all the major news stations, as well as a few regional and international reporters.

"First of all," I said before pausing to clear my throat. "Mayor Burke and I thank you for being here today." I looked back inside the station, glaring, hoping the mayor could feel my stare, even though he was probably already back home at his mansion, eating prime rib and watching this on television.

The horde of media mouths flapped wildly.

"*Wait* a damn minute until I finish, at least," I roared.

They quieted down.

"To date, Crooked Creek Township has recorded four unusual deaths in a short period of time. Mayor Burke and I are equally committed to solving these crimes."

The press roared again.

"People?!" It was a question, an exclamation, and a threat . . . all wrapped up in one. "Jeez," I breathed once they'd quieted down. "The sheriff's office has reason to believe all four murders are connected, and we continue to work with the FBI and officers from the surrounding area to track down all our leads."

I took a deep breath, which was a mistake because that silence was filled with even more incessant questions.

"*Shut the fuck up!*" I bellowed.

Instinctively, and perhaps in shock, everyone shut up.

"Now," I continued, "do you want to hear what I have to say, or do you want to talk over me? The choice is yours. I can go home and sleep fine tonight, but if you want to write your stupid news articles, you need the information I have. Up to you."

The reporters were all a bit wary at this point, taken aback, but I was too upset and didn't notice, and I didn't back down.

"Who has a question now?! Huh?! Which one of you wants to ask a question next and can you *get* your fucking microphones a few inches further back out of my face?!"

I was possibly the worst police spokesperson in all of history. But I was happy to be relieved of the appointment.

The audio clip of me saying "You need the information I have. Up to you." led every single national nightly news program that evening. For a few hours, I was the nation's most hated man as I berated the innocent journalists with my swear words.

By morning, the FBI had sent a trained media specialist from Chicago to handle all press conferences moving forward. I wasn't offended. You might even say I'd done it on purpose. Because I had.

I wasn't even worried about the audio or possible footage of me making the rounds. I knew what most had yet to figure out: Americans had short attention spans. Long-term, no one would remember me or my comments. And I'd more than accomplished my own goal with that press session, which was to get out of the responsibility of being the spokesman for the investigation.

I briefly wondered what Cindy had thought of my performance— though my insecurity reminded me that she may have rekindled things with her husband after I sent her back to him in Indy. There was no telling if she even saw the news of my tirade at all.

I was spending more time thinking about what Cindy was thinking than I had expected to, that was for sure.

● ● ●

Of course, I was forced to spend about thirty minutes listening to the mayor scream at me. He said a lot of fancy words and phrases, and some pretty ugly ones, too, but everyone knew he couldn't remove me himself. He couldn't even punish or demote me without city council approval *and* a vote of the citizenry.

Yelling at me was literally all he could do, and so he was doing a bang-up job of it.

I smiled the entire time. I'd never been happier to get yelled at. Seeing me smile only made him more irate, which only made me smile more. Honestly, we're both lucky we didn't get caught up in a never-ending spiral.

When he was finished, face red, sweat rolling down his cheeks, I stood and headed for the door. "I appreciate the opportunity to learn and grow, sir," I said, not meaning a word of it.

"Fuck off!" he bellowed, just as I'd opened the door. And just as I'd hoped, it was loud enough for everyone inside the building—and even a few microphones outside the building—to hear. "Go home!" he bellowed after me.

And while he had no authority to send me home for the day, I felt I'd earned some time off. And also, I'd forgotten to feed Zacchaeus this morning.

So I strolled home and took the afternoon off.

I enjoyed walking under normal circumstances, but with all the media vehicles driving around looking for footage of the killer, I adopted a brisk pace.

I stopped by the gas station a couple blocks from home to grab dinner and a six-pack.

After feeding the cat and eating a cold can of beans, I fell asleep in front of the TV, only to be awoken by dozens of phone calls after my interview had aired on the national news. I finally took the receiver off the hook, unplugged the phone from the wall, and went back to sleep.

CHAPTER 21

CORNFIELD

I STILL NEEDED SOME TIME to myself and wasn't ready to go back to the office. And I was sure Mayor Burke was still on the warpath.

So I called my mentor and asked if he wanted to get out for the day. His family had once owned nearly a third of all the farmland in Crooked Creek, and I knew I could get him to wax nostalgic while I also did a little light reconnaissance.

Father Warren's family had once owned the west side of Crooked Creek, land that was now owned by more than a dozen different families, most prominently the Dicers, the Watkinses, and the Griffiths.

There was a lot of acreage between those three families that I couldn't get my eyes on under normal circumstances. But under the guise of "taking an old farm boy out to his familial land for nostalgia's sake," I could not be denied by any gracious soul.

"It smells exactly the same." Wendall breathed in deeply and slowly, then out again, over and over for several minutes. Even an action like speaking required him to catch his breath these days. "Exactly." I could hear the smile in his voice without even turning to look at him.

He was so happy that I contagiously started smiling myself.

All this farmland used to belong to Father Warren's grandfather, Abraham Warren. He was an original founder of the town. Three different roads around Crooked Creek were named after him.

Wendall had asked me to drive him out to the land and then wheel the wheelchair as far as necessary. He wanted one last visit to his childhood stomping grounds.

I called the landowners whose driveway we'd used—the Prestons—to ask permission, but they hadn't answered the phone. They'd never said "No" to this request in the past, so we just went ahead with it anyway.

Father Wendall was struggling. He was clearly in his last months—I hoped for maybe a bit longer. He could no longer walk, even short distances. A nurse came by every day to check on him, but he could not afford to check into a senior-care facility. He was too proud to do so anyway. He'd rather die alone in a burning house than call the fire department for help.

I used to park nearly a quarter mile away, and we'd walk together to this specific spot. We'd done this before, many times, when he was able to walk on his own or with the walker. But this day, his mobility was so limited that I just drove right on up to the edge of his favorite small hill.

This would be our final time making the trip, and we both seemed to know it. Even Bones, his old dog, seemed content to stay in the vehicle this time.

Father Warren coughed a bit, but then it turned to laughter. He was sick, so it was probably laughter to begin with, but you couldn't really be sure. "Do you know how much trouble I got into out in these fields?"

The corn stretched as far as you could see in nearly every direction. The fields were mostly flat but covered small rolling hills here and there. To the east there was a single line of trees, mostly oak. Off to the west there was a patch of woods.

But otherwise . . . just corn.

He had told me a lot of stories about these lands over the course of our friendship, but never had he mentioned being a troublemaker.

"You?" I asked jokingly. "You got in trouble?" I couldn't believe it; I assumed he was joking or exaggerating.

"Yes, son." He wheezed and laughed some more. "Except . . . I didn't get caught much," he barked between hacks.

"Because you were so sneaky, or because there was so much land?" I was suddenly as curious as I'd ever been.

"When the corn is this high," he said, gesturing to the rows next to us where the corn stood about three feet tall. "About here," he added, moving his arm and hovering his hand just beside my waist. "That's the time. 'Cause for a kid . . . just tall enough to allow free travel to and fro. . . ." He coughed some more. "Corn that high, in that season—the season we're in right now, actually—corn at that stage don't need much attention. Farmers don't have to tend or check it much. Leaves the grounds free for mischief, mayhem, and even occasional larceny."

As much as he was struggling to breathe, let alone speak, I was surprised at how clear his memory seemed to be. I wanted to ask for more information, but I didn't want to cause any excess coughing. Curiosity won out.

"What kind of stuff would you and your cousins get into out here?" I asked, goading him on while also secretly hoping to glean a few clues.

"Oh, you know," he demurred, before spilling the beans. "We'd shoot dice, and shoot BB guns, bury unauthorized time capsules, build forts . . . all kinds of stuff. It was just the wild west out here during this part of corn season." He sounded nostalgic.

"Sounds like it," I said, mostly just to participate in the conversation.

"That's what you've got right now, son," he said, choking a bit on his words. And then he stopped.

"Sir?"

"The wild west," he wheezed. "Trouble. Evil, even." He hacked into his handkerchief a few times. "Tip-toeing around in your crops at a time when no one typically pays attention." He turned to face me, which I know wasn't easy because his neck was in serious pain. "He's not hiding time capsules or playing childhood games. You have to find this guy, Solomon. He aims to kill us all."

"I will, Father," I assured him. "I will."

● ● ●

After driving Wendall back home one county over and driving back to Jerusalem County alone, I was pretty hungry. I decided to swing by M Spot's and grab some chicken to take home.

As luck would have it—or maybe it was Murphy's Law—it was filled with members of the national media, who had only a few local places to choose from for dinner. I should have known this; I'm sure the Stoplight Diner and Umberto's Italian were equally full of out-of-town customers.

"Stupid," I whispered to myself as I walked inside.

I mean . . . I couldn't open the door, show my face to these people, and then leave like a coward, could I? No, I had to power through.

I walked slowly to the counter, confident that every eye in the place was on me. There was no conversation happening, no customer buzz, no sound at all. In fact, I could hear the flickering of the dying fluorescent bulbs in the ceiling.

"Sheriff Lancaster," Becky Mason shrieked. "We haven't seen you here in a while. How are you doing, honey?"

"I'm great," I said, trying to remain discreet for some reason.

Becky Mason was the daughter of the restaurant's founders, Cory and Liz Mason, and had been running M Spot's since her folks retired a few years back. She had their trademark southern slang, hospitality, and kitchen skills. The food had never been better.

She also lacked subtlety. Any hope I had that some media members might not recognize me was dashed once Becky spoke up. Oh, well.

"What'll it be?" she asked, a cigarette in one hand and a pencil in the other.

"Just give me a three-piece meal to go," I said quietly.

"THREE-PIECE MEAL!" Becky screamed toward the back of the kitchen, betraying the very concept of stealth.

"THREE-PIECE MEAL," a male voice screeched back at her.

I sighed, knowing I was still the center of attention for all reporters in the room.

"That'll be five fifty—"

"CHICKEN DOWN!" the male voice bellowed from the back.

"CHICKEN DOWN!" Becky shouted back, apparently acknowledging the update. Then she turned back to me and continued speaking calmly as though she'd never been interrupted. "That'll be five fifty-three."

I paid and received my change, and for an agonizing six minutes I was left to stand there waiting for my food. The last thing I wanted to do was face the media members gawking at me. But even staring at the floor got old pretty quickly.

I cleared my throat a few times. I stamped my feet. Finally, without the full permission of my brain, my eyes glanced over at the dining room.

Voices erupted in unison, each of them asking a question at the same time. Red lights went on around the room as tape recorders were activated. "Where have you been all day?" "Did you get fired?" "Were you reprimanded, Sheriff?" "Why did you cuss at us?" "Are you planning to resign?" "What did you order?"

All these and many more questions were hurled at me, in unison. I didn't hear any single question. Mostly I heard shouting, with only individual words coming in clear here and there.

Becky's voice finally cut through the cacophony. "Here you go, Sheriff." She handed me a to-go bag and smiled.

I walked to the exit, all the while still being bombarded with queries. I briefly wondered what I was even wearing, and if I would look like a slob in the photographs being taken.

At the last moment, I opened the door, and then solemnly turned to face the dining media members. There was a murmur as I cleared my throat, and then, finally, silence.

"No comment," I said plainly.

I turned and left the building, smiling.

As soon as the door slammed shut behind me, I cursed myself all the way back to my car. "You could have just gone home for a can of beans, but *no*, you had to get fried chicken, like every other person in this fucking town, you goddamn stupid fucking moron. Christ, does it get any stupider than you?"

I heard someone clear their throat just as I arrived at my vehicle. I looked up to see Stanley, one of the cooks and busboys for M Spot's, camped out at the corner of the building smoking a cigarette.

"I . . . I'm sorry you had to hear that," I offered meekly.

"Are you kidding, Father?" he asked. "You just made my entire week!"

"Well, then," I replied. "Let's just keep this incident between the two of us, shall we?"

"For sure, Father." He smiled. "I'm just happy to know you're human like the rest of us, Father." He sounded sincere.

"Good night," I offered as I got into the sheriff's SUV and headed home.

It didn't hit me just in that moment, but this comment would end up echoing throughout my brain in days to come: "I'm just happy to know you're human like the rest of us."

Where had I gone so wrong as to be seen as more than human due simply to the priesthood? Was the fault mine, or did it lie in the system? Or in the man making the observation?

CHAPTER 22

NEW FBI PERSONNEL, INCLUDING KID ANALYST NERD

THE DIRECTOR OF THE FBI, Tim Talbot, had had enough. He was tired of the news stories, the daily questions, and the protests outside his Washington, DC, office. The national media exposure had been the last straw.

So he sent the farm to Crooked Creek, Indiana, population two thousand. In the span of a few hours, our little corn town received two hundred new FBI personnel. Our city had grown in population by fifteen percent just from the influx of reporters and law enforcement.

They came with their own tents and pop-up shelters, their assault rifles, and their training. And I was sure they'd be of some assistance in controlling the crowds and citizenry. But would they help us catch the killer? No. Not a chance.

The only real use of these reinforcements was in terms of traffic control and overnight patrolling.

Unfortunately, foot soldiers were not the only reinforcements the FBI sent. They also sent a few analysts, one in particular with an obnoxious sense of self-importance. His name was Damien Gentry. He was a computer whiz, math expert, and all-around bedsore of a guy, in my opinion. He had dozens of ideas on how to solve the case—all of them involving numbers and data—and he had enough enthusiasm for three men.

I hated him.

Damien's philosophy for finding the killer lay in a complex algorithm he himself had written. If we knew enough data points about the victims, he argued, raw math could help us narrow down the list of possible culprits, and maybe even help us find and arrest him. How many victims were women? What were their ages? What time of day were they killed? Every detail was assigned a series of values pertaining to various traits he believed the killer would have.

It was interesting stuff, if it was being discussed in a classroom. Applied out in the field during an active murder investigation? Madness. I had more respect for Mayor Burke than I did for this mathematics punk.

Damien estimated it would take his program a few days to spit out some kind of actionable information; so, fortunately, after answering some questions, I was rid of him for a while.

The rest of the FBI? Not rid of them at all. They were everywhere. Every few years, one of many cicada broods emerges from their hibernation cycle and terrorizes the town for a few weeks until they all die again. We had more FBI agents in Crooked Creek than any brood of cicadas I'd ever seen.

At lunch I walked home from the station, just a few blocks, and passed a dozen agents out and about in cars and on foot—even a few on horseback: though, in true government form, they were local horses being rented. The FBI horses didn't travel, apparently. *Maybe the FBI doesn't even own or employ horses at all*, I wondered.

I even recognized one of the horses and called him by name. "Hey, Windbreaker!" Unfortunately, that caused the horse to leave his position—rider in tow—and cross the street to visit me. I couldn't help but laugh, although the agent riding Windbreaker seemed less than pleased.

As the horse approached, I embraced his neck, stroking his mane and whispering to him. Windbreaker had been Father Warren's horse until a few years ago. Wendall was finished farming and couldn't afford the physical toll it would take to continue taking care of the horse. So he'd sold him to the Watkins family. Clearly the horse still remembered me.

Finally I broke away and stepped back. I looked up and saw only sunglasses. "Agent," I acknowledged before turning to walk home.

Despite the heavy law-enforcement presence, life in Crooked Creek largely went on as normal. Benji Tomkins was still throwing his tennis ball against the steps of the old Methodist church. Ginny Dupree was still out overwatering her garden. The town's only two Little League teams were practicing at the city park.

Just . . . everything was now under the watchful eye of the FBI. It was the same, but different. Comforting and upsetting.

I rounded my last corner to see Cindy and her husband standing on my front porch three houses away.

"Oh . . . wow, fuck," I breathed to myself. Then I put on a huge fake smile and waved animatedly at them as I increased my stride.

This was almost certainly trouble. I'd been sleeping with Cindy for weeks, then basically banished her for a week to the city where her husband worked, and now they were both here. And yet, until I knew for sure that I was busted, I had to act normal.

I tried to briefly lock eyes with each of them, looking for anger in his gaze and pity in hers. Instead, I found both of them impossible to read. His eyes were neutral, but he was a therapist: surely he'd been trained to look neutral. Her gaze was something between panic and concern, which did nothing to help my anxiety.

"The Baxters," I called out when I was just a dozen steps away. "To what do I owe the pleasure?"

"I just had to see you in person, sir," he said as he trudged down the front steps to meet me. "So I could thank you."

My heart jumped at the news that he was not here to kick my ass. He likely still did not know about our affair, and I was dangerously giddy as I spoke. "Thank me," I repeated, giggling. "Whatever for?" I tried to compose myself.

"Even before this serial-killer nonsense, I've been working so much down in Indy that my wife and I haven't had much time together. But you sending her to town to research flower shops? Why, it was a godsend, Sheriff . . . Father . . . sir. We saw each other every single night, and

I just cannot thank you enough!" He grabbed my right hand and shook it vigorously.

"Ah, well," I stammered. "Just . . . following every lead, you know." I chuckled. "Glad to be of help."

"You sure were, sir," he replied, before an awkward few seconds of silence. "All right, then," he continued, "I'm gonna take her back to the B&B and head on back downtown. Just wanted to meet you in person and thank you for helping rekindle our marriage."

I nodded as they both walked down the steps to the car. Had I done myself in? Had I sent my lover right back into her husband's arms?

I waved as they drove off and then turned back to head inside. It was probably for the best. Perhaps my subconscious actually had sent her back to her husband on purpose, as a way to end an affair I didn't have the willpower to end myself.

I went inside, fed Zacchaeus, and ate a can of cold beans for lunch while watching an episode of *Perry Mason*.

● ● ●

By now, the police station was far too tiny. Even the extra room we'd allocated at the church wasn't enough to hold even one quarter of the law-enforcement officers now in town. Thankfully it was summer, and school was out, so we took over the Jerusalem County High School gymnasium complex—which actually had two full basketball courts, and twice that much space once all the bleachers were retracted.

Just meant I couldn't walk to work anymore. Well, I could walk to the station; but if I wanted to be any part of the FBI investigation, even only as an observer, I would have to drive out to the high school.

I decided to swing by the station on my way out to the school so I could check on Maggie. Turned out my whole outfit was here, at least the ones scheduled to work today. Deputy Travis Kent sat at his desk, head down, pouting. Maggie was at the copier, cheerily humming to herself. And Deputy Gene sat in the kitchenette, eating the leftover stale donuts.

"What's going on?" I asked, mostly just to get everyone's attention. "I thought the high school was the new police headquarters."

Travis just sighed and looked out the window.

Maggie gave me her patented "don't even think about asking me" face.

So Gene meandered over and gave me the bad news. "They said they don't need us. Said to go back to doing regular police work and let them handle the murder investigation." He tossed one remaining bite of powdered donut into his mouth, shrugged, and walked toward his desk.

"They don't know anything about this area or the people," I argued.

"Said the field director's staff had been here long enough to pick it all up," Gene called back over his shoulder without turning his head.

"Goddammit," I muttered.

Maggie made eye contact with me, then glanced at the swear jar on her desk.

"Not now, Maggie! Shit!" I turned, fully intending to storm out of the station and beeline to the high school so I could give Director Rathburn a red-hot piece of my mind. Instead, I stopped in my tracks as I saw all our neighboring county officers emptying out of their loaner SUV, dejected faces on all of them. Huey, Dewey, and Louie were as dejected as I'd ever seen them.

Those three and Cindy walked in and informed us that they, too, had been deemed unnecessary to the murder investigation. The FBI had turned them away at the Jerusalem County High School gym.

I herded them into the conference room and told them to wait. I noticed two non-law-enforcement things at this time: Cindy making eyes at me, and Greg making eyes at Cindy.

I dialed the number Maggie had been given, and some perky schmuck answered. "FBI Field Office, Jerusalem County, how may I direct your call?"

"You can put Rathburn on immediately or I'll reach through this phone and pull your ribs out one by one through your chirpy face," I spat.

I had no idea what I was doing, as this was my first ever time playing Bad Cop, but it worked.

"Rathburn," he barked. "This better be good. I don't have time for—"

I interrupted him. "Sir, Sheriff Lancaster here." I didn't pause long enough for him to speak. "Are you really going to ignore all our local knowledge and the local knowledge of the loaner officers in this investigation and shut us out of it?"

There was a slight pause. "Yes."

"These four loaner officers, at least," I said, exhausted, "the city has already paid for them through two more weeks. These are well-trained, seasoned law enforcement officers who know the state and the general area, and I can't believe you just want to throw away that resource in favor of your suit-wearing city goons."

Another short pause. "Believe it. If you don't wanna send 'em home, put them to work in your office. The FBI is handling all aspects of this murder investigation from this point forward. Good day." He hung up.

I wasn't really a violent person by nature. I wanted to love people and help them love each other enough to get to Heaven. But this man made me want to punch him in the face, and I added it to the list of eventual confessions to Father Warren.

I slowly made my way back to the conference room to deliver the news. I relayed my phone call with Rathburn almost word for word, because I wanted them to know what a dickhead that guy was.

"I am not sure we can make good use of you for two full weeks, but I plan to try. It is, after all, the taxpayers' money that brought you here, and I believe they should get something for it. That being said, all of you have performed admirably and have given us several weeks of your time away from your homes and families. If any of you would like to leave early and return home, I am willing to discuss it." I looked around, but not one hand went up. Not a single loaner officer seemed ready to leave.

"Good," I said, smiling. "And don't you think for a second that the local police in Crooked Creek are done investigating these murders, no matter what the FBI or the media might say."

CHAPTER 23

ONE MORE TRYST

CINDY AND I HADN'T HAD A CHANCE to be alone together since her return. And, being a loaner officer, she could be sent home any day now, though neither of us said it.

All we managed during and after the latest briefing was some nonverbal communication. She smiled, indicating she did not hate me for sending her to Indy. I shrugged and cocked my head and pointed at my watch, hoping to convey "Wanna come over later?" or, at the least, "Do you forgive me?"

She smiled again and nodded from across the room.

I felt a rush. Knowing she was going to come over later made me flush, and I was momentarily distracted from the briefing. What had happened in Indy? Had she seen her husband? Had they made love? Was that even any of my business?

A thousand questions raced through my mind, but chief among them was "Does she still like me?"

I would find out in a few hours.

● ● ●

Cindy had brought pizza from Umberto's, which was a minor miracle since none of my nonverbal communication at the station had included mention of my being famished. But I was indeed famished. It was as if she knew. I didn't even ask how long she'd waited in line for the pie.

She'd returned to Betty Q's with the other officers, and even sat around enjoying afternoon tea with Wayne, the officer from Huntersville

County, and Betty herself. Shortly before dinner, she'd feigned exhaustion, excused herself for the night, and snuck out the back door. There she found the bicycles Betty Q left out for guests of the bed and breakfast who might want some exercise, and she set off quietly for downtown Crooked Creek.

She'd gone to great lengths to keep our secret. I opened the door with a huge smile and a raging appetite.

We sat down at my kitchen table—which was just a fold-out card table—and devoured the pizza while laughing and talking. Often we would watch something on television after a shared dinner. Usually it was *Andy Griffith* or *I Love Lucy*. Tonight, however, we were both too revved up after more than a week apart while she hunted flower shops in Indy. We didn't even throw the pizza away before heading upstairs. We just left it on the table for Zacchaeus to chew up.

We didn't leave clothes along the stairs like breadcrumbs, the way they do in movies. Sex for cops is a little different, at least the disrobing part. You can't go grabbing and writhing and rolling around with firearms on your belt or handcuffs that dig into your back.

Cindy and I had turned our cop-based disrobing into a game of sorts. Whoever got naked first got to call the shots. Cindy usually won, but I will admit that often this was because I didn't care to win and, in fact, much preferred the sex—no matter the style or position—when Cindy was directing traffic.

I don't mean to suggest it was wild sex or anything. We didn't talk dirty or anything approaching that. Our sex was pretty vanilla . . . at least from what I can gather. Again, I have very little frame of reference. It wasn't my first time or anything, but I was on the near end of the experience spectrum. But from the confessions I'd heard, I knew sex could get a lot more "out there" than what Cindy and I were doing.

But Cindy was in charge. I didn't care much beyond that. I just liked knowing that she had the choice, which meant we were doing things that she would enjoy and get pleasure from.

Most of my previous relationships had been when I was a student. I held a girl's hand in middle school; I think her name was Carmen. I had kissed exactly one person on the lips in my life: a girl named Jennifer at the tenth-grade dance, and I'm reasonably sure she'd been paid to do it anyway. I had no idea what a normal adult relationship was supposed to look like, but this felt perfect. I even began to wonder if I could justify these actions . . . to God or at least to myself.

At this point the bed-and-breakfast officers assumed she was spending her nights with her husband somewhere between Crooked Creek and Indy. They'd even begun to tease her about her sex drive and the late-night rendezvous in dirty roadside hotels. Any time she showed up and walked in the front door in time for breakfast, they'd give her a good razzing while passing around the eggs and sausage.

She took it in stride, because the teasing meant the guys considered her part of the team. I'd learned how important that was to her, the only woman on the force in her entire county. She'd worked very hard to earn the respect of the male officers without becoming one of them in terms of the jokes or machismo.

But it was clear to me that my affair with Cindy was a huge mistake . . . my biggest mistake to date, perhaps. I was by no means perfect, but I hadn't made very many big mistakes in life. I'd always been cautious and careful. Calculated. Small mistakes, small improvements.

Even my faith was very math-like. I'd even used the transitive property of equality—if A = B and B = C, then A = C—in a sermon once, in an attempt to help parishioners better learn to see Jesus in the actions of everyday people around them. It was not a successful sermon, by any stretch, and resulted in many questions and letters.

But the point is that I was a thorough and thoughtful man. That is, until I'd let Cindy get close, which was ultimately quite dangerous. I can't even count the many reasons why, but chief among them was that I had allowed someone to get close to me—something I'd vowed never to do again after breaking free of my parents. With closeness comes sloppiness. It was only a matter of time.

But she smelled so sweet. Her demeanor was so calm, so even. And she smelled . . . like lilacs. Her smile so slightly crooked. Her perfectly imperfect teeth. Her stilted, halting laugh.

How does a man of the cloth fall in love with another man's wife? Answer: one day at a time . . . but also pretty easily, as it turns out. I suppose, in hindsight, we were perfect for each other at the right time. I was craving intimacy just as hers had been taken away by her husband's absence. It was a perfect storm.

It helped that the personalities clicked. And that we spent so much time together on the case.

In another life . . . if we'd crossed paths earlier in life . . . we'd already be together. So even though it was sinful and felt incredibly wrong, there was this draw . . . this utter rightness about it. It felt so correct and destined that both of us allowed our guards to drop. Our morals as well. We justified: she about cheating on her husband, me about cheating on the faith . . . betraying the very role of the priesthood.

But you don't know all the details. You can't. You can't know how adorable she looked sleeping in only those pink panties. You can't know how she smelled. You can't know how oddly natural the whole thing felt.

We felt meant to be, just . . . in a different life. Almost as though we'd been robbed of our opportunity together.

And when you bond to another human that strongly, you start cutting down fences without even realizing it, letting them look further and further into your life, your past, and your psyche.

You stop locking doors and secret cabinets.

Which only means that, inevitably, she will open them. It's just a matter of time. But until then, I was certainly enjoying the sin. Maybe even trying to extend its window.

We were beginning to know each other very well. That should have been a sign for us to stop. I knew that she kicked her feet at night, and she knew I snored if I slept flat on my back. I knew she hated brushing her teeth, and she knew I hated sleeping with socks on.

I loved her normal attributes. She wasn't skinny or overweight, but a normal, average size. I enjoyed the curves where I found them, but was mostly happy that she wasn't obsessed with being model-thin. She was confident in her body, which only made her more attractive. Her freckles and moles, while sparse, were perfectly placed, like stars mapping a journey for the blindly adventurous. God, I loved exploring her, at least as much as I ever loved exploring the Bible.

She was curious. Prone to blurting out questions unrelated to the topic at hand. Often she was probing to learn more about me, quizzing me on my own life's trivia. She was a sponge. I realize now that she was falling in love with me, voraciously exploring me the way all new lovers do.

Eventually . . . inevitably . . . she got too curious.

● ● ●

I was always a light sleeper. Always. It was how I caught my father sneaking in and my mother sneaking out. It was how I knew my sister had nightmares before even she did. I suppose it didn't help that I had spent years sleeping alone.

Zacchaeus didn't sleep on the bed because he was a gluttonous fool that couldn't make the jump. So every movement in my bed was me. At least until Cindy came along.

Now, every time she coughed, rolled over, or even breathed a little heavily, I woke up. I didn't mind, of course. I loved it. I loved being woken up by the nightly idiosyncrasies of Cindy. It just reminded me that she liked me enough to sleep here, overnight, in my bed.

On this particular night, however, Cindy was overly restless. I don't know if the pizza had given her indigestion . . . or maybe the travel back from Indy had given her anxiety. Whatever the cause, she tossed and turned and couldn't find a rhythm.

I was on my side, so I didn't have to snore to fake being asleep. For more than an hour she tried a new position every ten minutes. But nothing seemed to work.

A few times I almost spoke, asking if I could help. But I also had come to know Cindy fairly well these last several weeks. And every time I had asked if she needed my help—for any reason, sleeping or otherwise—she had gotten upset at the very suggestion.

Eventually she swung her legs over and got up out of bed, walking downstairs.

Now, there was a half-bath here on the second floor, so I knew she wasn't just wandering off to pee. I thought she might be in pursuit of a glass of water or an aspirin. Within a few minutes, I saw shadows dancing up the stairway, powered by the light she'd turned on in the living room below. For a brief spell, the TV was on.

But then I heard an unmistakable sound, one I had hoped never to hear outside of my own actions: the slow, excruciating screech of the basement door being opened. Its joints were rusty and creaky. The bottom of the door scraped and squealed as it rubbed against the linoleum. One could hear that door opening from literally any spot inside the house. I'd never oiled it, specifically so I would hear it if anyone ever opened it besides me. It meant Cindy was about to explore the basement.

And it meant that I was done listening and now had to act.

I sat up and tossed my legs over the edge of the bed, sighing heavily. I sneaked downstairs quietly and made for the basement door. From below, I heard the sound of the ripcord light bulb being turned on down there, then a short pause, and then the sound of the far-corner basement door opening.

She'd found the hydroponic garden. Perhaps my biggest secret.

You see, it's not possible to freeze flowers long-term. Very quickly they lose their color, and eventually their shape. So if you want to leave a fresh flower at a crime scene, you have to go fresh. Frozen is out of the question. I'd been dabbling in hydroponic gardening for several years, and even entered a tomato in the local county fair half a decade ago—I won third prize.

The entire water garden was hidden inside the shell of a traditional deep freezer. I'd just retrofitted the giant insulated box to suit my own needs.

The next few seconds seemed to take forever, and yet I was upon her before either of us knew it.

By this point she'd seen more than enough, but she still reached in and pulled out a completely-out-of-season bunch of pansies, staring at them in awe.

The blade went in slowly, because part of me wanted to savor it even as the rest of me wanted to escape to a delusion. I killed for a very specific reason—to send pure souls to Heaven—but that didn't mean I didn't ever enjoy it.

She gasped as it glanced off a rib and hit her lung.

"I'm so sorry, Cindy," I said, whispering in her ear and meaning every word of it. "I was really hoping I wouldn't have to kill you."

Keeping the blade inside, I pulled her body back away from the garden just in time for her to start choking and spitting up blood. She turned and locked her eyes on me as she fell to the ground gasping. She had so many questions.

"This is for your own good," I breathed. "I'll see you again on the other side." And I meant it.

There would be no more words between us.

CHAPTER 24

VICTIM FIVE

CINDY BAXTER WAS MY FIFTH VICTIM, and she was found outside Betty Q's Bed & Breakfast, spread across the threshold of the front door, wrists and ankles tied to the corners, disemboweled. She was missing two toes on her left foot.

It was an utterly gruesome scene that no written description could do justice to, and it took several officers to restrain her husband when he arrived.

In her hair had been a small bunch of pansies, tied with a pink ribbon.

As soon as I saw the body, I threw up in the ditch. I don't know how to explain it: looking at a body during the act and looking at it after the act are two different experiences. When the soul is being freed, it's beautiful; but a soulless body is quite an ugly thing indeed.

I knew I was doing a noble thing, I had zero doubt; but the details were somewhat hard to keep down at times.

The Lord never said serving him would be easy. In fact, he said the opposite. I was ready to have Saint Peter label me a murderer and send me to Hell, so long as the souls I'd rescued in a timely fashion all made it to Heaven.

And the euphoria . . . the raw adrenaline when I released a pure soul from its bodily confines . . . well, that could not be explained to anyone who had never experienced it. But clearly it was the Holy Spirit pouring out a blessing upon me as it passed by, ushering the soul up to Heaven. How could such an overwhelmingly positive sensation be anything but confirmation of my mission?

Unfortunately, Betty Q's would have to shut down for several weeks, if not longer, while the murder was investigated. And they were not happy about it. Betty Q herself kicked in the taillight of a police cruiser before her husband, Bart, managed to pull her away.

On top of finding Betty and Bart a place to stay, I also needed to relocate the half dozen loaner officers who'd been staying there. Recent lessons having been seared into my brain, I would not be volunteering to host any officers at my own home. In fact, there was reason to be concerned that these officers would simply be summarily dismissed and sent back home.

Instead, the city took the highly unusual step of purchasing a home on the active market, using municipal funds. I would later do more research than I care to admit down at the county registrar of deeds, but I never found another instance of the city of Crooked Creek literally buying a house on the open market. It was unprecedented. And corrupt.

The Grady house, which was only a few blocks from the station, had been on the market for several months, mostly because it was priced too high. Well, that and the fact that the previous owners had died violently just outside the property on the state road, so it was considered a bit of a cursed piece of land, but only to the loony.

Perhaps most importantly for the situation at hand, it was already furnished—the Gradys had died in a tragic car accident when a tractor-trailer drifted across the median on the highway and hit the family station wagon head-on. Everything left in the house at the time of the accident was being sold along with the house.

The Grady home was being sold by the family's lawyer, Benny Burke, who apparently did have a real estate license and who also just happened to be the younger brother of the honorable mayor of Crooked Creek, Mr. Sean Burke. So, in providing housing for our loaner cops and displaced citizens, the former of whom were going to be sent home in a few weeks for certain, the Burke family was also able to make a nice profit that was, on paper, completely legal.

Never underestimate anyone's pursuit of money. Anyone.

I wondered . . . had there not been an angle, a way to make money . . . would the loaner officers have just been sent home instantly? They were already considered superfluous by the FBI, after all. Betty and Bart might just as likely have been sent to stay with relatives as given a place rent-free in downtown Crooked Creek.

To their credit, Betty and her husband didn't miss a step. They didn't act like the victims they were. Instead, they kept on operating their bed and breakfast, just in a new building. They got up early each morning and made breakfast for anyone in the house who wanted it, tidied up between breakfast and lunch, and ultimately took care of those officers every day from the time they moved into the Grady house, and they never once complained.

Briefly, I allowed myself to joke internally about wishing I'd killed one of the other loaner officers sooner, then Cindy could have been on the same block as me all this time . . . but I felt guilty before I even hit the punchline, even if only in my mind.

Some part of me also missed her greatly. She was the human I'd allowed myself to get closest to in all my life, and now she and that closeness were gone.

I knew she'd expired on the positive side of things. She'd discovered my secret, and her heart was primed to expose me to others as a killer. Though she misunderstood my motives, I knew her heart had been in the right place when she'd passed.

She was in Heaven with her creator.

Still . . . I was sad. I was upset. I was angry.

I was even a little jealous.

●●●

No one was as angry as FBI Director Tim Talbot, who could be heard screaming through the receiver at Field Director Rathburn, wondering how any murder—let alone one so gruesome and one where the body was found on a building fifty feet from a main state highway—could possibly have occurred just hours after more than a hundred FBI personnel had come into the city and started patrolling.

It was all I could do to keep from smiling, for a few reasons.

Most everyone in the gymnasium was eavesdropping on the call—it was nearly impossible not to—which became obvious once Rathburn slammed the receiver down and the noise of it echoed through the silence for fifteen seconds. He whipped around to face us, fangs out and ready to pass along the ass-kicking he'd just gotten from his own boss.

"What the fuck have any of you been doing with the last five minutes of your lives, except listening to my phone call?" he screamed. "You think it's funny to listen to me get yelled at?" he bellowed. "Well, let's see how funny you think it is when I deduct *every one of your paychecks* to account for the time spent eavesdropping!"

A slight murmur went up from the group before Rathburn stamped it out with even more fire. "*Shut the hell up* with your murmuring asses! You have time to listen to my calls, that's time you could have maybe caught the killer. Fuck it! I'm docking all you bitches a half day. Sue me in court, and maybe you'll win in six years after several appeals. You bunch of insubordinate pricks!"

It's safe to say tensions were running high in Crooked Creek, as everyone tried to help solve the crimes while also carving out their own escape clause for whenever things inevitably went south. Personally, I'd been carving out my own escape route for months, and it was foolproof . . . at least, if everything went according to plan.

Killing Cindy was *not* part of the plan, yet I was still confident that the overall strategy would still play out in my favor. And I had a few tricks up my sleeve just in case it didn't.

● ● ●

Cindy's funeral was taking place in her home county, and many of the Crooked Creek and loaner officers had made the trip. Actually . . . everyone who wasn't on duty back home was there.

Cindy's husband read a poem; apparently it had been her favorite. It struck me as entirely unremarkable, and nothing about it reminded me of her. I guess he'd known her longer than I had, so I'm sure he knew what he was doing.

I tried to keep up a solid frown, suppressing the joy I got from knowing that the entirety of the FBI group was back in my hometown looking for a killer they didn't remotely understand. It wasn't too difficult; I really had cared about Cindy. I truly was sad that she was gone.

Then her parents hugged me. And her college roommate. And then her husband's parents. Like . . . I felt guilty enough already, you dicks.

Of course they didn't know, and couldn't know, my internal conflict regarding Cindy. And they certainly couldn't know for a fact, as I did, that she had gone to Heaven. They hoped, of course . . . they even spoke in the language of confidence.

But only I knew for certain.

I'm sure Heaven is great, but it would have to be a euphoric, psychedelic paradise to even come close to the feeling I got from sending a soul there.

At the burial ceremony, it started to rain. It was so metaphorical that it was kind of cliché.

Before the coffin was lowered, Cindy's mother spoke, recalling a little girl insistent on playing cops and robbers with her Barbie dolls. Then she sang Cindy's favorite hymn—"What a Friend We Have in Jesus"—even though Cindy had told me she hated church music and felt a great distance from God during her time here.

Funerals are mostly marketing. An attempt to convince the living that the recently dead had been a great person. We gloss over the flaws and imperfections, no matter how glaring, and speak only of the good qualities. And we don't do this out of respect for the dead person or to avoid speaking ill of them; we do this because we hope everyone will do the same when *we* die: gloss over our failures and over-glorify what few successes we had.

As a young boy, I once went to a funeral for a man everyone knew to be a violent criminal. And the priest spoke of time as though it were a completely flexible concept, suggesting that in the moment of someone's death they might convert ... that they might even have a conversation with God himself ... and that many, given those circumstances, might choose to repent before their final and complete death.

That funeral stuck with me, and it never made any sense. If we can just ... talk to God when we die and repent then, what's the point of living a holy life during our human time on Earth? I get that we want to give hope to the surviving family members, but at what point do we cross the line from supporting grief into generating fiction?

Obviously, you don't use a funeral homily to list the dead person's shortcomings and flaws. But there has to be a place somewhere in the middle, where we honor their humanity without making them sound like saints.

Because so few of them *are* saints.

● ● ●

We'd taken both of the Crooked Creek Police Department SUVs to come to this funeral, piling everyone into two vehicles. One of the SUVs was my daily vehicle, so I was driving. In my car were Skip, Gene, and Maggie, and they spoke of nothing except memories of Cindy. It was the most excruciating hour of driving I'd ever experienced. I figured the other SUV was the same, so I just tried to drive really fucking fast to get it all over with.

When we returned to the police station, I merely dropped everyone off and drove out on my own. I was tired of their words, I was tired of mourning Cindy, and I was just tired in general. I also needed some alone time.

I drove west out of town, waving at half a dozen FBI agents on patrol as I went. On Penn Street, it's really only a few blocks before the subdivisions become cornfields and you're out in the country again. Penn Street becomes County Road 1150, and you can keep going on this road for five hours without ever seeing another town.

I got off on Wallenby Road and took a left. When I hit Watkins Drive, I turned right. I was now on private property. Watkins family property. They weren't fans of the police and even less tolerant of trespassers. But when you own two hundred acres of land, it's impossible to monitor it adequately, even with fourteen children.

Way back in the corner of the Watkins land, butting up against the farm next door, was an old rundown greenhouse. When I'd found it a couple of years ago, it was overgrown with trees and shrubs, shielding it from view. I doubt the Watkinses even knew it was here, since they'd bought the farm from old man Simpkins. The greenhouse was in the middle of a couple of acres of trees, and if you didn't wander inside the grove, you would never even find it. I presumed it had been used to grow cannabis a decade or two ago.

I'd spent months fixing it up, careful to come infrequently and irregularly, as well as quietly. Under my care, the greenhouse was once again flourishing with plant life. Regardless of season, flowers of all kinds from all over the world were blooming and smiling at the sun. There was enough clearing around it for the sun to get through, but also enough foliage and overgrowth to keep it hidden. Seriously—unless someone walked directly into the tiny grove right at the border between two farms, no one would ever find it.

Before I could blame a person for my own murders, I would need supporting evidence to back up my claims. The greenhouse was the first step. If I could establish a potential source for all the out-of-season flowers, that alone would sway most critical thinkers. In a way, it was like bluffing in poker: I knew I could win so long as the other guy never saw through my bluff.

As for attaching the flowers to the victims with various methods, I was simply satisfying a compulsion to physically tie the meaning of each flower to the victim's body. It wasn't art, but it was sort of like that. Each crime scene became a canvas, and upon each, I left a unique victim and an emotionally resonant piece of themed memorabilia.

CHAPTER 25

SYMBOLISM

THERE WAS VERY LITTLE REASON for me to keep driving out to the high school and pretending that I was a part of this investigation. That is, with one exception: I was the killer, so I needed to have some idea of what the law-enforcement officers knew. But no one on the FBI's team was really pretending to take me seriously anymore, and that was okay. It might actually end up working in my favor.

This morning's briefing was being led by Damien Gentry, the wunderkind out of Chicago. As I mentioned, he was supposedly good with numbers and charts. I was, as you might assume, skeptical. How does a computer tell you what you need to know when you have utterly zero field experience? How can you even dare to revolutionize investigative methods before you even understand them?

And yet even an old skeptic like me can still be surprised now and then.

The FBI pissant turned out to have some skills after all. He was over-eager, obnoxious, self-important, and shrill. But he definitely had brains. Most importantly, he got us thinking about the meaning of the flowers left at each crime scene. We were definitely on to the flowers and investigating them from several angles ... but we hadn't yet thought to consider their meanings in popular poetry and literature, and to wonder whether those meanings had any ties to our victims.

And they did. And I certainly hadn't counted on anyone figuring out that particular piece of my process, at least not so early on.

Tina Hillary had given thousands of dollars to the church in her lifetime. Just a few months before I killed her, she'd made a $10,000 donation. And she'd also confessed to me that she had a terminal illness and hadn't but a year or so left to live. So I'd chosen white lilies for her, to symbolize the rejuvenation of her soul and its rebirth in Heaven. I'd woven one into her arm as a nod to how woven she had been into our local faith community.

Of course, lilies were also symbolic of love, femininity, weddings, purity, and grief—all of which Agent Gentry had included in his report. Multiple meanings for flowers meant that the true reasons that I chose them would be harder to discern.

Katie McGuire got daffodils because, like lilies, daffodils also symbolize rebirth and new beginnings. And Katie had recently decided to keep her baby from an accidental pregnancy, turning her back on the abortion option. And, yes, her unborn child had still died, but not at the hands of a monster . . . not because of an abortion. That child was given a direct ticket to paradise because of his mother earning a direct ticket to paradise. I knew the difference between abortion and this, even if others would fail to grasp it. Earth was a Hell all its own, filled with too much temptation for most to resist. In order to save souls from Hell, I had to save some of them from experiencing Earth.

I had long ago made peace with this.

Vernon Yarbrough had gotten black-eyed Susans because they are among the most robust and adaptable-to-their-environment flowers. And Vernon had more than adapted to his environment: he'd made the environment his. He was the only truly independent farmer in the county, refusing affiliation or partnership with any other small farm or large farming conglomerate. Vernon represented the very best of what the people of Crooked Creek could be. Yet he was nearly bankrupt, and the larger farms were inching closer to taking him over. And I couldn't let that happen to his legacy.

Vernon Stamper received magnolias at his death scene, stapled to his jacket, because magnolias represent a love of nature. And Vernon so loved nature. Most of all, he loved animals. Specifically, he loved dogs. The man took nearly every penny he saved above his living expenses and donated it to the local vet clinic.

Magnolias also were known to suggest themes of femininity and beauty, or even perseverance. Honestly, as I ran through all the victims and the flowers I'd left at the scenes . . . and the reasons . . . I began to realize that most flowers had multiple meanings or thematic uses.

Maybe the FBI pissant hadn't stumbled onto the amazing lead he thought he had?

For Cindy Baxter, the latest victim—the one I hadn't planned on killing—I had chosen to leave a small bunch of pansies in her hair. This had been a foolishly specific choice of flowers, as pansies are almost universally used to suggest feelings of love and romance. They do sometimes get associated with the concept of free thinking and independence, so maybe there was a bit of wiggle room.

I missed her so much already. And it wasn't the sex. Believe me, a single man can find ways to be sexually satisfied all on his lonesome, and the ultimate payoff isn't much different than it is when another person is involved.

Sure, the sex with Cindy had been incredible. But what I missed was the bond. The emotional intimacy had been what I had enjoyed most. Being vulnerable with another person is love, I don't care what other labels you want to throw on that behavior, and Cindy and I had been vulnerable with each other. We shared as many pains and secrets as we did kisses. I tried to take comfort in knowing that Cindy was with Jesus, and that I had played a part in making that happen. It helped, but the wound remained.

Before Cindy, my only real relational bond for the last ten years had been with God. Or with Father Warren. One was my mentor, and one was my savior, so it wasn't exactly easy to be completely open with them on an emotional level. I didn't talk to Wendall about my sexual urges, and I was confident he was all the happier for it.

Damien's presentation was thorough, and he'd gotten his information about flower symbolism from multiple sources. If nothing else, the kid was proving he'd be valuable as an FBI researcher for years to come. What he laid out for us amounted to someone setting up all the edge pieces at the start of a jigsaw puzzle: it was valuable and important work but wouldn't help us solve the puzzle. We still needed someone who could see the interior pieces for what they were. We needed someone with experience in getting inside the mind of a serial killer.

And, as fate would have it, such a man was but one single day away from arriving in town, though none of us knew it yet.

"Any questions?" Damien asked, turning off the projector and releasing the pull-down screen and sending it back up into its container.

"Well, what are your conclusions?" Rathburn barked from the back of the room, still clearly expecting the bulk of the work to be done for him.

"Sir," the kid replied, "the data support no conclusions as of yet. More analysis is needed. I suggest that we start by—"

"Then why did I spend thirty minutes sitting in on this meeting?" Rathburn interrupted. "Why am I even here right now?" He was the typical bureaucrat, unable to see value in incremental progress . . . only in Hail Mary situations—football, not Catholicism.

"It will help serve as a guide when profiling the killer," the kid responded meekly. "It's not a formula that can tell us who the murderer is."

"Why not?" the field director screamed before throwing his clipboard at the front of the room, shattering it on the chalkboard. He stormed out.

As I felt a swell of empathy for the agent on the receiving end of such a diatribe, I quickly reminded myself that all these agents were trying to find and capture me. None of them was my friend, despite how poorly they might treat one another. They were all on the opposing team.

It had been a mistake to even let Cindy into my world and onto my team, even a tiny bit. She was only dead now because she would have reported me or arrested me. I had let the opponent infiltrate my ranks with a spy.

I couldn't let it happen again.

● ● ●

After Damien's briefing, the FBI agents were feverishly photocopying the list of flowers and their various meanings, passing them out to everyone they saw, law enforcement and citizens alike. No one even noticed when I slipped out the back and headed home to take the rest of the day off. Or if they noticed, they didn't care. None of them would miss me.

Zacchaeus definitely noticed when I came home early.

In a way, I was testing things. I would need this kind of invisibility with the FBI at some point down the road soon, so it was good to see that it was working already. There were so many of them, each with important jobs, and only one of me, who'd been largely relegated to the sidelines.

This afternoon, I had two important tasks: put a lock on the door leading to the basement and, to hedge my bet, put a lock on the deep-freezer door down there. I didn't plan on having another affair or even having anyone come inside my house, but I was still feeling incredibly stupid about how Cindy had learned the truth . . . and feeling a lot of guilt.

If I'd better guarded the incriminating evidence, she would still be alive. Maybe she'd be asking questions about why the basement was locked, but she'd be alive . . . and I'd have time to change things up to avoid getting caught.

The freezer held everything necessary to burn me as the murderer, but everything was there for a reason. There were two dozen varieties of flowers—enough to give me options when it came to pairing a flower with a victim. In addition to the plants, there were also human remains and a few personal belongings: most notably Tina's wrist flesh, Katie's hands, dirt from under Vernon's fingernails, the other Vernon's wallet, and Cindy's toes and underwear.

These weren't souvenirs or keepsakes: they were pieces of evidence that I intended to plant on someone else in order to make an arrest and close the case without incriminating myself.

But after Cindy wandered down here and found this shit on her own, I realized it was time to take some extra security measures.

CHAPTER 26

PROFILING

(ANGRY PERSON KILLING KIND PEOPLE BECAUSE HE NEVER RECEIVED KINDNESS)

PERHAPS THE MOST UNDERSTATED arrival in Crooked Creek was a man named Gavin Thomasen. He arrived in a small rented car at a time when no one expected him, because no one had been expecting him at all.

He was a *New York Times* bestseller, though no one who'd even read his book could remember his name. He was an expert and a ghost; a somebody and a nobody. He was known to some in law enforcement as a profiler—the original profiler. His skill set was perfect for reading case files, studying evidence, and then producing an accurate, detailed profile of the killer in question.

He was known to get details right, such as gender, age, and even preferred victim type of the killer. He was considered a bit of a psychic by many in law enforcement—specifically those who thought he was a poseur and a waste of time.

And he rode into town with as little fanfare as possible, parked a block away from the precinct, and sat calmly in the waiting room for nearly an hour before Maggie got ahold of me and I returned to the station.

I rushed into the building, and Maggie pointed at the only other person there, sitting in the row of chairs we called the waiting room.

"My apologies, Dr. Thompson," I said earnestly.

"Thomasen," he corrected me.

"Oh, no, double apologies!" I laughed nervously. "Dr. Thomasen?" I pronounced and asked all at the same time.

"Very good," he said, nodding. "No apologies necessary, Sheriff. I know you have your hands full these days. That's why I'm here."

"Come in, come in," I said as I opened the door to my office and acted as a doorstop, waving my hand through the entryway.

As he moved past me into the office, I glanced at Maggie with a look that I hoped conveyed "What am I supposed to do with this guy?" while she responded with the world's most casual and unconcerned shrug. Maggie was excellent at her job and even better at letting us know where that job began and ended.

As Thomasen settled into the folding chair opposite my desk, I scrambled around to my own chair, all the while quickly scanning the desk and the room for any case-sensitive information that might be viewable. "So, Doctor," I began, "what brings you to Crooked Creek?"

"I believe I can help narrow your search for your killer," he replied plainly but confidently.

Several seconds went by while I considered that statement. "Well," I finally replied happily, "that is really good news, sir. We have been struggling with this case, as I'm sure you know, so any insight you might offer would be greatly appreciated."

"I have developed my own model," he continued, not recognizing my sarcasm one bit, "using case data from more than a thousand murder cases, to help predict the kind of person you are after . . . to create a loose profile that will help you ignore many potential suspects and focus on the ones most likely to be the guilty party." He smiled widely.

"Predict?" I said aloud, dropping the sarcasm for genuine surprise.

"That is correct, sir," he replied. "It is not unlike the algorithm that sophisticated bettors use when evaluating horse races."

"Mm-hmm." I nodded, but I was clearly confused, so he continued.

"I apply behavioral science in much the same way meteorologists apply weather science. It's predictive and based on multiple data points, but it's still prone to error due to the volatile nature of the subject of study."

I blinked a few times, running his words over and over in my mind. I was also still evaluating. This all seemed like academic hogwash to me still, and yet I knew that this kind of work—evaluating crime scenes and predicting suspects—was an emerging field. I'd read a few books about the science of crime.

"Why did you come to me instead of the FBI?" I asked.

"The FBI is here?"

"Oh, Jesus," I breathed before stopping myself. "The FBI has actually taken over the entire investigation and has set up headquarters out at Jerusalem County High School." I pulled open a random drawer, trying to give myself something to do besides look this man in the eye. "I think I have a map around here somewhere."

"And you think the FBI will listen to my theories?"

"Well, no," I blurted out before my brain caught up. "The FBI, from my experience, does whatever the fuck they want to do, pardon my language. You seem to have a decent theory, and you are welcome to share it with them. I just don't want you getting your hopes up, is all."

"I don't have any hopes," he replied flatly. "Just data." With that, he stood and reached out to shake my hand. "Now, can you tell me how I might find this high school that the FBI is using as a modified headquarters?"

I reciprocated the shake and added, "Maggie, my receptionist out there . . . she'll give you directions to the high school."

"Thank you, Sheriff," he said, with the enthusiasm of someone who's just gotten an amazing job offer for a dream position.

● ● ●

Later that afternoon, after Dr. Thomasen had gone through several FBI background checks and convinced enough of the gatekeeper agents that he had valuable data, there was a briefing in the high school auditorium. Thankfully, I heard about it in time to attend . . . mostly thanks to John the Janitor—a school custodian who attended my church and enjoyed gossip.

And before you get offended by the name "John the Janitor," he picked it himself. He said he thought of his position in life as every bit as important as John the Baptist's, only with more puke and poop. It was a disgusting analogy that scripture didn't really support, but I never challenged him on it because I didn't see much point. Nevertheless, he was a shameless gossip, and I had a pretty good regular update going on how the FBI was proceeding without me.

I couldn't resist showing up for the presentation for several reasons, not the least of which was to continue sticking it to the FBI. They'd barked me off of many elements of this investigation since they'd arrived, but I needed them to know I wasn't some wimp who could be bullied . . . and that I would be continuing to investigate this case until the end of time if it suited me.

It was also helpful to know what concrete information law enforcement had about the killings, so I could continue to avoid detection and arrest.

As sheriff, I was curious to see what insights Thomasen might have into the killings that would have otherwise escaped me. I knew I wasn't a natural detective, but I liked to think I'd come a long way during my tenure here. And as a killer, I was clearly curious to learn what his profile had gotten wrong and right about me. I found it hard to believe that a person could use books and previous case data to narrow down the suspect list in this case to—basically—me.

But I was in for a rude awakening. Or, I should say, half a rude awakening.

It was astonishing how much the profiler got right, compared to how much he got wrong. Truly mind-blowing. And I don't mean that facetiously. He was uncannily intuitive, and his overarching theories made complete sense. But every one of his direct hits had a companion wild miss. It really did feel as if he were firing arrows blindly, and doing so during one of his earliest archery lessons.

"We are dealing with a meticulous individual," Thomasen said. "Nothing sloppy, nothing left to chance, everything with a purpose."

False.

I was sloppy as hell and had left many possible clues, despite my sweeps over each and every crime scene. It was ultimately a wonder of forensic science that I hadn't been caught based on crime-scene evidence alone. But crime-scene investigations around this time were wildly incomplete, and no one ever went back to look at these murders from a cold-case perspective until well after I was gone from the crime scenes.

I was also plenty sloppy on the "home cleanliness" side of things. I'd been here, living in the same church-owned house for ten years, and I had never once vacuumed. I mowed the lawn now and then every summer . . . but only when I felt I was nearing a neighborhood complaint.

The point is: I was relatively lazy in the grand scheme of things.

"This person is male, between thirty and fifty years of age."

True, though this seemed like kind of an easy guess.

"The killer is right-handed."

How the fuck?

"He believes that he is standing in for God . . ."

. . . true. Shit.

". . . sentencing his victims, the perceived wicked, for their crimes because God was too inactive or too lenient."

The exact opposite of true. Interesting.

Dr. Thomasen continued: "This person was almost certainly raised by abusive parents who instilled early a warped sense of black and white."

False. My parents were hippies who ditched me at a commune in California when I was nine. No one is sure if they did it on purpose or because they were high. Neither they nor any of my subsequent foster parents ever laid a hand on me. I suppose there was the occasional verbal abuse, but that's stretching things to match an assumption. My upbringing was largely harmonious and free of pain.

"The suspect is likely driven by pent-up sexual tension and has been ignored by the opposite sex for so long, he began ignoring his own sexual urges."

Ha ha ha ha ha ha! I was growing less worried about this professional profiler by the minute.

"He was possibly in love with one of his victims . . ."

Goddammit.

". . . quite probably all of them."

Phew.

"Gender, age . . . these things mean nothing to this man. It's the souls he's drawn to."

Fuck.

Back and forth it went like this until I had a revelation: no matter how wrong this book nerd was about me, even his getting a few things right could still narrow the pool enough to be a danger to me, considering how small the town was.

He could say the killer was blonde, and that would narrow the list down to 25 percent of the population. I was one of a couple thousand.

Knowing I could be included in a narrowed-down suspect pool regardless of my actual innocence—and by innocence, I mean guilt—was troublesome. This was not a threat I had planned on.

● ● ●

I hung around after the presentation, pretending to look deep in thought or bored, while mostly I was eavesdropping to try and find out how seriously the FBI was taking this man's mathematically based prediction concepts. Turns out, they mostly thought he was a joke. Granted, I wasn't able to get a read on every agent, but the conversations I heard were all mocking the poor bastard and his theory.

This was a huge relief, since roughly 40 percent of his predictions were correct. Sure, *some* could be attributed to luck, but not 40 percent.

I made a mental note to learn more about suspect profiling, if only to keep myself one step or more ahead of my pursuers.

The poor guy stuck around for a few hours, desperately hoping for one of the senior agents to take his theories seriously.

It never happened.

Slowly, and with shoulders slumped, he loaded all his notebooks and slide decks back into his car. I watched him hand-write a note, fold it, and place it in one of the temporary makeshift mailboxes set up for the agents on loan. Most of the agents got cards and love letters, but at least one of them would get a note containing the very final thoughts of Dr. Gavin Thomasen. Because, as luck would have it, the doctor died just outside the city limits in a car accident.

The only person who had taken his theories seriously had been the killer, and he'd learned a great deal about how not to get caught next time.

CHAPTER 27

I DIDN'T SIGN UP FOR THIS

If I was going to get away with my crimes, I would need someone to pin them on.

Having been a sheriff for many years now, you'd be surprised how many criminals attempt to get away with their crimes by simply hoping the cops think someone else had done it. I knew enough not only to stay out of the spotlight, but also to give the police someone else to focus on.

I had the greenhouse on the Watkinses' property. I had my keepsakes in the garden down in the basement.

I just needed a fall guy . . . and I had a few in mind.

A few of the Watkins children would have fit the bill, but with the greenhouse there on that property, I thought it was a little on the nose. The human brain is wired to accept *some* odd coincidences when the stakes aren't too high—like two men named Vernon in a town of a few thousand people—but in murder investigations, odd coincidences were usually red flags.

Buzz Martinson was an easy target, and one almost no one in town would bat an eye at for crimes such as these. It was almost too easy to use him.

Finally, there was out-of-towner Merritt. He'd been here a few months now, mostly working odd jobs and doing handyman work. But no one knew anything about him. A stranger is a blank slate. I could say whatever I wanted, and most of it would stick.

I had other options, of course. But these were my top three targets at present.

I had time; there was no reason to decide now, and I wanted to leave myself open to any last-minute "eurekas." But regardless of which person I eventually chose to frame for my crimes, the plans all hinged on that remote greenhouse. This meant that I had to tend to the plants and flowers there on a regular basis, lest they all die.

Ideally, I'd get out there every day. Plants were sensitive things, prone to complication at the very slightest change to their environment. I had to settle for twice a week, if I was lucky. Just to get out there, I had to drive out into the back country, then switch to horseback to get over the ridge, and *then* do the final thousand feet on foot to avoid the horses making noise.

On this particular night, I was fifty feet from the greenhouse when I heard the hounds.

The Watkinses were very concerned about poachers, encroachers, and anyone who might be using their land or stealing their shit. They'd often called the station, reporting vague sightings of intruders on their property; but by the time officers arrived, no one could ever be found.

We assumed they were insane or were just fucking with us. The jokes around the station were mostly Bigfoot-related. But tonight, the family's motivations ultimately did not matter. The Watkins clan was out in force, chasing an apparent spy. The Watkins family, like many large farms in the county, believed that "Big Farm" corporations were spying on them and actively plotting to take over their lands or even poison their crops. They also feared that neighboring farmers were sneaking onto the property to somehow inhibit growth or otherwise damage the Watkinses' crops.

The family held stock in all sorts of theories, and none of them needed to be true for me to get discovered by a Watkins posse while I was snooping around without permission on their sovereign land. Fortunately for me, the Watkins clan was as dumb as nails. Not one of them knew how to train or manage a smell hound. A scent dog is only as good as its handler, and these handlers were supremely stupid.

In addition, these weren't scent dogs. They weren't purebred, and they weren't trained even a little bit. These dogs couldn't even sit or stay on command, let alone follow tracks or a scent. They were a pack of seven mutts who liked to bark and run when their owners got worked up.

So while I had very little time to act, I had some advantages. All I really needed to do was give the dogs a distraction . . . something momentary but long enough to give the Watkins clan reason to doubt the dogs . . . and I might just get by.

I knew the dogs might smell my presence if there wasn't something more potent for their noses to take in. So, I slipped my pants down a bit and urinated on the ground, spraying near and far as best I could. Perhaps I could distract them with such a scent, like countermeasures against a torpedo in a submarine movie. Perhaps not. I was too desperate to be completely logical about it.

For extra measure, I pulled the pepper spray from my belt, covered my mouth and nose, and sprayed that shit everywhere. Pepper spray was a relatively new tool in the police officer's arsenal and incapacitated suspects by inducing labored breathing and tear-duct issues. The statewide training made a point of mentioning not to use pepper spray if you had a canine partner, because it did a number on a dog's ability to smell. I hadn't had any hands-on experience with the device, but things were desperate enough that I'd take all the help I could get.

I was smart enough to have trudged out here in stocking feet, so as not to leave a shoeprint, so I hoofed it from the urination spot directly toward the tiny grove that contained the greenhouse. My footprints could still be a giveaway; but this was unfarmed land, partially grassed over, and I had to hope the scent was driving the hounds more than any visual evidence was standing out to the humans.

In case the greenhouse was discovered later, I chose to climb a tall maple tree next to it, rather than hide inside with the flowers. Once I was up the tree, I began to think of this as a stupid thing to have done. If they found the greenhouse, one of the dogs or humans would surely look up and see me in the tree. But it was too late to climb back down, and there weren't any better hiding spots anyway. Either the dogs would pass the grove by, or they wouldn't. I'd done all I could do.

The dogs approached, followed quickly by the Watkins family members—most on horseback but three on four-wheelers and one on a dirt bike. Through the leaves, it looked like maybe ten people, give or take. I couldn't be sure.

The dogs circled and barked a bit, seemingly concentrated on the odd mix of human urine and pepper spray I'd left behind. They backed off a bit but still circled.

For several seconds, a choir of jarring sounds rang out . . . gasoline engines of the four-wheelers and the dirt bike . . . horse hooves pounding the ground . . . men yelling . . . like three different movies playing through the theater speakers at once.

Someone shot a flare gun, but, in typical Watkins fashion, it had been fired laterally to the ground. It ended up stuck in the dirt, ass out, fifty yards away, hissing viciously as it went nowhere and did nothing but illuminate a ten-foot circle around it.

Then, only a few seconds later, the posse took off, headed east and away from my position, the horses and motorized humans following the dogs; the dogs following . . . nothing in particular.

It was as though the small corner grove had been blocked in their minds as even being part of their own land. I mean . . . whoever they thought they were chasing . . . even without hounds . . . you'd think they'd have checked out this small grove of shrubs and trees that is super-nearby and totally perfect for hiding in. But no . . . they just kept on.

Somewhere in the next thirty seconds, I passed out from panic and anxiety.

I would later learn that the Watkins family had been chasing what they thought was a pig poacher, only to eventually end up catching a sickly coyote—who had probably tried to poach a pig, if we're being honest here. They'd killed him and claimed victory, considering their land once again sovereign and free of interlopers.

I'd lucked out again. I wasn't a cat, but how many lives did I have here? I knew the Lord approved of my mission, but even he couldn't openly defend me at all times.

Or could he?

● ● ●

I awoke just before dawn, cranky and with every joint creaking from having slept in a tree. I assessed the time based on the imminent sunrise and determined that I had a half hour or so before the common local farmer woke up and got to work. That was just enough time to tend to the flowers in the greenhouse.

Climbing down proved harder than climbing up, mostly because the adrenaline was gone and had been replaced by aches and pains and general body reality.

A thousand feet away, two farms over, and technically in another county . . . I was amazed to find my horse, Barley, still standing where I'd left him. I'd only half-heartedly looped the reins around the tree like I typically do for short stays. He could easily have broken free and wandered away. But he hadn't.

I said a prayer as I rode back toward the truck, asking God to help me be less stupid in the future.

And I think he heard my prayer and answered it in the form of Harold McKee, leaning casually against my squad car like he owned it, smirking like a dickhead.

"Hey, dickhead," I said as Barley and I sauntered up.

"Why are you always so hostile, Father Sheriff?" Father Sheriff was his favorite nickname to try to shame me for one of my jobs by invoking the other.

"Why are you always a dickhead, Harold?" I climbed off the horse and started leading him into the trailer.

"Don't tell me you're out here because of that wild goose chase the Watkins clan was on." He was probing. Guessing. He knew something was slightly off, but he wasn't sure what it was. Honestly, he was easier to read than a first-grader.

"As always," I said flatly, "I am not at liberty to discuss police business. And even if I were, you would be the last guy I would discuss it with." Barley trudged up into the trailer like he had a hundred times before, and I lifted the gate and locked it behind him. "In other words," I summarized, "no comment."

He smiled the way dickheads smile when they think they've scored a point even though they haven't. Then he waved as he climbed into his beat-up vehicle.

My middle finger got loose of the rest of my left hand momentarily and stood tall to salute the dickhead as he backed out and drove away.

● ● ●

I pulled onto the side of the street around 4 a.m. and parked, turning the engine off immediately. It wasn't a populous part of town, but I was more concerned about the noise than the headlights.

I could have put a crude bomblike device on his car. One could argue that I should have, if only to avoid possible links to myself and the victim. But I couldn't help myself.

None of my victims deserved their pain quite so much as Harold McKee. And tonight he'd earned his ticket to Heaven by ultimately discovering me at the Watkins farm from which it should have been easy for him to deduce my involvement in the killings. I had some connection to the deaths. From there he would clearly go on to follow a discovery path that put me in the spotlight, which would take me out of the Lord's service permanently.

And I couldn't have that.

And while I wasn't intending to make Harold an obvious victim of the local serial killer, I still wanted his actual death moment to be personal. I wanted him to know it was me. I wanted him to know he was right . . . just before he died.

So, I knocked on his front door.

He opened it.

"Hey, dickhead," I said just before I jabbed a knife into his jugular. "Time's up."

I had my gloves, my windbreaker, and even my plastic shoe booties on, so I just followed him into the house even as I was laying him on his back to bleed out.

"That's it," I said condescendingly as I shut the front door. "You're going to bleed out very soon, and then you'll be on the road to Heaven. And you can thank me for that, since I decided to take your life just after you'd made a noble decision. The decision to turn me in."

He choked and coughed up blood, his eyes wide with sudden fear.

"You never would have gone to Heaven of your own accord, Harold, and you and I both know it. Your soul has long been poisoned with the salacious drive for edgy news and the money and attention that comes with it. Satan probably rents a room in this tiny fucking house. But I caught you . . . caught you in a moment of pure righteous anger . . . and so you'll end up with Jesus for eternity. You better thank your fucking lucky stars, son," I barked.

And then he died.

He bled out for another half hour or so, which was fine with me because I needed that time to set up the flashpoints for the fire.

I'd never set a fire intentionally before, but I considered it a useful skill and one that I was probably overdue to learn. Most of my library research told me to ensure proper accelerant coverage. So I sprayed gasoline in every room, upon every surface, and even the walls and ceiling. For fun, I decided to light the fire with matches from the sacristy. Killing someone in order to save that person's soul seemed just as worthy a use of blessed matchsticks as lighting liturgical candles.

Because I didn't want Harold's death being discovered as a murder soon, and definitely didn't want it connected to the serial killings, I took the body into the living room before I left, propping it up in the La-Z-Boy facing the TV. He'd burn enough that the knife wound would disappear, and his death would be considered accidental and one that had occurred outside the scope of the federal investigation.

As I drove back toward my own house, I did the math. A neighbor of McKee's would probably spot the fire and call it in after just a few minutes. Many would be asleep, but at least one would see, smell, or hear the fire pretty quickly. Let's call it fifteen minutes.

Then that call would go out to the local volunteer fire department. That group consisted of ten local men and women, but they would all first go to the volunteer fire station just north of town.

The county fire department would also receive the alarm and set things in motion. Their headquarters were technically in Crooked Creek, but they were so far south of town, on the very edge of the city limits, that it would take them fifteen minutes to get to the site of the fire.

All this meant that no one would get to Harold's home in time to find anything other than what I wanted them to find: a charred-out home with the corpse of a lazy dead man.

I knew Terry Riley, the local fire chief, and he was a better EMT than he was a firefighter. He was certainly no fire investigator. And the man absolutely hated paperwork. This fire would be ruled accidental quickly enough for Terry to get home in time for eggs.

CHAPTER 28

CONFIDENTIALITY

A FEW DAYS LATER, I was in the high school gymnasium after another profiling briefing from the pissant when I felt a hand on my elbow. I turned around to see Lt. Irwin, distress on his face. He jerked his head to the side twice, indicating a desire for a more private conversation.

I nodded my agreement and followed him into a nearby hallway.

"You—you're the local priest around here, right?"

"I am," I said cautiously.

"And you have a doctor/patient confidentiality thing there, with the confession and all, correct?"

"That's true." It wouldn't help the current conversation to bog him down with the specific rules of confession at this point; the man was clearly looking for an outlet, and I intended to provide him one, even if it wasn't by the book.

"So you can't repeat to no one what someone confesses to you?"

"That's also true," I lied. Technically, I did have discretion in these matters, and if someone confessed to a crime, I could choose to report it to the authorities. But in my experience, no one asked questions like these if they weren't looking to unload an absolute whopper of a transgression. And, as the resident evil in this-here county, I was curious to learn what kind of sin could make a federal man tremble this much.

● ● ●

"Father, forgive me, for I am a total fuckup," he began. "Oh shit," he immediately followed, "I'm definitely not supposed to cuss here in this little booth."

It was Lt. Irwin's first confession, and it showed.

"It's okay," I assured him. "I promise I've heard much worse."

"I seriously doubt that, Father," he said, shaking with fear.

"Whatever you have to say, son, I promise that this is a safe place. This chamber, and even this entire building."

Several seconds of silence followed before he finally blurted out his true thoughts. "I have evidence that one of my fellow members of law enforcement is—"

"Stop right there," I barked, immediately contradicting myself about the confidentiality. "Don't even finish that sentence until you hear me out. I am required to keep everything you and I talk about confidential . . . *except* criminal activity. If you tell me about a crime that you have participated in or witnessed, even secondhand . . . I have to report it to the police."

Startled and confused, Irwin replied spontaneously: "We are both the police, though, are we not?"

"I don't think I have enough time here, honestly, to explain the difference between the priest as an individual and the priest in confession as a conduit to God. Point is . . . I have to report it to my own authorities—state police, in this case—if I believe you have confessed to a crime in this booth."

"I'm gonna burst, Father. I have to tell someone, and I was counting on you to be bound by confidentiality." His voice grew even more panicked.

"Son," I tried to sound comforting, "you need to find an attorney or a psychiatrist. They can give you the confidentiality you desire—"

"I'm sorry, Father, but I can't wait any longer! I can't do it: it's tearing me up, and I—"

"Easy," I tried, like an idiot, as though he were a horse, "easy, there. Don't take this personally, kid, but I'm going to leave the—"

"His own daughter!" Lt. Irwin began sobbing.

Aww, shit, I thought to myself. *This is unrelated to the murders and is going to be a whole other thing I have to navigate.*

"Whose daughter?" I asked reluctantly.

"I didn't know," he said loudly. "I didn't know until it was too late. I didn't know he was capable . . ." He sobbed and trailed off as the tears took over.

Ultimately, I would learn that he was talking about his father's abuse of Irwin's own sister, something that would disturb anyone who heard even the most fringe details.

Most folks carry this kind of pain. It's not always so severe or carved quite so deep, but everyone carries some manner of childhood pain or trauma. But Irwin couldn't carry his pain any further. Choking and sobbing, he started with this childhood trauma and then moved forward in time as his memory inched through the history.

As a teen, he'd dabbled in petty crime, mostly robbing the elderly at knifepoint. In his early twenties, he'd hit a sort of rock bottom when he narrowly escaped arrest in a large-scale drug heist that went bad. Most of his crew had been killed on site; two had been arrested and sent to prison. And that's when Irwin went straight. Apparently, he'd been carrying this pain and guilt his entire life, never unloading it on a spouse or therapist . . . just . . . existing with massive grief and remorse.

I ultimately felt sorry for him. He had overcome massive adversity to become a decent human being. For a brief moment, I considered killing him to ensure his soul's place in Heaven. But I didn't feel completely at ease with the idea of a murder scene inside the confessional—let alone inside the church—so I abandoned the idea. I tried to let God guide these kinds of decisions, and it just didn't feel like I was getting a "Yes."

He wasn't Catholic anyway, but I also didn't give out traditional Catholic penance, so I encouraged him to seek redemption in some form of volunteering with area prison ministries and other convict-outreach programs.

He sobbed lightly as he left the confessional, and all the way through the sanctuary until he'd left the building, and I assumed for a good while even after that.

● ● ●

The situation in Crooked Creek had reached maximum national interest. "The serial killer of Indiana" was nightly national news, and everyone was scared across the entire mid-state. The leading nickname at this point was the Gentleman Killer, because the killer always left flowers at the scene.

I thought it was horrific and perfect.

Universities hours away—like Purdue and Notre Dame—were canceling classes, despite every murder so far occurring in Jerusalem County. Truckers were passing through overnight instead of stopping along our main highway to sleep or grab a bite to eat. Farmers were waiting for more pure daylight before getting out into the fields. Even the newspapers and mail were being delivered a bit later than normal, and in broad daylight only.

In Jerusalem County, people were downright paranoid. The single grocery store in town, Clemmon's, was packed every day as folks began stocking up for a protracted long stay at home. Key items began running out rather quickly: bread, milk, toilet paper, canned vegetables, and, oddly, potatoes.

We had only the one gas station inside the city limits, and it kept sporadically running out of gas every third day in between intermittent emergency deliveries, even though no one in town really ever had anywhere they needed to drive to.

It wasn't helping things that the town's population had nearly doubled due to visitors. We had federal agents, journalists, and gawkers alike. Most of these people were sleeping in tents or vehicles, but their impact on the local supply of food and essentials was devastating. And many of the gawkers—fans of chaos, as I called them—were also openly flouting local traffic laws or causing noise complaints every night, using up federal resources like FBI agents just to create a memorable moment or take a dangerous Polaroid.

It was absolute pandemonium for a community that thrived on repetition and boredom. Nearly every citizen's life was thrown off in some way or another.

I didn't have a ton of power in the main investigation just now—I was more of an as-needed consultant—so I decided to check in on some locals to see how they were holding up. I decided to start in my own neighborhood, so I walked two doors down to Ms. Field's. Ms. Field was a widow whose husband had served in the Korean War. He'd come home with a healthy touch of what they called "shell shock" and began acting irregularly. Eventually he'd driven his car off the bridge over the widest section of Crooked Creek and died from his injuries.

Since then, Ms. Field had kept largely to herself. She went out for gas and groceries and her weekly bridge game, and that was about it. She had two Siamese cats that hated me and hissed at me anytime I got near the property, and she had a huge clothesline out back—big enough for a family with five kids.

She saw me coming and stepped out the front door onto the massive porch before I was halfway up the walk. "Sheriff," she said flatly.

"Ms. Field," I responded while I continued up the sidewalk.

"It ain't Christmas, so I know you aren't here for donations for that church of yours that I don't even attend."

Ms. Field also had a way with words that was succinct and usually a little mean.

I just laughed. "Yes, ma'am. That's the truth."

"Then what can I do you for?" she pressed, crossing her arms firmly and defiantly.

"Just checking in, Ms. Field," I responded. "Just going through the neighborhood, seeing if anyone needs anything. No reason to get alarmed." I paused, then continued. "Do you have any needs, ma'am?"

"I live a block away from Clemmon's and half a block from the gas station. You think I need you for anything?"

I sighed but tried to turn it into a laugh. "No, ma'am. Just checking. You have a great day now," I said, waving as I walked back to the main sidewalk.

"See you at Christmas," she barked before slamming the front door shut.

I made a mental note not to kill Ms. Field, since her soul would most definitely end up in Hell. I was developing quite a list! On both sides of the ledger!

• • •

The Kinnemans were next on my list. They were a block west and had attended Mass a few times. I knew they had a newborn as well as a couple of young kids. My main concern was their survival: did they have enough food and diapers, could they get by for a week or two if the store ran out of things? Thankfully, they were all set in that department. But where they seemed to need help was the spiritual and emotional area. Both husband and wife—Matt and Jane—were overly stressed. Both worked forty-hour weeks, with Matt's mother watching the kids during the day.

Jane Kinneman worked as a receptionist at the school board's office, and Matt was a farmhand full-time and a part-time coach of the high school baseball team. He'd worked for the farm long enough to have earned a small ownership stake—some farmers with lots of land will give their best workers a direct stake in the success of the farm. Eventually their kids would be old enough to help out on the farm and give mom and dad a break, but that was a long way off, and I often worried about their family.

Because the FBI was using the high school as a headquarters—and the high school was where the school board offices were located—Mrs. Kinneman was at home, along with all her children. Matt, it seemed, was still needed for his farming job, even though the high school baseball season had been suspended. So he wasn't home today.

"What do you need? What are you lacking? How can I help?" I peppered her with questions as I tried to remind myself that doing God's work involved much more than sending pure souls to Heaven at the right time . . . it involved doing the very basic kindnesses for the "least of these" among us.

How much have I lost track of my own daily priestly mission?

Jane looked at me for several seconds, not a change on her face. Finally, she started laughing. "What do I need? What do I need?!" She cackled, the baby bouncing in her arms. "What *don't* I need, mother-fucker?! I need diapers. I need nannies. I need tampons, wipes, baby gates, and ground fucking beef. I need frozen shit and canned shit and all the shit to fill my fridge. I need stamps, textbooks, day-care dues, and gas money. I need *everything*, Mister Father Sheriff. Now how much of that can you give me? Or are you just here to feel better about yourself and not actually do anything constructive?"

I'd been worried about the FBI or even the local cops getting wise to my act; I'd never expected a common citizen—a neighbor—to see through me so easily and thoroughly. I actually stammered aloud for a few seconds.

Before I could speak, she slammed the door on me.

She's a pure soul, I told myself immediately. *She's as pure as you've met.* This would change my plans.

I was an organized killer, and I prided myself on meticulous planning. But the nature of the victims—those who had most recently demonstrated a purity of heart and selflessness—meant that I couldn't plan very far ahead. All my plans were subject to change at a moment's notice.

And this woman—this entire home—radiated goodness and kindness. It was an energy one could not miss. I knew I had to kill her, not because she'd seen through me and cussed me out, but . . . also . . . definitely because she'd seen through me and cussed me out. The question was how to do it while keeping her children safe and cared for.

I'd have to plan this one out, hoping that she maintained that righteous anger until I was ready to execute.

Through the door, I raised my voice a bit and promised to send some supplies and check back in a few days, and she continued yelling at me as I walked away. I knew she was right, but I couldn't let her know, especially now that I had added her to my list.

Next door down was a home known to belong to Pete Preston. No one was sure what he looked like. He never came out. His groceries were delivered, along with the rest of his needs. But he paid his bills on time and didn't do anything to annoy his neighbors, so the area residents were basically fine with his presence, though, it should be noted, no one let their children ring his doorbell on Halloween.

I'd made attempts in the past to talk with Mr. Preston, so today I just waved toward his house as I walked by and moved on to the next approachable human. That turned out to be the Duckmans.

The Duckmans were also incredibly private. They lived here in Crooked Creek, but they drove hours out of their way on Sundays to go to their preferred church three counties away. The talk about town was that the Duckmans were Pentecostal, and their church's worship service included ribbon-dancing and speaking in tongues. There was, of course, no proof of this. All anybody knew for sure was that they didn't attend any church in Crooked Creek, and they often went for Sunday drives that lasted for hours. People filled in the blanks themselves, and over time those explanations became canon, and eventually no one even had questions about it.

We did know there was a father and mother—Gerald and Janice—and two daughters—Jessie and Gwen. The girls were enrolled at the local high school, and they were both known to be shy and quiet. Gerald, the dad, worked as a factory foreman over in Ft. Blaine, while the mom, Janice, was a nurse at a local doctor's office.

I walked up to the porch and rang the doorbell. I heard the soft echo of the bells resonating throughout the inside of the house. There was no discernible movement inside the house, and the repeating sound eventually died off. Despite my inner conscience, I went up on my toes and peeked inside the small glass window of their front door as I hit the doorbell again.

Nothing.

They were either not home or not remotely interested in talking to me. Both possibilities were equally likely, as far as I could figure.

I sighed as I walked farther up the block. *I'm not going to do any good this way,* I thought to myself. *I'd do more good eavesdropping on FBI briefings at the high school, giving my two cents to any agent there who would listen. This here . . . is useless.*

I turned for home, dejected. But then I remembered I did have a new victim, a new job . . . a new soul to save. And I was whistling and walking more briskly within seconds.

CHAPTER 29

JANE SAYS

JANE KINNEMAN HAD THREE CHILDREN under five, the youngest being three months old. She would normally be answering phones and performing general office tasks for the school board, but because the out-of-town law enforcement had taken over the local high school—which housed the school board offices—she was stuck at home with the kids.

Normally Jane's mother, Agatha, came over for the day to watch the kids. Agatha was a widow and was perpetually bored, so she was still coming over every day despite the lack of need for her childcare services. This only made Jane's days more frustrating.

This situation was going to take a little bit of observation and planning, as I was pretty sure God didn't want me killing any children if I could avoid it. But the mother was a different matter. Was she being selfless by constantly coming over to watch the kids, or was she serving her own needs?

I settled on the mom being selfish and therefore not of interest to my pursuits. I would be killing only Jane.

Now I just needed a way to either get Jane's mother and children out of the house all at once, or get Jane herself out of the house all alone.

Matt had taken on several double shifts at the farm for the summer. He worked too many damn hours to be a factor in my plans or in his own family's life—though I ultimately found a way to use him to my advantage.

● ● ●

Around nine the next evening, roughly an hour after all her kids had gone down, Jane received a phone call from me. I put on my most serious voice.

I spoke slowly and solemnly. I made sure to crack my voice now and then and pretend to choke back tears. I explained how Matt, her husband, had been in an accident out on the farm. That it was bad. That she should leave the kids with her mother and come immediately, by herself, to the farm site to say her last good-byes.

I will admit that it felt a bit cruel to make Jane think her husband was near death, but I reasoned it was worth it for the end result: Jane going to Heaven. So far, God seemed willing to overlook an awful lot of fringe behavior, so long as more pure souls were showing up at the pearly gates.

After the fateful phone call, Jane called her mother and breathlessly explained the situation. As soon as Agatha showed up, Jane grabbed the keys from the wall and dashed off into the garage.

The farm that her husband Matt worked on was miles outside the city limits, and it only took a few moments for Jane to be driving on empty roads. She sped up a bit, certainly hoping the FBI in town had better things to do than chase speeders.

About halfway to her husband's workplace, Jane slowed for the upcoming stop sign at State Road 48. When the car finally came to a stop, I bolted up from the back seat of the vehicle, pulled her back into her seat via her forehead, and slashed her throat wide open with a shaving blade.

I lurched forward and threw the car in PARK.

I leaped out the back door, opened the driver's door, and reached in to turn the keys in the ignition to the OFF position. The car shut down, and everything went dark.

I stood back up and looked long and hard down both roadways, searching for headlights. There were none. I sighed in relief. I didn't need much alone time here at the scene, but I needed some.

I reached into my jacket and pulled out three pink peonies. I carefully carved a small opening just below Jane's shoulder blade and slid the flower stalks in as if into a shirt pocket. The peonies represented everything Jane deserved and had earned but never received: romance, a happy marriage, compassion, and honor. These would be restored to her in Heaven.

I took just a moment to admire and inspect the scene, concluding that I was happy with things the way they were.

With that, I was off and running full-tilt toward the small grove of oak trees a half-mile away. I ran without looking back; the plan would be derailed if anything behind me went awry, and I didn't have time to face that possibility. If any cars showed up while I was running, there were plenty of other directions for me to go to get out of sight.

I was running against the rows, the cornstalks smacking my arms and my face. I fell several times as the corn plants tripped me and the rows of mud disrupted my stride. I cursed the grove for being located against the grain of the corn rows instead of in line with them.

After what seemed like hours, but was only about six minutes, I arrived at the small oak grove where I'd stashed my police SUV ahead of time. Yeah, do the math on that one, if you dare; I put the vehicle there and then *walked* back to town the entire five miles, mostly through various fields and groves.

Did I know how to sell a bit, or what?

I considered just staying put, sitting in the police SUV and waiting for the call to go out over the radio. Why drive all the way back into town, only to drive all the way back out here again? But the problem was that I had no idea when someone would find the body or when it would hit the police band. Fact is, traffic out on these country roads at night was close to nil—that's why I'd chosen this spot. So I had no choice but to drive home and wait for the call like everyone else.

When I got home, I turned on the TV, made a plate of nachos, and curled up with Zacchaeus while waiting for the phone call. But it never came. I fell asleep.

I didn't awake until well after 7 a.m., and there had still been no call.

Maggie would definitely have called me about any new murders, even if the FBI guys decided to leave me out of it. And there was also Reggie at the county hospital, who had promised to let me know about any new admissions to the morgue.

Zacchaeus stretched and looked up at me in a blissful haze.

Has no one found Jane Kinneman's body yet?

It seemed impossible. Yes, the back-county roads had less traffic, but it's not as though they had *zero* traffic.

A sudden panic set in. After all, a killer never knows he has been found out until it's too late. Had I made a mistake in this last kill, or maybe even prior? Had I given myself away? Was the FBI just waiting for me to show up for work today before pouncing on me?

This is the guilty conscience that the truly law-abiding citizen will never know. Once you break the law seriously enough, you never stop looking over your shoulder or waiting for the other shoe to drop . . . no matter how good you are.

If the jig was up, there was no avoiding it. I was probably already being watched if they'd found her body and made me as the suspect. I wouldn't even be able to skip town. At least not right now. I played out a few scenarios in my mind, but it all came back to one truth: I had to act as if everything was normal until I had proof that it wasn't.

So I showered, shaved, and put on my uniform. I fed the cat and walked outside to the SUV, glancing to and fro as I went, looking for signs I was being surveilled. Then I drove the minuscule distance to the station, careful to come to a complete stop before turning onto the main road.

At the station, I was not immediately surrounded by FBI personnel. I was not bum-rushed upon getting out of my vehicle. Instead, everything appeared to be operating normally.

I walked inside and was greeted by a collection of familiar sounds. Maggie was answering a citizen complaint call, Skip was explaining his latest Sasquatch theories, and Gene was there to greet me with a handshake even as he took a bite out of his toast-and-egg sandwich. Everything was normal.

If Jane had been found, and I had been implicated, I would have been arrested before now. I was in the clear . . . for now. This took such an emotional weight off me that I had to spend a few moments breathing intentionally just to avoid an anxiety-release attack.

"Lancaster!" Irwin barked as soon as he entered the station, jarring me out of my meditation. I'd been so focused that I hadn't seen or heard him coming. I sat up, shook my head, and waved him into my office.

"Lancaster!" he yelled again after entering my office. "We need your help! Lady from here in town went missing sometime last night, and she hasn't come home yet."

"That's terrible," I feigned, knowing he was talking about Jane Kinneman. "Who is it?" I asked, assuming this would be the next question a cop who is *not* the murderer might ask.

"A Jane Kinneman."

"Oh, I know her. She's one of my neighbors."

"Everyone in this town is one of your neighbors," he said dismissively.

"Why didn't anyone here tell me? Didn't they call 911?"

"No. The husband was out looking for her, got panicky, and saw one of our patrol units and flagged them down."

"I see."

"We've got him out at the high school right now, along with the kids and the woman's mother, just routine questions while our boys check out the house for evidence."

"You're taking control of this investigation?" I asked, shocked. "This is a missing-persons case, Lieutenant, not another victim in the series of murders. Am I correct?" Maybe I could find a way to check things out regarding Jane and her car if I could put myself in charge of the investigation.

"We got permission from your mayor as well as my boss to treat her like another victim," he explained curtly. "Just a victim we haven't found yet."

"Goddammit," I spat. "I suppose you're going to be handling all the speeding and jaywalking citations as well, in case they go on to be killers or victims?"

"We'll leave those to you." He smiled smugly. "For now." He started to leave.

"Well, can I at least help you guys look for the woman? Where are they concentrating their efforts?"

"Sheriff, you can go looking for her as much as you like. We'd appreciate your help. Just so long as you remember it's our case, and if you find something it needs to be reported immediately."

"Of course," I said, not meaning it.

"We're focused on mostly the north and west parts just outside of town. Apparently she got a phone call saying he'd been hurt at work, and she raced off and left the kids with her mother. But the husband's fine. Now his job is out east, but we've already checked out there and found nothing. She has a sister up in Elkhart. Guessing if she's not a murder victim, maybe she went there. We got all our agents keeping an eye out, but that's where we're focusing." And with that, he turned and left.

What in the world had happened? Had I not actually killed her? Did she survive long enough to get the car off the road or make it to some nearby home? Did someone else come along behind me and then manipulate the crime scene?

There were only so many possibilities. At least I'd made that phone call from a phone booth instead of my own home phone.

I turned off the light and opened the door to leave my office.

Skip and Gene were ready for me.

"Are you going out to look for Jane? She's my god-aunt, you know, my godmother's sister," Skip spewed all in a single thought.

"I would love to help," Gene agreed. "Known Jane since she was a toddler."

"That's great, guys, but who's going to deal with the parking meters and noise complaints?" Parking violations and noise complaints were the two most frequent calls we took. Many were fraudulent or easily resolved, but every one of them had to be chased down by a member of the force.

"Aw, Sheriff, one of us can handle that on his own," Skip countered.

I looked at Gene, and he shrugged, seeming to suggest he was fine with me letting Skip go along.

"All right, Skip," I replied. "You can help me look. We know this area better than them FBI guys, so let's focus on the local knowledge and lean into it, okay?"

He nodded excitedly.

"All right, Skip, you take the southeast. Take Pearl Drive out to 71 and then take that toward the county line. You're looking for her car, for sure, but also for anything askew. Anything out of the ordinary. Any signs of foul play."

"Yes, sir."

I said, "I'll go east down Uria Avenue until it turns into State Road 4. Let's keep in touch on the radio, and maybe we can find her out there."

With Gene witnessing the conversation, and therefore able to relay the contents to Maggie or any FBI personnel, the two of us set off and left the precinct. As soon as I was out of the residential area and there was no other traffic around, I sped like hell out to the previous night's kill site. I had never driven so fast before and have never done so since. I was the very definition of desperate. I absolutely had to find Jane's body before anyone else, if only to ensure that my own involvement in the death would remain a secret.

I came up on the intersection in question but was still in too much of a hurry to apply the brakes early enough. So at the last minute, I slammed them on and screeched and skidded into the middle of where the two roads met before finally coming to a stop.

With no regard for any potential oncoming traffic, I exited the vehicle immediately and ran full-speed to the spot where I had left Jane and her car just nine hours ago. The car was gone. Jane was gone. It had rained—poured, really—for a few hours overnight, so I couldn't even see any tire tracks or blood spots. Nothing. It was as though she and the car had disappeared into the ether like ghosts.

CHAPTER 30

GOING BACKWARDS

"I FOUND HER," the radio chirped. "This is Skip, sir. Sorry, sir. But I found her. Oh, God, it's awful . . ." he trailed off.

Skip found her? Skip? In the southeast?!

"I'm at the cliff here near Zeller Creek, sir. You better come take a look at this." He sobbed for a couple of seconds before remembering to let off on the button to his police radio.

I was standing right on the spot where I'd left the dead woman and her vehicle, and yet somehow the first person to discover her was my dimwitted deputy a mile or two to the southeast?

What the fuck happened?

Everything had been washed away on the street. The same must have been true for any tire tracks on land on the far side of the intersection; I couldn't see any indication that a car had driven away from here on the roads or through the fields.

But something had happened to that car!

The storms had just done too much to the landscape.

I walked back to the SUV and climbed inside. "Zeller Creek?!" I said aloud, before looking around in all directions, trying to get my bearings. Then I decided to throw it in REVERSE, backed up about thirty yards, and then stopped, looking out to my right. And sure enough, there was a swath of damage to the cornfield, meandering and winding away from the road in the general direction of Zeller Creek.

"Reverse?" I said to myself.

• • •

Skip was correct: it was an utterly awful sight to behold. I'd left Jane for dead, throat slit, in a public place, but the scene Skip had come upon was worse than it would have been to find my intended crime scene.

Let me try and explain what had happened, as best as I could tell from my own observation as well as the eventual coroner's report.

When putting the car in PARK, I guess I ultimately hadn't quite moved the lever all the way there, leaving it somewhere between PARK and REVERSE. Jane's dead body must have slumped forward some time after that, notching the gear lever back into REVERSE as well as pushing her right foot down onto the gas pedal. The car then lurched backward in a straight line for a handful of seconds before the body on the steering wheel started moving in reaction to the motion of the car, leading to a back-and-forth kind of chain reaction, causing the car to weave a bit and then leave the road and enter the nearby cornfield.

The car reverse-jumped the roadside ditch and bobbed and weaved its way through cornfields and other terrain, which was all quite flat.

Jane's corpse continued to inadvertently direct the car through the fields by slumping left and right in reaction to bumps and slopes, ultimately pointing it toward a small area known as the Lower Gorge. It was a sudden series of rocky cliffs extending down about twenty feet below to Zeller Creek.

Once the car reached the edge of the gorge, it leaped up momentarily, before flipping and landing in a crumpled heap against a large boulder at the other side of the creek. The rock had smashed a good portion of what had been Jane Kinneman's body, not to mention the car. Blood was everywhere, along with numerous other disgusting-looking substances that I presumed to be organs and muscle fragments.

I threw up immediately, though a large oak helped me hide the sight from Skip.

"It's okay, boss," he yelled as I vomited. "I puked too. A couple times."

The obvious first question I had was whether or not the flowers had survived the trip, which would denote this as another one of our serial killer's victims; *my* victims. Second, I thought about the body, and whether the knife wound on the throat had been obscured or undone by the general mutilation of the crash into the rocky cliff.

"I already called the FBI," Skip blurted out.

Goddammit, I silently spat. "Good," I lied. "Good job, Skip." I was completely out of control of the situation, and it had me on edge.

All my plans had become unreliable since I'd started going off-book for spontaneous murders. Cindy was the start of it all, but it had continued since then. And I was now a liability to myself.

"Good job," I repeated, for lack of anything else to say.

● ● ●

Ultimately, there was too much damage to Jane Kinneman's body for the FBI to treat her demise as anything other than a wild accidental vehicular death.

The flowers I'd planted in her shoulder had flown out the window sometime before the car careened into the creek's crevice. Enough of Jane's body was slashed and smashed by the rocks and the metal car pieces that no one even suspected that the wound on her throat had occurred pre-accident.

Just another dead body in Jerusalem County. Like they were frequent. Regular. Which, lately, they actually were. Though another death not connected to the serial killings would, oddly, make most of the locals breathe a sigh of relief, I surmised. Even though some small, twisted part of me still wanted the credit for myself.

I even sent Gene and Travis back along the tire tracks looking for clues, certain they would find and return with the flowers. Instead, they came back shrugging their shoulders and laughing about some kind of stupid inside joke they'd developed on the journey about mud shoes.

Certainly, I was relieved to not come under any scrutiny on account of this new dead body. I was definitely tired of feeling anxious and accused. But having spent so much time personally on the circumstances—only to have them turn out so nebulous and uncertain—well, now, that was frustrating. Infuriating, you might even say.

I'd done far less work to cover up far sloppier murders. I guess you could say I was mostly mad at my overall lack of recognition. Even though I knew my mission required no recognition—and, in fact, was railing against the idea of recognition itself—I still wanted some fucking credit for my many and varied actions to improve the collective existence.

But now we'd lost the reporter and Jane Kinneman, both killed for the same reason as all my other victims—because they demonstrated holy selflessness deserving of eternal life. Of course, one I had covered up because I thought it would look too suspicious, and the other one looked incredibly suspicious despite having not been covered up even a little bit. So while both would go to Heaven, their deaths would lose significance in the overall narrative of my actions, should that narrative ever be told.

The FBI was beginning to lose patience.

And suddenly . . . I saw my way out.

I'd drawn so much heat to this tiny town that I was destined to get caught if I kept it up. But if I could cause the FBI to lose interest . . . if I could make the trail go cold . . . I could live on, change locations, and keep sending holy souls to Heaven.

I decided to give them one last hurrah. There would be exactly one more crime scene attributed to the Flower Killer, and then he would go silent.

● ● ●

"Forgive me, Father, for I have sinned."

It was a voice I didn't quite recognize at first.

"I am the Flower Killer—" he said before bursting into laughter.

It was Timothy Givens, teenager, prankster, and well-known idiot.

"Sorry, Father, I couldn't keep it together on that one."

"Do you think it's humorous to pretend to be a serial killer?"

"I don't know," he replied. "Yeah. Kinda."

"What brings you to confession today?" I decided to stick to the priest role and leave this kid's parenting to someone else.

"My parents made me."

"I can't remember hearing confession from you recently. What happened to make your folks think you needed it today?"

He sighed and slouched—yes, a trained listener can hear a person slouch.

"You don't have to talk to me if you don't want to," I added. "You just . . . can't be absolved if I don't hear your confession."

"I stole money from Mom's purse again," he finally exhaled.

"Why did you do that?"

"Aren't you supposed to just listen to my shit and give me my sentencing?"

"If that's what you prefer."

"That's what I prefer," he barked.

"Very well," I conceded. "Twenty 'Hail Marys,' and I'd like you to visit the county jail for four hours and talk with inmates convicted of theft."

"What?"

"Listen, kid," I said sternly. "You don't have to listen to me. You don't have to do what I say as long as all you care about is pleasing your parents. You did that by coming in here. But if you want to please God, then you have to go beyond confession."

"Man, screw God," he spat through the screen before storming out of the booth.

I heard his every stomping footstep as he stormed out of the church and slammed the door.

It was safe to say that this kid was not on my list of potentials for my final victim in Crooked Creek.

I waited another fifteen minutes before I heard the exterior door open and close again. It wasn't my job to hurry folks into confession. And I'd heard the door open and close before, only to open and close again without anyone's visiting the confession chamber.

I was here for those willing to confess and no one else. And the great majority of my parish members were so pious that they felt confession was beneath them. Which it was not. But I'd grown less concerned with the rank-and-file attenders of Mass and much more interested in the truly selfless individuals in our community.

This particular confessor took time making his way through the sanctuary up to the confessional. Even once he'd arrived, it was another ninety seconds of silence while he pondered whether or not to enter. Or maybe he pondered what to confess. Regardless, after much consternation, he finally entered and closed the curtain behind him.

"Forgive me, Father, but I think I have sinned." I didn't immediately place the voice, but it did sound familiar to me.

"Go on, son."

"I've known something for weeks, but I ain't told no one yet. I think I sinned by keepin' quiet, your honor."

Stanley! It hit me. Stanley, the busboy from M Spot's who'd witnessed my verbal vomiting weeks back. Stanley . . . Goodspeed. I think his last name was Goodspeed. *Wait. What did he just say?*

"You've known something?" I replied.

I was living in constant fear of being found out. By man, not by God. I knew where the Father stood on my actions and had no qualms about having to pay an Earthly price for them. But I still served him better as a man who was not in jail. So my first instinct at Stanley's declaration was to assume he meant that he knew I was the killer.

But then I realized that he would be an idiot to tell me that he thought I was the killer, with only a thin wall and a screen between us. But then I realized that he was exactly that big of an idiot.

I needed more information.

"I know about something. It's a crime. I'm sure it's a crime. I just wanna get right with God without going to jail, sir, and I know you're kind of, like, in charge of both them avenues around here. No?"

"Why don't we focus on you for now," I parried. "What is it that you know? What have you seen?" I was reasonably sure he didn't mean my cussing spree outside the diner. And his tone suggested true remorse, so I began to think he wasn't here to talk about the serial killings or evidence in that case at all.

He shook with fear, or maybe guilt. He shook so much, it made his words come out like aural roller coasters. "Buzz Martinson," he began. "You . . . y-y-you know Buzz. Right?"

Everyone knew Buzz, but I didn't want to rush this kid. I was suddenly concerned about his emotional and mental state. "Yeah."

"You know how he makes hooch and stuff. Right?" The shaking continued, his words chopped by the breaks as he convulsed.

I legitimately did not know that Buzz Martinson was making moonshine. Moonshine was pretty fucking far down my list of concerns as a sheriff and as a priest. People who like to drink are gonna drink, and that's all you can do about it. So I was not terribly surprised. But I pretended to be in the know, just to keep the information flowing. "Of course," I replied. "Everyone knows that."

"I thought so," he said, sounding relieved. Then he took a couple of deep breaths before continuing. "Well, what not a lot of people know is that he has a partner. His neighbor, Matthew Wright."

I exhaled audibly in shock before I could stop myself.

"That's right," Stanley replied, "Mr. All-American himself. Running hooch for his beer and stripper money."

I knew where the local kids got their beer, but I hadn't heard of any regular stripper activity and wasn't sure which larger city they were driving to for that particular endeavor, as Crooked Creek didn't have any nightclubs. I also didn't care right then. "Go on," I said flatly.

"I hate them dudes; they ain't never been nothing but mean to me, truthfully. But I ain't gonna lie, man; they got the best shit around for miles. So I buy from them every now and then—only when I can afford it and when I know my stepdad's gonna be out of town for a bit."

His stepdad drove a tractor-trailer for a living; his mother worked the overnight shift at the brake factory next county over. Neither wanted him drinking hooch, of course, but there were pockets of time every week when they were unable to stop it from happening.

"I was over there about, say, near seven or eight weeks ago, I think it was, buying a couple gallons from Buzz. The way they do it is, they make you give them the money, then, while you wait on the porch, they go back and get the stuff. Ain't nobody out there watching, so I never figured why I couldn't just go inside while I waited, until this one day."

I was on the edge of my seat and didn't even reply with words. I merely breathed in and out, waiting for more details.

"So Buzz, he takes my money and then he goes back to get the hooch, you see, only this time he left the front door open—only the screen door closed, and usually they close both them doors. So he goes off outside the range of where I could see, you know, to get the liquor, and that's when I seen Matthew Wright stomp up the hallway. 'Buzz,' he yelled, 'you left the fucking door fucking wide open!' And then . . ." he trailed off, choking on his words.

"And then?" I nearly shouted.

"And then he opened a bedroom door." He sighed heavily before continuing. "And before he closed it, I seen inside that room, sir. And I seen Deena Jaines in that room tied up to a bed, sir, and some other girl, too." He began to cry. "And I ain't told no one because I was afraid!" He was now sobbing and quickly turned into a pile of shuddering flesh and bone.

Deena Jaines? Deena Jaines?!

"Deena Jaines? Deena Jaines? Are you sure?" I was skeptical at best that Deena Jaines was even still alive, let alone still here in Jerusalem County.

"It was her," he cried. "She used to be friends with my little sister, man. It was her. But I was too afraid . . ." He was then reduced to a blubbering mess, admirable in his emotions if not in how or when they manifested. "I think she saw me too! Oh, God, Father, what do I have to do to not feel so guilty anymore?"

Deena Jaines being alive and still here close to town was huge. She was the biggest story to come out of Crooked Creek prior to these recent killings. She'd gone missing ages ago, and we'd even made a bit of national news at the time, though nothing like what we had now.

This was pretty huge.

My first thought was that this could serve to heal my reputation as sheriff. Imagine bringing in the suspect in the most famous crime in county history.

And just maybe she could bring things full circle for me. If Buzz really did have a kidnapped Deena Jaines on his property—or any captive female, really—I could probably make him my patsy. It's not so big a stretch from kidnapping to murder, after all, at least in the eyes of regular folks who'd never commit either crime. Plant a few items, and suddenly the sex creep looks like a mass killer.

Matthew Wright being involved here kind of complicated matters, but not so much that it would hinder my ability to spin things. But it did mean the kid had been mourning his dead pregnant girlfriend around the same time he was keeping her best friend as a sex slave for everyday extracurriculars. And Matthew having been an early suspect after Katie died would only help sell the public on his overall guilt. Or even co-guilt.

Suddenly I had options.

It was all lining up perfectly, which made me question it obsessively. And yet, even as I doubted that the string of luck that I was on would be a permanent sort of phenomenon, I had to admit that I was still doing the Lord's work, which tended to afford one a little extra grace.

CHAPTER 31

A GIFT

Before telling the FBI about Stanley's confession, I needed some time to plan and set things in motion. I would need to plant some evidence, at a minimum, but I also wanted time to rehearse my lines and prepare my various emotional responses so they'd seem as genuine as possible in the moment.

And I needed to set up the reason for the information exchange in the first place.

I was no longer technically under the rule of the Vatican, but our parish still treated the act of confession as an absolute privacy between confessor and priest, even in cases of crimes being committed. I couldn't risk the extra pressure of a congregation angry at me for breaking the oath in addition to all the other balls I was trying to juggle.

But I could apply some pressure from the sheriff's side of my life. At least . . . if I could catch Stanley in a crime.

And I was able to do just that a mere few minutes after his confession.

I radioed Skip and had him set up a speed-check zone on the main road Stanley would use to get home from the church. And because Stanley was a cocky, mildly aloof teenager, he was prone to speeding. In fact, he'd had several citations within just the last two years.

It was enough of a reason for Skip to bring Stanley in. And once the boy was in the station, I kept him in a holding cell for a couple hours before talking to him. I had used that time wisely. But eventually I had to start questioning him.

"Stanley," I said with mock sympathy. "Stanley, Stanley, Stanley. You're in big trouble here, son." I sat on the table so as to remain physically above him in a position of authority—a trick I'd learned from watching the FBI boys interrogate suspects. "You've had one too many speeding tickets, kid."

I splashed all nine of his moving-violation reports onto the table at once.

He lowered his head in shame.

"You are now eligible to have your license revoked *permanently*. That means you won't be able to legally drive yourself anywhere, at any time, for any reason. You could be on your way to the hospital with a pregnant mistress like you tend to carry, and I can still stop you for driving without a license and haul you off to jail without you ever even meeting your brand-new child. And then your girlfriend will find out!"

"I was just all revved up from that confession, sir," he tried.

"Confession?!" I shouted, tilting a little more heavily than usual toward the bad-cop side of things. "Son, if there's one thing I know about Catholicism, it's that a man's confession to his priest in the confines of that little booth are off limits! Kaput! No access! That is privileged information!"

"I know, but I'm just explaining why I was—"

"No one here cares *why* you were speeding, son. You done been caught doing it too many times for the reason to matter. You're the boy who cried 'wolf' ten times after the town got angry about you doing it. You beat the dead horse. You're done driving in this town, kid."

"Well, how am I supposed to get to my job, then?"

"Take a tractor. Ride a cow. I could give a rat's fucking diseased fucking ass how you get to work. Crawl on your hands and knees for all I care. What I *do* care about, Stanley, is all these killings we got going on here in town. Those are big crimes. I need to arrest people for some big crimes. Do you know anything about any bigger crimes, Stanley—any information that would help me bust some big criminals in exchange for your freedom?"

He looked right into my eyes as he realized what was happening. Then he looked up at the camera in the corner of the room and then at the microphone in the center of the table.

"Don't worry, Stan," I smiled. "That shit ain't on, kiddo. None of it is recording." It most certainly *was* recording. "The FBI is all out at the high school looking for serial killers; there's no one here but you and me. You literally only have the one way out of this, and I think you should take it. Why don't you tell me whatever you know about any kind of local criminal activity, and you can be home watching the soaps tomorrow at lunchtime with your ma."

"Father Lancaster, how can yo—"

"*Sheriff* Lancaster, boy. Know the difference. And the greater good is being served here, even if you're too fucking stupid to see it. Now tell me all the shit you know, and maybe I can let you keep your license!"

●●●

The search warrant was sworn out inside of an hour later. I'd called the county judge, who was definitely an idiot. But that was a better move than calling the city judge; he was more than ninety years old and would sleep through any late-night phone calls, as I had learned the hard way. He also hated me.

We threw Stanley's crying ass back into a holding cell for his own protection as we sounded the alarm to the FBI.

It was late, well after 10 p.m., and it took a while for everyone to get up to speed, but by eleven we were silently swarming the outside of Buzz Martinson's house, communicating with hand gestures while on radio silence—there was a concern that these boys had a police scanner. And just in case he wasn't here at Buzz's house at the moment, we also had a team surrounding Matthew Wright's house.

Of course, at this point, I should probably let you know about my extracurriculars from earlier in the evening.

While Stanley was in holding awaiting interrogation, I drove out to Buzz's place. I left my car on the road and went in on foot. I smelled the pot a hundred yards from the house. Matt Wright and Buzz were both getting high in the living room while watching TV. It sounded like a game show.

I worked my way around the outside.

Halfway around the house, I found a bedroom with boarded-up windows. It seemed to match the location of where Stanley had mentioned seeing the girls. It made sense that they would block out that room's window.

I moved to the back of the house, where I saw a cellar door. I needed to get access to the girls without the men finding out. *Perhaps I could get inside through the basement? Are these two smart enough to have any kind of countermeasures in place, like noise alarms?* I'd have to take the chance if I wanted to get inside undetected. I put on my gloves so as to avoid leaving fingerprints.

Turned out the men were way too stoned to notice an intruder, even if I'd walked through the front door and announced myself. This would've made my job easier, had I known it at the time of entry.

Instead, I crept into the house via the basement, moving mere inches at a time, sensitive to every scuff and scrape of my shoes on the cement flooring beneath me.

As I reached the main floor and entered the hallway, the crowd on the TV game show went wild over a particularly humorous player response. There was no laughter in the room. The suspects were surely asleep or catatonic—the smell of weed was oppressive.

Somehow, I resisted the urge to peek around the corner to visually confirm the status of the suspects. If they were awake, they could see me. If they were asleep, I was still going to be extra-quiet from here on, so the peeking was useless. And apparently they hadn't heard any sound I'd made so far, so the odds were in my favor.

Thankfully, they'd left the television volume up loud enough to give me plenty of sound cover. So, instead of peeking, I merely stepped across the hall and entered the room Stan had described seeing from the front porch. Once inside, I quickly swung the door back to the edge of the latch and carefully closed it the rest of the way.

I flipped up the light switch and instantly put my fingers to my lips to hopefully keep the girls from making any sound in reaction to my presence, loud enough to wake their captors outside.

Both girls were chained side by side to a large king-size mattress. There were no sheets. The room smelled of sickness and poison to me, and I had to cover my face with my hand. There was a connected bathroom in the corner, with a massive pile of towels and clothes in the doorway. A rickety fan in the corner spun so slowly, I could count the revolutions.

There were more restraints on the dresser top, along with what could only be described as surgery utensils. It didn't take a lot of critical thinking to figure that this was a place where two twisted men were repeatedly having their way with two captive women, in a variety of disgusting ways. This was a redneck backwoods version of a prison camp, and I nearly lost my stomach contents over the whole sensory experience.

Thankfully, for the sake of modesty, these women were somewhat clothed, though in the most generous definition of the word. One wore underwear, and the other appeared to be naked under a robe.

It would be difficult to get these women clothed, coherent, unchained, and ready to make a stealthy getaway from this prison. Fortunately for me, I had no intention of helping them escape. In fact, I'd come here to kill them.

Catching these two men in the same house as a couple of dead bodies of kidnapped people would tip the scales at them so hard that everyone in the county would think they had been the serial killers all along. The perfect patsies. In fact, thanks to the fortunate timing of Stan's confession, I was on easy street. I was absolutely as giddy as could be.

I had just one single moment of pause: when I de-gagged Deena Jaines with a finger to my lips, still pretending to be a rescuer, she quietly gasped "Thank God". . . shortly before I put the knife into her. But it was a quick pause, just a mere half-second long.

I'd never knifed someone while looking into their face before; it was strange. "It's okay," I assured her, covering her mouth back up with my free hand. "I know you were expecting a rescue, but that's actually what this is . . . a rescue for your soul. You're going to go see Jesus now," I beamed as she started coughing up blood.

If you've never stabbed someone in the gut who wasn't expecting it . . . I doubt you could understand the look Deena gave me. But it was a deeply satisfying look, I can assure you, so long as you were reasonably sure that that person's soul was going to Heaven. I smiled at her the way I assumed St. Peter would smile when welcoming her to the pearly gates: kindly and with excessive warmth. The last thing she saw was my smiling face, and I figured that had to count for something.

She was too weak to make much of a response, but as her tiny gasps escaped, I pretended that she was thanking me, like an actor winning an Oscar.

No, I had not come to save Deena, but to exploit her for my own gains. Terribly sorry to disappoint anyone who hasn't been paying attention up to this point. And Deena herself. She'd seemed so relieved to see me come into the room, sheriff's uniform on, gun drawn. She didn't notice the latex gloves, or at least hadn't questioned them. She'd naturally assumed I was there to save her.

And I *had* been there to save her. Just not in the way she imagined.

The other gal was a stranger to me, and she was passed out the whole time. She may have come from a nearby county or maybe even this county, but just not from a family whose children ever crossed my path. I slit her throat quickly and then set about placing the evidence.

Chrysanthemums were tossed about the room, a flower often understood to reference death or betrayal, but also known to signify good-bye. And this would be my final kill, at least as far as this town would know. This was my farewell to the police and FBI trying to find and catch me. It was a little on the nose, but most of these country-raised folks would never know until long after the fact, if ever.

I left the knife on one of the pillows and got the hell out of there.

●●●

The FBI surrounded the house, and, getting no response from repeated attempts to communicate, both by phone and loudspeaker, they decided to move in.

And they moved in from all directions. While the front entry team quickly discovered the stoned occupants and restrained them, the rear entry team was finding the women's dead bodies. Then finally the cellar entry team arrived on the main floor. It was absolute pandemonium for a good three or four minutes.

Ultimately, Matthew and Buzz were both awake and relatively coherent when they were cuffed and read their rights, and more than a few FBI agents got sick over the sight in the home's master bedroom.

I watched from a hundred yards away as the FBI personnel ran around tying up all my loose ends and doing my job for me.

It seemed as though literally every law-enforcement employee was out there at that moment. And some hadn't even been requested. They just wanted to check out the final crime scene. Word had gotten around quickly that the Flower Killer(s)—the "S" was new—had been caught. People wanted a glimpse of the action.

CHAPTER 32

THE FRENZY

HAVING TWO MEN IN CUSTODY who had been found at the scene of a double murder that included flowers . . . well, this essentially closed the case on the Flower Killer, at least as far as the media and the local FBI brass were concerned. The two young men were denying most everything regarding murder left and right, but the evidence was overwhelming at this point. It was only a matter of time.

When I'd been inside the home, killing the girls and moving about freely, I'd left enough evidence to convict them both with very little difficulty. The souvenirs I'd been collecting from every victim were finally paying off. Fingertips, organs, hair, other body parts . . . I had a piece of every person I had killed in my deep freezer in the basement.

Cindy had had to die when she'd discovered my hydroponic garden, but she'd have been just as marked if she'd gone five steps further and opened my deep freezer to discover my macabre collection.

Anyway, I'd brought those keepsakes to the Martinson house, along with all of my flowers.

Buzz's house didn't have a deep freezer in the basement, so I'd shoved all that shit in the freezer atop his fridge in the kitchen, going so far as to throw a half dozen frozen steaks and several TV dinners from his freezer into my trunk for later use, and also to make room for flowers and body parts.

Now, as I mentioned previously, flowers kept in the freezer for a while will eventually lose some of their color, even after thawing. I'd learned this the hard way in my previous town. But the flowers I was shoving into Buzz's freezer wouldn't lose color before the FBI found them. And if anyone stopped to ask about the flowers being in a freezer . . . if any scientist mentioned the coloration issue . . . why, that would be months after Matt and Buzz had been given multiple life sentences each.

I'd managed to luck myself into a perfect finale.

Actually . . . honestly . . . God had surely guided that outcome for me, due to my repeated obedience. He had led me all along, and I would continue to trust his guidance.

● ● ●

The interrogators from the FBI split the boys up, asking them similar questions but then insinuating to each that the other had sold him out. It was a classic routine, and the boys were unfazed by it, continuing to insist that they were innocent. And they *were* innocent—of murder, of course—but they were guilty as fuck of the kidnapping.

Neither would be caught in a contradiction, because both had the same story: I got stoned and fell asleep.

"We got so stoned that a bunch of crazy conspiratorial shit happened all around us in a short period of time without us knowing it" is a hell of a way to try to prove one's innocence. Few juries ever buy the "it's a massive conspiracy against me" defense. It didn't ultimately matter that, in this instance, their defense happened to be true.

The boys insisted on their innocence. But as soon as they'd been arrested and arraigned, the entire county turned on them. Yard signs that used to say "Catch the Killer" or "I'm scared to leave my house" now switched to saying things like "Fry Them Both" and "Kill the Killers!" I even saw a sign that said "Set them on fire and laugh as they burn."

Virtually no one was wondering if the real killer was still out there. *Of course the real killers would claim innocence*, they told themselves. *Classic line of defense.*

I wondered if I should be ashamed at how easily I'd manipulated the situation. But, honestly, that moment passed rather quickly.

The press proceeded to dig up all the demons on both boys, starting with Buzz and the accident that had killed his friends. They also started asking questions about Katie again, wondering how authorities could have questioned and let go of Matthew during that investigation. Thankfully, that was the interrogation directly *after* I had been relieved of my control over the investigation, so all it did was make the FBI look even worse. It didn't impact my reputation whatsoever.

Everything was coming up roses for Solomon Lancaster these days. Every time I was interviewed, I could smile and hide behind the fact that ". . . it was the FBI's investigation, and I was just a bystander." True, I'd called in the final bit that had brought the entire house of cards crashing down, but I was still just the messenger. It was the FBI that had done all the real work.

I was willing to give them the credit so long as they also took ownership of all the case-handling shortcomings.

• • •

The media frenzy only increased from there, at least in the short term. Every national news entity that didn't already have a presence in town arrived, along with reporters from all the major cities. Cameras in Crooked Creek quickly outnumbered the humans, two to one.

The lead anchors showed up in tour buses, complete with makeup and PR personnel. They came with lights and boom mikes and multi-camera coverage. They converged on the city to suck up whatever gossipy juice might be left in this sordid tale. They came for the blood; they came for the ratings; they came for the advertising dollars. I wished they had pure hearts just so I could have an excuse to take a few of them out, but they were all vulturous opportunists.

Everyone who was anyone in news was here, including dozens of international reporters and news teams from places like Brazil, the United Kingdom, France, and South Africa, as well as many more. The capture of the now-plurally-dubbed Flower Killers was international news, and everyone around the globe was looking forward to watching justice happen in the name of the victims.

I got quite used to saying "I *am* the local sheriff, but I was taken off the case as soon as the FBI was called in." I did find it interesting how different that phrase sounded in all these foreign languages after the translators got done with it. The translator from Japan seemed to imbue the phrasing with an air of frustration, as though he was taking my words and trying to emote as he spoke them, which I appreciated.

But the bulk of the media attention was focused on Buzz and Matt. As usual, the story was more about the killers than the captors. I was thrilled, if I'm being honest, to learn that the focus of most national media had turned from law enforcement back to the perpetrators.

Thrilled.

Regional Director Rathburn and Lt. Irwin were taking their media victory laps, sure, even appearing on the late-night shows. They were free to make these appearances because the bulk of the FBI forces had pulled out of town almost as soon as the arrests had been made. There was a new serial killer in California, as well as a developing militant religious cult in Texas, and the FBI really only went where the active crime was. Their job here was done. They'd caught the killers. Time to go catch more someplace else.

But no one was talking much about that in the media either. The bulk of the news coming out of our little community was about the two young men arrested and charged with the killing of nearly a dozen local civilians. Everyone just seemed to assume the two were guilty, so every question started from that perspective, which quickly framed the public debate on them in a negative light.

It took maybe a day or two for the bulk of public opinion in America to swing against them.

• • •

In the days leading up to the trial, I was running through my usual daily routine for the most part, trying to go through all the motions and remain innocent-looking for as long as possible. I didn't want to seem too interested in the case, but I didn't want to seem too *dis*interested either. It went on like this for me for a good several weeks as the case progressed through the various formalities and official congregations.

That is, until one Thursday when I received a call from the county hospital in Del Plaines telling me that my friend and mentor, Father Wendall Warren, had been admitted to the hospital's intensive care unit after suffering a stroke. I was listed as his emergency contact.

I relayed the details to Maggie, dropped everything, and raced off to the hospital. Father Warren was more than a father figure: he was the father I'd never had. He guided me while loving me; he critiqued me while loving me. He molded me . . . while loving me. The thought of losing him to illness caused me to exceed the speed limits excessively as I drove toward the hospital.

I accosted the main nurse upon arriving at her station. "Father Warren," I panted, depleted from my rushing there. "Can you tell me where he is?" My breath was thin enough that the sound of it did its own begging.

A doctor walking by overheard the exchange just as the nurse pointed at him. He graciously walked toward me and engaged me, even though I'll bet he wasn't required to.

"You're here about the old priest?" His voice was friendly and soft.

"I am," I replied, still edgy.

"He's going to be okay," the doctor replied, "but only for a few months more."

My head went down in sadness but not surprise.

"You had to know his time was near," the doctor continued.

I merely nodded.

"He will get to go home again," he offered hopefully. "But it might be the last time." The implication was loud: the next step would be to put him in a group home, which I knew he would never accept. I was pretty sure the doctor also knew this.

So we would be sending him home from this hospital stay with the implied knowledge that he would die soon. Some part of me had even been planning for this.

"Can I talk to him?"

"Sure," the doctor replied, "but he won't hear you, and he can't answer back right now."

"Just make sure I'm called on the day he goes home, in case he needs a ride," I barked, struggling to hold back tears. "Put it in his file on the first page, okay?"

"Certainly," he responded, nodding his head to give me extra confidence.

I entered the room, immediately taken aback by how many of the machines keeping him alive made weird noises. One was ticking. Another beeped. A couple had a low hum of a unique frequency. One sounded like bubbles in water like a fish tank.

People sometimes talked about being uncomfortable in hospitals because of the sights . . . or the smells, even. But for me it was the sounds. It was auditory anxiety, bouncing off the tiled floors and back down off the cheap-material drop ceiling . . . dancing off the windows. A wall of unusual noises encircling me at once, perpetually.

I finally shut my ears off, mostly, and turned to my eyes for information.

He lay there looking dead. Eyes closed, skin pale, no signs of life. My father figure was dying right in front of me. It wasn't fair. It wasn't fair because I still had so much more to learn from him. It wasn't fair because he had been so kind that he deserved more time on Earth.

And it wasn't fair because I still had one more confession I needed to give to him before I could feel complete absolution for my actions. I knew my actions were righteous—sanctioned by The Most High, even—but I would still need a bit of absolution to make my own trip to the pearly gates go as smoothly as I hoped.

"I'm not ready for this," I said aloud as I paced back and forth at the foot of his bed. "I need more time. I can't have you leave like this, Father. I can't . . . confess to you like this. And I can't confess to anyone else. And I'm going to need to confess soon. A lot."

I stopped pacing and talking and put my hands on my hips and just stared at him. It was strange that I was feeling more anger than sympathy in this moment—something I knew I would end up correcting with prayer and penance, and yet I could not stop feeling it.

How dare you go unconscious right before I need your help? I ranted silently. *I have managed to overcome every single obstacle to my mission here, and you go and do this? Now? If you really loved me—if you really loved God—you'd come back and do it quickly.*

Because he and I have work to finish, Wendall!

I had the ending all planned out for my story here, and it was completely ruined if Father Warren wasn't around to play his intended part. I was feeling truly helpless for the first time in years.

I was wary of hospital employees. I was concerned he wasn't able to hear and remember in a coma. But something came over me . . . something I could not deny or control. I lunged forward, clasped his limp right hand, and blurted out an awkward speed-confession. "I've killed a bunch of people but all for good reasons and they're all going to end up in Heaven because of it." Just as quickly as I'd approached and grabbed that hand, I let go of it.

I knew inside that this had not been a true confession. But I was stupidly hoping it would be enough to show St. Peter that I had tried my best under the circumstances in the event Wendall died before a proper confession could take place.

Besides, I didn't have many options. A fake half-assed confession was better than no confession. And even though I'd been following divine instructions all along, I also knew I'd crossed the line a few times in doing so and would therefore need absolution. Even men called by God were sometimes required to sin to reach their responsibility. And that's why confession and absolution existed in Catholicism in the first place: to allow people to be human and make mistakes while pursuing something greater and more pure.

But in the end, this one-sided confession had failed to result in absolution because my conduit to God had been in a coma.

I sighed deeply.

This is gonna have to do.

I crossed myself, nodded at the old man's body, and left the room.

"Who is taking care of his dog?" I asked the nearest nurse.

"He has a dog?"

CHAPTER 33

THE JURY

BONES WAS NOW LIVING WITH ME temporarily while Father Warren recovered. The old dog didn't need much more than food, water, and a small patch of yard to do his business. The rest of the time, he was curled up on the floor near my feet.

Bones knew me. And he knew that he was now outside his normal home environment, being watched over by a friend of his owner. But even so, the dog was still uneasy, occasionally sighing or whining; he was clearly missing his longtime companion.

Zacchaeus was having none of it. The cat began hiding out under my bed upstairs as soon as Bones came to stay with us, sneaking out only at night to nibble some food, use the nearest litter pan, and then skitter back under the bed again. He was wary of a new creature, at least for a while. I would have felt sorry for him if Bones hadn't been such a harmless old softie. There was zero reason to be afraid of him.

But old Bones and I got into a routine pretty quickly.

I'd fire up some nachos and turn the antenna so that we could catch the channel that played the *Lucy* and *Andy Griffith* reruns every night. I'd toss a bite to the dog every now and then because he wasn't my dog and he was ancient and near death and I figured a corn chip with cheese on it wasn't going to kill him any more than all the other shit that was constantly threatening to kill him.

And the dog was old. Older than any dog you ever met. His owner was in the hospital, but the dog was probably still closer to death than his owner. I wasn't going to have the dog's last days, should they be with me, be anything short of . . . well . . . decent. Human food for sure, and that seemed like all Bones had the energy for anyway. It's not like he was asking me to go for a drive so he could hang his head out the window. Or catch a frisbee. Hell, on the drive here from his owner's house, he'd stretched out on the back seat and slept the whole way.

Some dogs are chill like that, but Bones was just old, and the chill factor was a byproduct of his age. He just didn't have much energy on a daily basis. I got rather used to him during his short stay at my home and even had fleeting thoughts of maybe getting a dog of my own someday. Maybe when I had less to worry about and fewer overall responsibilities. Thankfully, he was well trained and really needed to be let outside only twice a day, which allowed me to spend lots of time at court during the trial.

Most of the FBI agents were gone, now that there was no one left to catch, but a good portion of the national media remained, eager to break any news that emerged from the trial. Most of them left me alone, but a few still picked at me for threads of information that they could unravel into a story. So as I left my home one day, I encountered two reporters on my front walkway.

They both started barking questions at me like carnival-game bosses, each trying to drown out the other through volume and enthusiasm. Both were looking for a quote they could turn into a headline. I approached both and stood inches away, stone-silent, until they shut up. Then I waited a beat and said, "The Lord be with you." Then I smiled, crossed myself, and walked away.

●●●

The jury would be composed of twelve Jerusalem County citizens. There was immediate concern over whether any local citizen could be impartial in this case, given all the local victims and the news coverage, both local and national. The defense attorney, Brant Stampler, argued for a change of venue, but the county judge, Judge Thorpe, quickly shot him down on precedent. Judge Thorpe was dumb as a boulder, but he respected the law, and I was happy about that.

A trial should be held in the jurisdiction of the crime's occurrence, unless there are massive extenuating circumstances. Knowing about a series of killings happening in your local area, Judge Thorpe ultimately ruled, did not automatically sway a prospective juror to one side or the other when it came to specific defendants and evidence. You could know of a crime but still objectively adjudicate it, so said Judge Thorpe at least.

Jury trials were exceedingly rare in this county, even more so in the city of Crooked Creek. Hell, cases here almost never went to trial, so most of the townsfolk had never even received a summons. Most had no idea how jury duty even worked or that it was a legal requirement of one's citizenship. Still, it seemed as though nearly everyone in town received a summons, which created a chaos you don't really want to know about.

Jury selection was laborious and long, with jurors getting dismissed left and right for even the slightest connection to either side of the case. At one point, the defense team dismissed a potential juror because he answered "Yes" to the question "Do you grow crops on your property?"

I myself even received a summons but was one of the first to get cut, because I was the local sheriff. And I was ecstatic not to have to serve on the jury in this or any other local case. Being sheriff was hard enough; being a juror was saintly.

I did sit in, however, on the rest of jury selection. I was fascinated by which jurors were objected to by which lawyer. I had a great deal of fun guessing as to the reasoning behind such decisions.

The prosecution seemed to want to get rid of potential jurors who had previously had a relationship with either of the suspects. The defense seemed to favor those same potential jurors, while attempting to oust any that spoke with an educated voice. They were looking for loners, the more ignorant the better.

Just how small is Crooked Creek? We nearly ended up with one of the accuseds' cousins on the jury. Of course, jury trials were ultra-rare here, as I just mentioned, but the fibers woven between these townsfolk were strong and old; nearly everyone knew everyone, but that didn't mean the area couldn't field a jury of impartial peers.

* * *

The other problem with a jury trial in a town this small was sequestering them. Crooked Creek had a single bed and breakfast, and even though it had recently been relocated and rebuilt, it wasn't large enough for twelve people. Outside the city limits to the north was the Jerusalem Inn. But it only had ten rooms. To the southeast, there was an eight-room motel.

We found much the same to the dead east, south, and west, until ultimately it was decided that the jury members could take over the now-vacated FBI cots and spend each night in the recreation hall at my church. It was important to keep them sequestered in the same space, which would ensure that they all had a similar experience even outside of trial.

But they had even more restrictions beyond just staying in the same place. They weren't allowed access to any news about the case, from print to radio to television. They weren't allowed even to talk to their wives and husbands. It was a total shut-off from the regular real world, and it was enough to make some of them start behaving strangely.

In addition to all that, they weren't allowed to talk to each other about the case. So, we had to constantly monitor their conversations like some kind of speech police.

I and my deputies became unwitting prison employees. It was as if I was the warden, and the deputies were the guards. We were now trying to contain mostly-innocent people, despite our vow to fight crime and track down lawbreakers. We were babysitters with guns, walking around the large room like lunch monitors, listening for offending words or phrases.

Basically, the jurors lived in the church fellowship hall in between group trips to court. (We did manage to confiscate a school bus from the parked summer fleet for our official jury-transportation vehicle.) We brought in food for them three times a day; all three of the local restaurants had been making money hand over fist since the FBI had come to town, and I was at least happy to see city money go back into city businesses. So the jurors got more than their fill of tenderloins, beef and noodles, and Italian fare. Most of them were used to this kind of food, though they weren't used to eating it every third day.

Eventually, some even started ordering salads and chicken entrées to avoid gaining weight. Others began ordering off the kids' menus, asking for chicken fingers and microwaved burgers, all in the name of variety.

This being rural Indiana, several well-intentioned folks actually baked and then brought cakes or casseroles to feed the jurors, though we were not allowed to accept that kind of thing as it might be seen as an attempt to sway the jury's decision.

You should have seen people's faces as we turned away the fruits of their labor on a technicality. "You don't want to eat my casserole because you think it could be poisoned?" should be a newly designated facial expression. Of course, they didn't express such feelings out loud; I merely inferred, based on their collective facial expressions. To soften the disappointment, I directed the generous cooks to the police station, reminding them that I had hungry overworked officers there who would love a free home-cooked meal.

I honestly felt bad for the jurors. And because I was in a couple of positions of power in this town, I decided to help out. During one recess, I ran home and grabbed my graphic novel collection—remember, this was only a couple blocks from the church. I then fired up the church phone chain by calling the first person on the list and emphatically asking for games and puzzles and magazines and books—the magazines, we had to check the date on and ensure the issues predated the trial, of course. I stressed the utter boredom of jury duty, since I knew so many locals were unfamiliar with it, and I think it paid off.

You wouldn't believe how many donations were made by the next morning. Never doubt the ability of religious folks to rally around a prayer-chain topic. We got clothes, games, decorations, puzzles, a bunch of food trays we had to re-donate because we couldn't accept food donations, and even some stuff you don't want to know about.

The jurors were suddenly noticeably happier while in the fellowship hall, smiling and laughing regularly. Many still missed their families, of course, but for now the boredom of the sequester period had been replaced with a bit of fun.

Having to judge a fellow citizen's actions sucks. Having to do it while spending large amounts of time away from your family and in the company of strangers . . . it's even worse. So I was glad to make it a little bit easier for the jurors. I had my own preferred outcome for this case, of course, for a few reasons, but I wasn't a monster. Quite the opposite; I figured Heaven's agents would view me as an angel.

But I needed these boys to be found guilty. There were only a few ways of ensuring that, of course, and they were all technically illegal. But I was still exploring.

● ● ●

I bought a bag of proper dog kibble—along with a few cans of wet dog food—at the supermarket on the way home. I was determined to get this dog to eat something other than my leftovers. I didn't eat very well for a human, and that shit certainly couldn't be good for a dog.

When I opened the door, I saw Zacchaeus cuddling with Bones on the living room floor. The cat was startled by the door and made like lightning back upstairs and under my bed, pretending to be scared again. But clearly the two animals had bonded in these last few days during the hours I was gone. And that was a win in my book, though Zacchaeus would never again cuddle up to or make nice with Bones in my presence.

It was a secret affair, I reasoned.

I tore the bag open and poured some of the dog food into a cereal bowl. I walked over to the old dog there on the floor and rubbed his head.

"Here you go, Bones," I said, setting the bowl down. He began eating almost immediately.

Next I opened a can of the fancy wet cat food. Zacchaeus didn't get those very often, and I was hoping to entice him out to at least occupy the same room as the dog by using a special treat.

It worked. The cat peeked around the corner at the top of the stairs, looked over at the dog, who was too busy eating to even notice anything else, quickly scooted back down the stairs, skirted along the living room wall, and was back in the kitchen as I set his food down on the linoleum.

Finally, it was my turn to eat. I had snagged a batch of Harmony Harron's famous Hoosier Chili. Harmony had won the town chili contest five of the last six years, and her Hoosier Chili was always the first dish to run out at potluck dinners. She'd brought some for the jurors, and instead of sending her to the police station, where Gene would surely eat every bit of it himself before I got some, I pretended to take the dish for the jurors but instead stashed it in my car when no one was looking.

Hoosier Chili is basically regular chili. It's not some wild variant with exotic or weird ingredients. It's just chili. Only, chili in Indiana is very mild—not a lot of spicy chili around these parts. Also, we use more meat than you do. However much meat you put in your chili, we put double that amount. We like meat, not heat.

I don't cook a lot at home, but I do reheat things often. I popped a bowl of that sweet meaty chili into the microwave for a minute or so and then sat down to enjoy it while I watched *Pinkerton P.I.* Unfortunately, this week's episode was a rerun. But I loved the show enough to watch even the reruns. I knew a lot of folks who skipped the reruns, but I find you catch details you missed the first time around.

This episode, titled "The Disappearing Man," was about a bank robber, like many episodes of this show. Only this one was unique in that the bank robber got away at the end. Typically, the Pinkertons would find their man and kill or arrest him by the end of an episode—usually kill. But not this time. This outlaw is the one who got away.

Between spoonfuls of chili and moans of satisfaction, I became obsessed with this outlaw. I knew he was going to get away because I'd seen this episode before, but I was actually anxious for him on this second viewing. And then the payoff at the end when he finally escapes . . . well, it was quite intense.

I identified with that outlaw. But this was not because I am a criminal, but because people would think I was if I were ever found out. I knew in my heart that my actions were pure, but I am enough of a realist to know that most of the world wouldn't share that viewpoint.

CHAPTER 34

THE TRIAL

A MURDER TRIAL IN REAL LIFE is a lot more boring than one on TV or in a movie. You cannot possibly understand unless you've been witness to one. This was, personally, my first. I was not prepared for the slow death of the very concept of time.

On television, it's all very exciting. There's shouting back and forth, and it moves at a breakneck pace. The jury never looks bored or exhausted, and the audience is engaged and focused. But in real life, most everything moves at a glacial pace. Sometimes there is shouting, but it's rare. The jury looks bored and sleepy on the second day of the trial, and the audience is largely reading magazines and newspapers.

And then there are the lawyers. On television, lawyers are charismatic, enthusiastic, and articulate. They give powerful speeches that win over jurors and audience members alike. They are magnetic and speak with authority. In real life, however, lawyers are dull and monotone, and they fumble their words. Their speeches are droning, repetitive, and full of jargon; they bore jurors and audience members alike. They remind one of bad teachers, and they often speak with a nasal sort of pinched staccato.

Exciting moments do happen in murder trials, but the waiting in between them can be interminable. And if you're on the jury, you get to be bored to tears for many days or weeks, after which you then get to determine the fate of someone's entire life.

Trials are mostly made up of the quiet moments in between, when various agents of the court are speaking. So one lawyer might make a motion—a boring one. Then the other lawyer might respond to that motion in an extremely boring way. Then there will be silence, sometimes for minutes, while the judge considers things. These silences in between segments of that trial could be deafening. After a motion is decided, for instance, it could be several minutes of quiet conferring before the judge announces the next order of business.

I say "silence," but what I really mean is "relative silence except for the endless shuffling of papers and people clearing their throats." It's not technically quiet. It's just not loud. It's like a football game on TV, right? If you take out all the commercials, time-outs, time between plays while they reset the ball . . . the game itself takes only an hour. But with all that filler, it's a three-hour-plus affair. And once you start noticing the downtime between football plays, you cannot stop noticing it.

● ● ●

The two local defendants continued to assert their innocence, even as the rest of the town—the rest of the world, really—had already decided that these dickheads were guilty. They were so guilty-looking that both the public defense attorneys in Jerusalem County had recused themselves. Eventually, the families raised enough to hire a big-shot defense attorney out of Ft. Wayne, a man full of bluster and blather named Brant Stampler.

Stampler was all show and no substance, so he came in blazing with motions for this and motions for that. He figured he could blind the judge with motions and eventually get a few of them passed just because His Honor would want some peace and quiet.

Only this judge, Judge Thorpe, despite his shortcomings, was a stickler for the rules. He hated being manipulated and tended to punish attorneys he thought were trying to trick him. So, while the multiple appeals filed by the defense did take up several days, the attempt was ultimately futile, and the case went forward.

Days went by as the prosecution laid out its case. They brought a handful of FBI agents to the stand. They brought multiple medical examiners to the stand, including the county medical examiner, Derrick

Dobbins. They brought psychiatrists, biologists, psychologists, and more to the stand. They brought character witnesses willing to testify to other illegal and generally mischievous behavior by the defendants.

They hammered the indisputable evidence of kidnapping, rape, and torture. And while those were all charges in this trial, the only charges that truly mattered were the murder charges. No one doubted that these two gutter-brains had captured and tormented the two women. Then the prosecution homed in on the physical evidence in the freezer, including the flowers that had been found at every murder scene and the physical trinkets the killer had collected at each scene.

The state's case was weak in only one area: motive. So the prosecution largely sidestepped that issue but for one witness—a psychiatrist who talked mostly about how serial killers, by nature, don't have a motive beyond a deep and undeniable urge to kill. There didn't really need to be any connection between the killer here in Crooked Creek and the victims, if the killings were serial and based on uncontrollable urges.

The motive, such as it was laid out, was simply that they had to kill because their brains could not envision any other reality or outcome. They could not quiet the demons in their heads in any other way.

● ● ●

Father Warren was released from the hospital just about three weeks after his admittance. I was happy to pick him up, with Bones in tow, and take him back home. It went largely unsaid between him and myself and the doctors, but it seemed agreed that he was going home to die. That being a consensus of sorts, I doubted how closely he would adhere to any health instructions, including those on the entire bag of medications being sent home with him.

His home, as I've said, was one county over, but he said almost nothing during the entire drive. He just rested his head, closed his eyes, and occasionally petted Bones, whose head was in Wendall's lap.

At first, I talked a bit, telling him about the latest news in town about the trial, as well as local gossip. But it soon became clear that he wasn't in a conversational mood, or perhaps he wasn't in a conversational capacity. I couldn't be sure, and I didn't want to annoy him. So I clammed up and turned on the radio, which was set to a talk-news channel. The host was railing against the Soviets and what he perceived to be the weak position of the United States on the global stage.

The Father remained quiet, eyes closed, for the remainder of the trip home, only stirring once I had turned into his driveway and his body felt the familiar dips and bumps.

I had arranged for a local nurse—someone from a clinic here in this county—to check on Wendall every other day, and he'd graciously agreed to show up today to welcome Father Warren home and to help the man acclimate to a life at home that came with restrictions and supervision. Wendall was proud, so having a nurse would bruise his ego; but his ego was no longer my concern as much as his heart and lungs were.

Bones went right back to his usual spot on the living room carpet, seemingly happy to be back home in a more familiar environment—though I was certain he would miss all the nasty, greasy food he'd been eating back at my house.

As I eased Wendall into his chair, a walker nearby, he whispered, "You haven't given confession …"—he coughed a bit—"… in months." He sighed as though even that one sentence had taken all his energy to utter.

I smiled. "I know, Father, and I plan to return for confession very soon. But I have to get back to court for now. There's dinner on the counter, just microwave it for five minutes—there's a note on the container. I'll be back soon," I added. "I promise."

With that, I left the old man and his old dog and returned to my vehicle. The defense was starting their case today, and I didn't want to miss too much of it.

● ● ●

A lot of murder trials—a lot of trials of all kinds—take a long time to complete. Some even take years and years. In Ft. Wayne or Indianapolis, the courts were backed up with criminal cases. But in a jurisdiction as small as Jerusalem County, that was not the case. And in Crooked Creek, we only had the one.

So the trial would take as long as it took, and that would be that. It would not face endless delays like a city homicide case might. It would not get shelved due to backlog. And so, the defense began their case roughly two business days after the prosecution had rested.

The defense's case could be summed up as "Just because someone does one kind of evil does not mean they are capable of *all* kinds of evil." And it was a flimsy fucking case, let me tell you. The defense attorneys needed to convince the jury that their clients were capable of kidnapping, rape, and torture . . . but somehow *not* capable of murder. It would be a tough sell. And the focus would be entirely on motive.

In legalese, these lawyers would end up standing in front of a jury and saying something along the lines of "If they'd wanted to be murderers, they'd have killed Deena Jaines instantly and would not have held her captive for months on end."

As I said, it was a tenuous argument at best. There was no question that these guys were looking guilty. Even the jury seemed to grow more and more angry as the defense's case waged on.

The lawyers called expert witnesses who talked about the difference between the compulsion to kidnap and the compulsion to kill, but I'm certain that all the jury heard was "They might be rapists, but they aren't murderers, you guys," which is a hollow argument to the common man who does not break the law in even the small ways. A great many Americans felt that crime was crime, and that the country was made up of law-abiding citizens and criminals, with no middle ground.

Neither of the defendants was called to the stand, which spoke volumes. That meant the defense attorneys didn't believe they could make their clients sympathetic to the jury members, at least not through testimony. It suggested that they could only incriminate themselves by testifying.

After merely a week, half the time the prosecution had spent, the defense rested.

● ● ●

The only portions of a real murder trial that come close to the TV or movie versions are the opening and closing arguments. Those are the only moments for which an attorney ever memorizes a full speech. They might run flash cards for various objections or even speed-prep questions and answers with pretend witnesses, but they don't do full memorization except for the opening and closing arguments. Remember, though, that most trial attorneys are terrible actors. Even when they've memorized the script, most still offer up a stilted delivery that undoes whatever conviction the words they wrote might have had.

The prosecutor, on the other hand, is not merely a lawyer; he or she is also a politician. This is typically someone who has been doing public speaking for years, has experienced live press conferences, and is not easily fazed.

So, you can assume how this went.

The prosecutor stood, buttoned his jacket, and proceeded to utterly nail his prepared argument for conviction. He emphasized all the right words at the right moments. He gestured—wildly when necessary, but mostly subtly. He punched words and phrases the way a trained actor would. He earned an Oscar in my book.

Then . . .

The defense attorney stood, pranced about a bit in practiced movements, and overgestured while sounding like someone reading a text for the first time. Don't mistake—he recited it all from memory—but he did so in a way that made him sound like a kindergartener learning how to read.

You could tell that some jury members were embarrassed for him, even as others seemed to be silently encouraging him. But when your words are a chore to get out, your message takes a back seat to the convoluted machinations of your mouth.

The judge instructed the jury as to what they could and could not consider, and how the deliberation process typically worked—which took about ten times longer in reality than the movies made it seem—and then they were dismissed for deliberations.

I'd spent many weeks with these jurors. I'd heard them all talk about their personal lives and their families. I'd been their monitor throughout all this jury-sequestering time, and I'd come to know each of them more closely, to varying degrees.

I knew on the bus ride back to the fellowship hall that the verdict would be guilty. We'd spent hours creating a special private room at the church for their private deliberations, and it was ultimately used for only five minutes.

The jurors took one vote and all twelve voted "guilty." The reading of the verdict in court was ultimately anticlimactic. Most of the audience expected a guilty verdict, so few people were surprised.

● ● ●

The sentence was for life, so the two guilty parties were sent to a high-security facility in Indianapolis to serve their time.

Matthew and Buzz would be in prison until they died.

And I made peace with their false murder convictions by reckoning that they both deserved life in prison just for the crimes they *had* committed against the two girls. They got the time they deserved, even if the record had them down for crimes that others had committed.

And by "others," I mean myself.

I committed those crimes and had done so with the express intention of getting away with it and having it blamed on someone else. I had lucked out. I should have had my fall guy or fall guys picked out from the beginning. Instead, I'd just followed my urge to kill and made the rest up as I went along.

Well, I wouldn't be making that mistake again anytime soon. From now on, everything got planned: the victims, the patsies, the homicide detective on duty . . . all of it. I would leave nothing to chance. Never again. Wherever I went from Crooked Creek, I would produce a more refined, careful, elegant version of myself. I was determined.

I was operating on a divine mission, but within an Earthly culture and system. Everything I could learn from this holy spree of killings was something I could apply to my future endeavors to speed pure souls to Heaven before they had time to sin again.

CHAPTER 35

THE HARVEST FESTIVAL

THE TRIAL WAS A FEW MONTHS behind us by this point, and most of Crooked Creek had finally returned to normal. The few lingering FBI personnel had left. The media hounds were gone. Even the true-crime fanatics had mostly moved on, though a few stragglers remained looking for unturned stones ... anything that might give them more false hope in their pursuit of understanding these crimes.

The community hadn't experienced a murder in two months, not since the last of the Flower Killer deaths. The corn and soybean harvests were winding up, and the talk was that most farmers in the area had experienced a high-yield year.

It seemed odd that the lack of a murder would be what makes things feel ordinary, but that was the case in that fucked-up town. It helped that kids were just going back to school—the Harvest Festival always served as a sort of "back to school" party for the entire county. It typically fell just two weeks after school went back in session and helped everyone let their hair down and have one last summertime jam.

The Harvest Festival was basically a street fair. It included food vendors selling sweet and savory snacks. Sweet corn was just in the first few weeks of harvest around here, so many of the food trucks were offering various corn-based delicacies like cornbread, corndogs, and kettle corn. But plenty of other non-corn foods were available as well. And, of course, other vendors offered a long list of desserts to be sampled, including elephant ears, funnel cakes, and all kinds of deep-fried delights.

And then there were the carnival games like ring-toss and throwing darts at balloons. There was even a dunk tank where people paid for the chance to throw a ball, hit a target, and dunk various local citizens like the mayor or the manager of the grocery store. I was asked every year to volunteer to be dunked, and every year I laughed in the face of whoever asked me.

Then there were the rides. There was a tilt-a-whirl, a small roller coaster, a spinny ride I called the Dizzy Maker, and a modest Ferris wheel.

So, the annual Harvest Festival came at exactly the right time. The citizens needed this kind of release after all they'd been through these last several months. And that release came in the form of a street fair that stretched exactly four blocks lengthwise and shot west one block from Main Street at every intersection. So it was a relatively small-scale affair. I was able to walk the entire perimeter—even while stopping to chat every now and then with citizens—in about forty-five minutes.

Gene Harris and Travis Kent were on duty and wandering the interior of the Harvest Festival. Gene would no doubt be eating constantly, but he was a seasoned-enough police officer that he would still notice any signs of evidence or importance, even while pursuing his next meal. Kent wouldn't be partaking in the carnival's wares. He was too practical, too serious about the job. It was why I'd hired him. His military experience meant he had above-average skills for reading situations and handling firearms. His youth made him trainable. He was any sheriff's dream officer, and I wasn't going to take him for granted.

● ● ●

I wish I could tell you we found and busted a serious criminal enterprise during the Harvest Festival, but that would be a lie. The entire event went off without a hitch. We didn't make a single arrest on any of the three nights of the celebration. Not a drunk driver or an aggravated assault or even a fucking parking ticket.

The county was showing its true colors. This was not a place for crime. This was not a place for lies or injustice. This was a simple place where people who worked hard were rewarded. This was Crooked Creek, Indiana. We were small, but we were huge. Harvest Days only served to prove that the community was ready to move beyond the murders and into the future.

We had Skip down at the dunk tank, and I heard he was getting dunked left and right. The rest of the local police force was actively participating in the festival—I personally won three stuffed animals at various carnival games and gave all of them away to kids standing nearby.

As I walked up and down the streets included in the fair, I couldn't help but reflect on these last many months. I knew these to be loving people, quick to defend their own. They were durable, both in terms of weather and in terms of bad news. I'd ended up here by accident, really... just by virtue of the man I'd chosen to kill and his intended destiny... but I'd fallen in love with this place ... these people ... the local values and priorities.

I couldn't help but stop as I passed my favorite carnival game. I paid the buck-fifty and stepped up to take my turn. The game was about baseball and guesswork. The player, me in this instance, would throw two pitches, each of which would be measured for speed by the on-site radar gun.

Then the player had to predict the speed of their third and final pitch. After the prediction was logged, the player threw the third pitch. If the player correctly guessed the speed of that pitch, he or she won a cheap plastic baseball helmet ... the team of their choice. If the guess was wrong, then, of course, the player earned nothing and went away sad.

I decided to play one final game before the fair shut down. I handed over another dollar and a half, took the three baseballs, and then took several deep breaths.

I thought back to my youth when I'd been limber and bold. Then I wound up and fired my first pitch.

Fifty-two mph.

The radar gun doesn't lie, though I wished like hell in the moment that it did.

I was old, of course. No longer in possession of my Little League abilities. Rusty, creaky, and in need of a ton of practice. But I didn't have time to practice.

I wound up again, feeling more determined, and let loose a fastball I felt really good about, even as it sailed slightly above the strike zone.

Sixty mph.

The gun was tempting me to attack and destroy it. That second pitch had seemed like everything I had in me.

And here's where most people who play this game make their fatal mistake: they guess the third pitch's speed will be directly in between the first two pitches. They split the difference. Something about the human brain causes them to think math or statistics has some kind of sway here in this moment in this game.

In reality, players are just getting warmed up. They've been riding roller coasters and eating fried foods all day. They haven't been practicing pitching. They haven't been warming up their arm. They haven't been stretching.

So, the brain forces most people to guess low, when in reality the thrower is still getting warmed up, and the arm is going to be more and more capable as the first several throws occur. If I were a normie, without the inside information on how the game worked, I'd have guessed my third and final throw to be around fifty-six or fifty-seven mph. But because I knew how the game worked and also knew that I was just warming up, I bumped my guess above the second toss's speed. I guessed sixty-three for my final throw, three mph higher than my second.

And I nailed it. Sixty-three on the nose.

Those in the crowd went wild with applause. Even the game master was surprised. And I walked away with a cheap plastic bright-red Cincinnati Reds baseball helmet valued at roughly three dollars and a mile-wide smile on my face that was invaluable, all because I understood the science of the human body more than the average contestant.

● ● ●

There was usually a bit of mischief after midnight every night of Harvest Fest as drunk folks made their way home. But this year there was nothing. Before twelve even struck, the streets were empty and eerily quiet. A few straggling carnival workers remained as they shut down and locked up their livelihood, but the streets were otherwise empty.

The fear in Crooked Creek was sensible now. No one was out super-late pushing boundaries, but no one was rushing off to lock up at sundown. The killings had left the town and the entire county better off. People were wary now, but also people here had grown closer to each other. They'd learned to count on one another, lean on one another, trust one another.

I'd set out merely to send a few righteous souls to Heaven, but in the process I'd strengthened an entire community. I would be leaving Crooked Creek, small as it was on the map and in population, better than I'd found it—a happy byproduct of my mission to find holy souls and help usher them to eternity.

CHAPTER 36

MOVING ON

I TOOK THE DEPARTMENT SUV out to Father Warren's house.

The media was gone. The FBI was gone. The case was closed. The guilty were judged and imprisoned. Every loose end was now tied off. And it was finally time for me to make a full confession for all the mortal sins I'd committed these last several months. I'd gone far too long without offering confession. I'd planned it that way, of course, but the confession itself was still a necessary component of that plan.

I pulled into the driveway and saw Bones in the front yard. He was barely able to lift his head, and he certainly didn't come greet me as usual. Pulling up farther than normal, right up next to the house, I parked and popped the trunk, sighing audibly as I exited the vehicle. I wasn't ready for this.

I grabbed the two large duffel bags from the trunk, nodded at Bones, and went to the front door. I rapped on the screen door with my knuckles and called out: "Father? You in there? If you haven't died yet, I'd love to visit with you and give confession." I grinned.

A few seconds went by—enough that I almost began to worry—before he coughed to life and offered a hacking reply: "Come in, you sinner." He laughed for a second before it turned back into coughing. He was nearer the end than I wanted to admit.

I entered and left the duffel bags by the door. "Hey, you old man," I said affectionately.

He was sitting in the easy chair, a single reclinable sofa-quality chair. It was old and worn, like him, but he loved that chair.

"You should've confessed the last time I saw you," he wheezed, pointing at the couch for me to sit down.

"The last time I saw you, I was driving you back home to here. The time before that, you were knocked out cold in a hospital bed."

"Well," he started, seeming confused. "You can't just skip months of confession at a time, you know," he added. "Unless you have been sin-free that whole time."

"I know, I know," I admitted as I made my way to the couch and sat down. "It's been far too many months. I have much to confess. But also, Father, you have to remember: I have been pretty busy lately."

He nodded. "And have you solved the murder case?"

"We did." I replied. "We even found two kidnapped victims all tied up and murdered. I'm surprised you didn't read about it in the papers."

"I can't read anymore, you jackass," he barked.

"It was on TV too."

"I can't see the TV!" he barked instantly. "If you'd cared to visit any time in the last three months, you'd know all this. I get my news from those who care enough to visit me!"

It didn't seem worth it to continue telling him that I had visited him in the hospital and had driven him home from the hospital as well, so I let it go without argument. The man I'd seen as a mentor all those years had morphed into something angrier. Perhaps there was no wisdom left in there to share with me.

Still . . . he was the only one around who could and would hear my confession.

"I've missed you," I tried.

"Missed what? Smelling the waste I leave in my own pants? Talking to a loony person? The long drive?" He was more combative today than I was expecting, but it wouldn't change my plans in even the slightest way.

I took a deep breath before responding. "Maybe we should just move into the confession, Father," I offered.

"Whatever," he barked.

Age and illness had taken away from him most of his personality and likable qualities. I wondered if he was even capable of representing me before God throughout my confession, but I was in no position to suggest such fears aloud.

I stood, knowing the routine, and I grabbed the divider screen with much enthusiasm, jostling it into place. I sat back down on the end of the couch, now hidden from his view. "Father, forgive me, for I have sinned."

"Yeah, yeah, yeah. Clearly. Just get to it already." He was growing more impatient with me by the moment. It was a side of him I'd never seen, and yet he'd never been this close to death before.

"I had sexual relations with the female police officer sent from Foster County. It went on throughout much of the murder investigation." He didn't make any obvious noises or movements, so I continued. "I lied about that affair several times. I also continued to perform all my regular duties as priest, including confession and Communion, despite the unconfessed sin in my own heart."

"And?" he finally coughed out, seemingly unmoved by my sins confessed thus far.

And so I continued. "I lied. I hid evidence from other officers, and I did some other sinful stuff, too, but it was all for a good reason."

"Yeah?"

"I figure . . . the math is all that matters; right, Father? If we get more souls to Heaven, then we're doing our job; right? So I just decided to stop waiting for people to die of natural causes . . . and started killing them right after a clear good deed. This way, you see, I can assume they end up in Heaven." I smiled in genuine pride. "If left to their own . . . humanity . . . they'd surely fuck it all up again. Right? I mean . . . humans are, by definition, fuckups. Why can't I even the odds a bit for some of them?"

I could hear his raspy breathing, so I knew he was still paying attention. I stood up and kicked the privacy screen across the room.

"So I started killing. I started killing every pure soul I could find. And there weren't many! I had to look pretty hard, actually!" I began to pace back and forth between his living room and kitchen, growing more vitriolic as I continued. So weak was the man . . . so helpless . . . I slowly became my true self to him as I ranted, completely unafraid of any recompense from him.

"I killed that old woman because she'd just given a ton of money to the church. Generous lady. I needed to make sure she went to Heaven. I couldn't risk something small like a speeding ticket or an unpaid water bill keeping her out of glory!"

I probably sounded insane to him, but I'd never made more sense to myself. Finally verbalizing these thoughts, out loud, was liberating. I was doing good work and was only just now finally getting to take credit for it.

"And the girl?" he wheezed.

"No one loved Katie more than I did," I responded. "But she'd been faced with the toughest of morality tests—whether to become a mother or kill a fetus. She had pressure from her star-athlete boyfriend to get an abortion. She sought my counsel. And after all that, she still chose the right decision: to keep the baby."

"A baby you killed when you killed her," Wendall whisper-spat. I wondered how many breaths he had left and how he chose which thoughts to spend them on.

I smiled broadly. "A baby and mother who are now both with Jesus in Heaven. Don't you get it, Wendall? By killing at the exact right moment, we can send more souls to the Father than ever before! If it costs me my own place up there, I am willing to accept that!" I paused for applause that I knew wasn't coming. "I sent people to Heaven who life's hurdles would have ensured went to Hell!" Still no reaction. "I probably did more for the kingdom than any of my preaching-only contemporaries!"

And Wendall started to cry. Not just small tears, but sobbing, convulsing tears.

"I knew you wouldn't understand. I hoped you would, but I knew you wouldn't." I walked to the doorway and dragged both duffel bags back to the living room. I stood up and spent a few moments scratching my head to try to extinguish an itch. "I just . . . I thought you of all people would understand."

He coughed a few times, weakly.

"It's a new era. The old methods are no longer effective."

Maybe I was just projecting, but I could feel the peace in the room. He knew he was on his way to meet his maker, and I think he wanted it.

I finished tying and then began positioning the duffle bags. "Those people who I killed. They're all with Jesus now. You can't . . . Father, no matter your feelings on my methods, you can't argue with my results."

I dumped bones on the floor before him.

I heard him gasp. Then he mustered up enough strength to speak again. "Who is that?"

I laughed as I began pouring accelerant all over the place. "You should know the answer to this question by now, old man. That," I paused for effect, "is Father Solomon Lancaster, your replacement at the Crooked Creek parish."

His eyes went wide.

I continued, still spreading accelerant throughout the tiny home. "I had a flat tire, you see, several counties over and eleven years ago. And a kindly young priest stopped to help. He was on his way to his newest assignment in Crooked Creek, and, unlike me, he wasn't wanted for any crimes.

"We bore a passing-enough resemblance that his driver's license became mine and worked just fine. I buried him once I settled in, but not too deep—I knew I'd need his bones eventually. And now his bones will close the loop. The story will be of the young priest and his older mentor, who died together in a tragic fire."

Wendall began looking around, using only his eyes, trying to find a fire.

"I haven't set it yet, Wendall."

Just then I struck the match, smiled widely, and dropped the match to the fuel-soaked floor. I walked out of the tiny farmhouse smiling. Relieved. This was the final piece of closure.

I pulled the vehicle up closer to the house, got out, and left it running. Then I made for the old 1940s pickup Wendall had always kept in his garage. It had no plates, but ... I had some spares. The battery was dead as hell, so I used the tractor to jump it. Then I lit a match and tossed it into the dry hay, hopping into the truck before the blaze engulfed the barn.

Two fires were better than one, I figured.

The old pickup sputtered and jolted forward as I guided it down the driveway. Suddenly I stopped the vehicle and hopped out to admired the blaze.

Crooked Creek was my second town, my second spree ... but that fire, that massive funeral pyre ... that was my best work yet. I memorized the image for easy recall.

My mentor, my namesake, and all the evidence of my existence ... all aflame ... rabidly lapping up at the sky.

I whistled. "Here, Bones," I called. The old dog pried himself up off the lawn with a bit of difficulty and ambled my way. I pointed to the truck cab, and he cautiously walked forward and tried to step up inside. He didn't know what was going on; he had no idea I was burning his owner alive. But he still accepted my assistance in helping him into the vehicle.

Because he trusted me.

Everyone in this town was ultimately undone by basic trust. Trust in the collar, and trust in the shield. Trust in God, and trust in the law. Neither were really very trustworthy, as it turned out. Though the townspeople would never know. All they'd find is two bodies matching two known area priests.

I set off on the country road—Zacchaeus in the back seat, wary but calm, and Bones in my passenger seat—a full gas tank and a new perspective.

I smiled ear to ear.

"How do you feel about Oregon?" I asked my dog companion, scratching his ear. "I hear they have some truly good folk up there."

Bones rested against my scratching hand as I steered the vehicle out of Indiana corn country once and for all.

"Shake?" I asked, holding out my open palm. To my delight, Bones responded by placing his paw in my hand. "Nice to meet you, Bones," I said. "My name is . . ." I paused, realizing it was time to take on a new identity. I'd left Father Solomon Lancaster behind forever. "My name is . . ." I wondered what profession I might dive into next. Would I go from priest to teacher? Or woodworker? Skilled laborer?

My options were endless.

"My name is yet to be determined. Let's go to Oregon," I announced to the rest of the car's occupants. "We'll figure out the rest on the way there."

THE END.

ACKNOWLEDGEMENTS

A book doesn't just happen through one person's efforts. I had lots of help, including but not limited to: my wife, who encourages me every day; the great people at Turner Publishing and Keylight Books; my friends at CinemaSins; my friends at MadeIn; my friends and family; my early readers; and especially Terry Foster, a friend who provided much needed insight into aspects of the Catholic faith where I was lacking understanding.

ABOUT THE AUTHOR

Jeremy Scott is a writer and entertainer from Nashville, TN. He is the co-creator & narrator of CinemaSins, a YouTube channel dedicated to movie-related comedy with over 9 million subscribers, and the author of *The Ables* series and *Original Sin: From Preacher's Kid to the Creation of CinemaSins*. A former online marketing consultant, Jeremy spends his time cohosting a popular film podcast, playing and listening to music, and being lousy at golf. He lives just outside Nashville with his incredibly understanding wife and their furry cats.